Lost in Spindle City

M. Lee Prescott

Published by Mt. Hope Press

Copyright 2014, Mt. Hope Press

Cover design by Ashley Lopez, E-book Formatting Fairies

ISBN: 978-0-9912855-2-5

All rights reserved. No part of this publication may be reproduced, stored or transmitted (auditory, graphic, mechanical or electronic) without the express written permission of the author, except in the case or brief quotations or excerpts used in critical reviews and articles. Thank you for respecting the hard work of this author. To obtain permission to excerpt portions of the text, please contact the author at mleeprescott@gmail.com.

This book is a work of fiction. Names, characters, places, and events are products of the author's imagination or are used fictitiously. Any resemblance to actual people (alive or deceased), locales, or events is entirely coincidental.

For my children and grandchildren

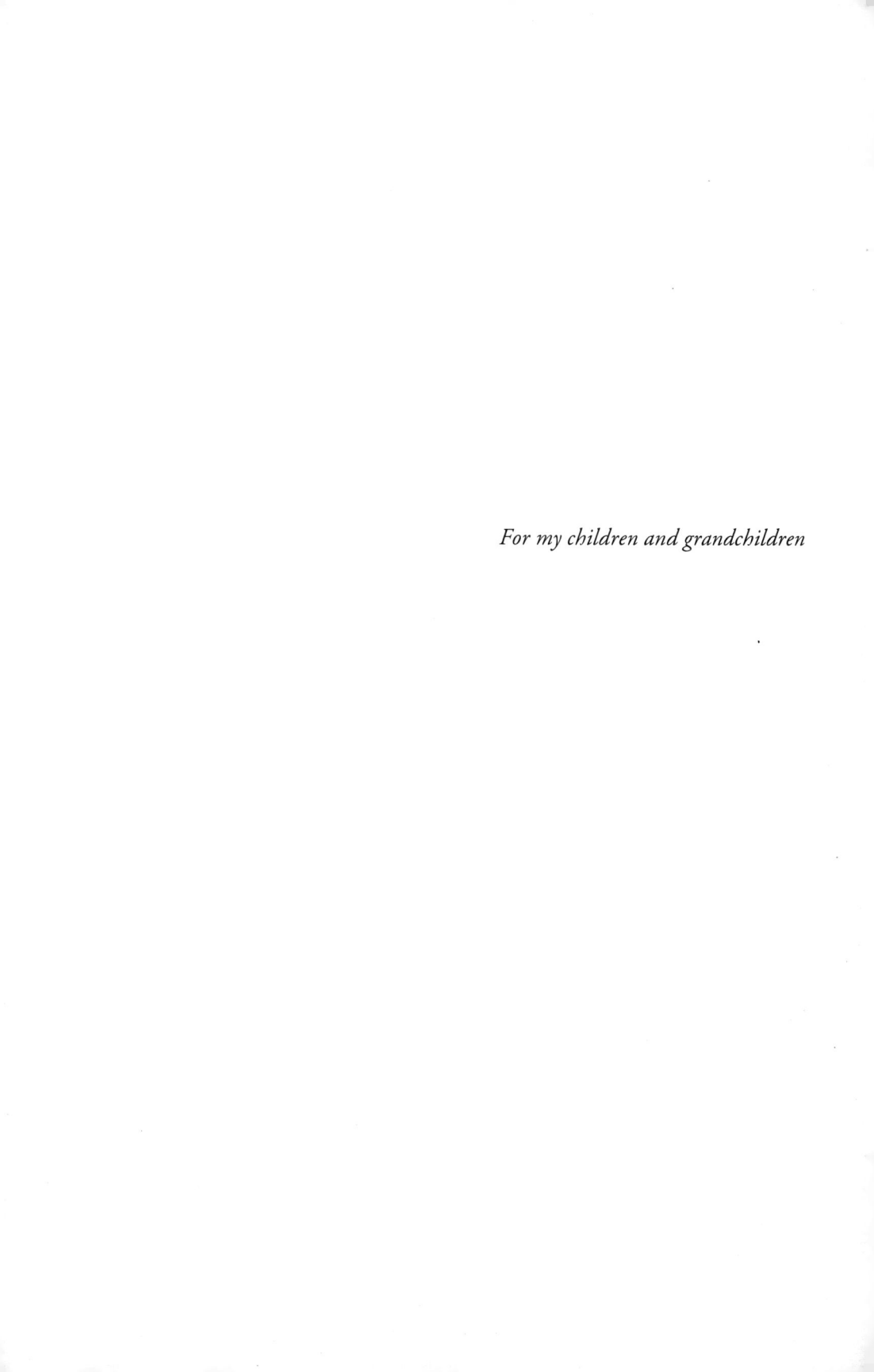

Chapter 1

Some days have less than auspicious starts. This was one of them. My third-floor office seemed light years away as I dragged myself up the stairs. My head was fuzzy, legs wet noodles, and my stomach churning. Other than that, I felt terrific.

Last night was one of the truly dumb ones where I forgot that I'm fifty eight not twenty eight I had just wrapped up a crappy case, and despite my best efforts to breathe deeply and let go, my shoulders and neck were locked tight as a tick. Instead of taking a bath and hitting the sack, yours truly had to play tough PI, belting back beers with the guys at the *Rainbow*.

A little hole in the wall bar frequented by the locals, the *Rainbow* is a block from my house. A small cardboard sigh taped to the inside of the grimy front window, "Food and Spirits, do drop in," is the only indication that it's a place of business. The sign, brown and curling at the edges, was penned in red. The ink, now faded, coordinated nicely with the grayish pink, peek-a-boo, half curtains, frayed and dusty, after many smoky years. One glimpse of its subterranean façade and no passer-by would dare "to drop in."

Once I got started on the beers and shots of tequila, it was all over. My neighbor, Vinnie and I played cribbage or maybe dice. There used to be an ancient pool table, but Jack, the owner, had it removed the previous year, fearing its imminent collapse might injure one of his valued patrons.

The walk home, a dim memory, I had slept in my clothes—never a good sign. I woke at 6:00 a.m. and the phrase "death warmed over" sprang to mind. After three aspirins, a shower, juice and muffins, I felt better, but that's not saying much. I'm supposed to have oat bran and lots of fiber to combat high cholesterol and triglycerides, but after ingesting platters of grease and empty carbs the previous evening, that was pretty much a losing battle.

A run? Out of the question. My daily yoga? Probably not wise to invert my body at present. Better to wait until dark to see stars. Maybe a short walk, then I'd treat myself to a coffee cab. The rest of the world calls them milkshakes, but around Spindle City, we call 'em cabs or cabinets. Yum!

I hate coffee, am a tea drinker, mostly Earl Grey and Yerba Mate, but I love coffee cabs and occasionally coffee ice cream, both of which serve as my primary treatment for the occasional hangover I experience as a middle-aged nincompoop. I keep a coffee maker in my office for clients and I've been known to swill a cup to be friendly, but coffee has never been part of my daily routine.

My name is Ricky Steele, given name, Dorothy. I've been married, but no kids, have one sister and a father who I see once in a while. I was married for about five seconds and have no children, the latter my one regret. I recently had, what for me, was a serious relationship that lasted about five months. It ended when he went back to his former live-in girlfriend. I had a history with Jay Harp, the lothario in question, and should have known better than to trust my heart to him again. We had a brief fling in our twenties when we were both members of a wedding party. As best man and maid of honor, we spent many hours together and one thing led to another. We kept things up for a month or two post-wedding, but then Jay disappeared, never to be seen again, until last year.

I was investigating the murder of his brother, Ron Harp when Jay and I met up again, and our former spark turned into a blaze. We spent some passionate, intense months with one another, and even discussed moving in together. Then Jay confessed that he had "unfinished business" with his former fiancée, Marty. What is it with men and "unfinished business" with old girlfriends? My reaction to his confession was to storm off and refuse to see him or talk to him. We speak on the phone every so often, but I always refuse to see him. I have to admit that I miss him. Our break-up hurt more than previous ones. My friends tell me I have a gift for choosing men who are dishonest and narcissistic, but maybe I'm not "girlfriend material?" Who knows? I try to stay positive and hope that the right guy will walk into my life someday.

I hold many odd jobs, from newspaper columnist for our local paper, to waitress and craftsperson. Most recently, I've been working as a private investigator, a profession, which I recently fell into thanks to my own foolishness. Then, to my surprise, I found I liked it enough to put in the hundreds of hours interning with two local PIs that were required in order to get my license. I'm a private person and this life suits my personality, if not my overall health, and I've let some of the odd jobs go, waitressing, in particular.

While I've stumbled into several murder cases, most of my work is fairly routine. A good friend, Bud Dixon, runs his own insurance business and throws me a fair amount of work. Insurance fraud is a full-time occupation for lots of folks so Bud's jobs help make ends meet. I also pick up a fair amount of work trailing errant spouses, since infidelity is epidemic. About half of this work is accomplished in the real world, the other half online, since the Internet is a cheater's best friend.

Over the past months, I've become the PI of choice for a certain Newport set. Having hubby followed and photographed as he goes about his tedious daily routines seems to be the "in thing" for bored housewives and those who have a vested interest in keeping close tabs on the checkbook.

My last case, which I tried mightily to stay out of, nearly got me killed. There are certain cases one does not take in this city, if one wishes to remain among the living. I was out of physical danger now, or at least for the next decade, but I was still emotionally shaken, hence last night's idiocy. I'm not a big drinker, the occasional beer and glass of wine is about the extent of it, but sometimes the amnesia of alcohol can be therapeutic. A day spent indulging myself with junk food and sugar and I'd be ready to face the world again.

As I reached the top of the stairs, my stomach flipped. Increased heart rate, beer and tequila definitely do not mix.

My office is in a restored mill building in the heart of the city's Flint District. It's a beautiful structure, the façade still strong and proud, despite acres of advertising splayed across its granite walls. In the city's hay day, its cavernous rooms once roared with the machinery of textile production, hundreds of workers toiling twenty-four hours a day. For years, the abandoned mill had sat, guttered and empty, left to ponder its fate as the once thriving city slipped into poverty, neglect and high unemployment. Now, although silent, the halls and passageways had been "repurposed" and housed a variety of enterprises.

The ground floor hummed with a ragtag collection of outlet stores and bargain kiosks hawking every type of merchandise, but right now the second floor is vacant, providing a buffer between Outlet Central and offices on the third floor. Bud, my insurance friend, began his business here and dragged me along, but as his client list grew, he moved to fancier digs downtown, leaving me with several other tenants on the partially renovated third floor. Not exactly a classy location, but it suits me. I have my own rear entrance, insulated from the comings and goings of the outlet crowd.

At the moment, there are four of us on the third floor. I'm in 308, a real estate appraiser I rarely see is in 312, a salesman for "Boats Afloat" or some nautical magazine is in 316. The writer in 320 comes most days at 10:00 a.m. and departs shortly before 3:00 p.m. He told me last week that 320 is his sanctuary, an escape from the bedlam at home. The remainder of the floor is vacant. An acre of empty is a lot of empty. They tell us there are sixty to eighty potential office spaces, but it takes a certain type to locate here. Cheap and bizarre. It's relatively quiet and fairly secure, at least during the day since they've hired extra security to keep the bargain hunter's thievery in check. Apparently for some, no price is cheap enough.

I slid open the heavy metal fire door and headed down the hall. The walls were painted dull, asylum grey, but they left the beautiful woodwork alone. I ran my hand along the dark mahogany chair rail, collecting dust. Unfortunately, the renovators had made no attempt to match the old with the new, so my cubicle and others had been slapped together, minus mahogany trim.

As a middle-aged spinster set in her ways, I have a little routine I like to follow which involves a cup of tea, a little bill paying, or ignoring, depending upon the status of my bank account, a little office tidying, record keeping, and whatever puttering I find to occupy me until I drink my tea. I do not like to be interrupted before 11:00 a.m. I have found this ritual to be important to my sense of well-being and willingness to face the day. I was not to enjoy my treasured routine today.

Chapter 2

I found her curled up against my door, a tangle of arms and legs. Her spindly legs were covered in snagged black netting that had been patched in several spots with nail polish. Bright red pumps, from all appearances, several sizes too large, adorned impossibly long feet.

Street people often camp out in buildings when they can slip by the airtight security system. In other words, they're regulars. I've kind of adopted one little lady, Irene, whom I suspect is around my age, but looks to be about a hundred. She's been sleeping in my hall for the past six months. If I forget to lock the office door, I often find her stretched out on my couch, catching up on her beauty sleep. Irene snores. Loudly. She's short and pudgy, not scrawny like this little gal with her bony limbs sticking out all over the place. I definitely did not have room on my couch for two.

I was contemplating how I might slip around my slumbering guest, when Terry, the appraiser, banged open the fire door and startled her awake. I turned to give him an icy glare, but he had already banged into his office, not a glance in our direction. Turning back, I found her rubbing her eyes, looking disoriented and none too happy. That made two of us.

She gathered herself up and ineffectually endeavored to smooth her hair as she inched up the wall like a spider. Her light brown hair, the consistency of my childhood dolls after I'd styled their tresses, stuck up in odd clumps, coarse, wiry and clearly in need of a wash. She wore a red skirt and matching ribbed top, the entire ensemble made of a hundred % unnatural fibers. Over her skimpy get-up, she wore an oversized man's gray sport coat in a herringbone pattern, brown suede patches on the sleeves. I suspect she had grabbed it from the outlet dumpster on her way in, to ward off the April chill.

Several strands of brightly colored beads hung from her skinny, ostrich neck, and she sported matching dangly earrings. Her left earring was missing its bottom red bead, giving her an off-kilter look, and I found myself listing to the side as I regarded her. As I gazed into dark, round eyes rimmed with think black eyeliner, I gulped. I was looking at a child, twelve at most, maybe much younger. Bud's fifth grader looked older than this sad little bird.

"Miss Steele?" She spoke tentatively, voice husky.

I nodded, thinking, at least she can read. My office door has my name emblazoned in stick-on black and gold letters. Very classy.

"I'm sorry to be crashed here."

I shrugged. "No problem, happens all the time. Must've been a rough one last night, huh? Shouldn't you be in school or something?"

"Not today. Sometimes we go, but not today. I needed to see you and I snuck in before the guard locked up so I could catch you first thing."

She began fussing with her hair again, pulling at her skirt, smoothing out the jacket. Clearly nervous gestures, a way to occupy her tiny, shaking hands until I responded.

I smiled. "Well, you caught me. Come on in."

I didn't have a good feeling about this, but what could I do? Besides, my solemn routine had been broken now, so what the hell?

Chapter 3

My office has two small rooms, no bathroom. The bathroom's down the hall and pretty grungy. About once a month, I scrub it out, as building cleaning service is practically nonexistent. Every couple of months I work on the plumbing. My fellow tenants don't seem to care about maintenance, but then, I've never set foot in the men's room, and never intend to.

My outer office has a couch, or guest bed, as some would call it, super comfy if you ignore the moths that fly out of the holes in the arms. I keep a woven basket of old magazines, mostly donated by Bud. As a waiting room, it needs work, but I rarely have clients waiting. There's also a small refrigerator, the table beside it holding a coffee maker, electric tea kettle, and a few assorted canisters filled with sugar, coffee and tea bags.

My inner office has two tall windows that look out over the parking lots and rows of mills beyond. In its heyday, the city had over a hundred granite mills dotted along the river. It's an incredible view. In the morning the sun streams in and the office is warm and comfortable, not so much in the late afternoon. I have a huge oak partners desk that I discovered in one of the yet-to-be-renovated spaces. The landlord sold it to me for ten dollars and Bud helped me drag it down the hall. After I cleaned it up, polished the wood and fixed a couple of broken drawers, it gleamed. Sitting behind it makes me feel established and solid, as if my business had a long, illustrious history.

A four drawer file cabinet, three chairs, a gray metal locker, and two steamship prints on the wall complete my décor. I store valuables and my camera equipment in the locker, but any two-bit crook could pop the lock in three seconds. I wasn't sure I should offer coffee to my visitor. Didn't it stunt growth or something? Instead I invited her in and she took the most comfy chair. I sat in my swivel chair, and scooted it around the desk to sit beside her.

"So, what's up?"

"I'm sorry to bother you so early in the morning, but Mrs. Silva said you could help me and I really need help."

Ebbie Silva, a friend of a friend, had hired me a few months earlier to track down her brother-in-law. He had skipped out on her sister and Ebbie wanted a word with him. A few quick phone calls and I managed to dredge him up. When I handed Ebbie his address, I almost felt sorry for the guy.

"How is Ebbie?"

She shrugged and fidgeted. "Don't know her too well. Lives near us, that's all. She told me you can find people. I need you to find someone for me."

"Oh?"

"My friend, she's gone missing."

"What did you say your name was?"

Her face reddened and she gave me a shy, kid's smile. "Oh, sorry, it's Natalie, Natalie Remy. I been so stressed about Lisa. That's who I'm lookin' for, my friend, Lisa. I so worried, I'm kinda out of it, you know? It's just she's been gone for a couple of days and I'm getting freaked."

She was trembling now, rubbing her hands together. I caught a glimpse of an incredibly thin arm inside her coat sleeve. I knew with certainty I was way out of my depth.

"Hey, are you hungry? I think better with food and a cup of tea."

"Well, I—"

I rose, smiling down at her. "My treat. I'll put it on my expense account. Come on, Dino's is right around the corner. We can talk while we eat."

She followed me out of the office and down the stairs, her heels clattering at every step. The buildings and lots along Quarry Street were quiet as we walked side by side, maintaining the silence except for the drum beat of Natalie's high heels. She hovered close, occasionally brushing against me the way good friends do as they walk and talk. This was a needy child. Where was her mother?

Chapter 4

Dino's Diner is a long, dark, narrow affair with high-backed oak booths, their seat covers upholstered in green, faux-marble naugahyde. The booths run along one wall and the counter, with ten swivel stools in gleaming chrome, same naugahyde seats as the booths run along the opposite wall. There is a mirrored wall behind the grill. I make it a point never to sit at the counter. That's all I need at 7:00 a.m., a good long look at myself. How to ruin a day before it even begins.

Dino was full of his usual early morning cheer, which I find amusing, endearing, or irritating, depending on my mood. This morning I found it disconcerting. Clearly, solicitous attention unnerved my companion when she clearly wanted to blend into the woodwork, or naugahyde. She clung to me as we retreated to a rear booth, away from the grill with Dino right behind us.

"How can a man be so lucky? Two of the most gorgeous creatures in the city, right here in my restaurant! Did they go to *Lizzie's*, *The Pier*, the *Q-Club*? No, they came to *Dino's*— together even."

"We love you too, Dino. How's Lois?" Lois, his wife, worked the lunch shift, keeping his fraternizing in check. At breakfast he was on his own.

"Why bring Lois up when we're having such a good time, just the three of us?"

"Dino, my love, we're in kind of a hurry, and real hungry, so could we please just order?"

"No problem, doll. We'll get back to this later." He winked at Natalie, her mouth agape. I had the maternal urge to say, "close your mouth or the flies'll get in" but I bit my tongue.

"What'll it be for you and your gorgeous friend?"

"Go ahead," I said, "anything you want."

Natalie ordered a full breakfast: eggs, sausage, toast and juice. She refused Dino's offer of coffee and asked for a large milk. At least some part of her is still a kid under all that. I ordered tea and English muffins, lots of jelly on the side. Dino winked, then swaggered off, leaving us in peace.

"So what's up?" I asked, as Natalie slipped out of her overcoat and began shaking again, rubbing those bony little arms. "You sick?"

"No." She shrugged. "Just a nervous habit, I guess." She forced her hands to her lap. "I'm not sure what to tell you. My friend, Lisa, she's just gone, no message, no phone call, no nothing. It's not like her. We always tell each other everything, you know? If we're in trouble, we always turn to each other. We ain't got anyone else really."

"What about your parents?"

"Lisa's mom hasn't seen her in a while. I mean, she's pretty much out of it anyway."

"What about your parents?"

"It's just my dad and he doesn't know Lisa very well or me either for that matter. Actually, I live with Lisa. My dad's kinda busy, you know? He didn't need a kid around, if you get my meaning."

I didn't, but I left it alone. "So the mom hasn't seen her. Anyone else that might know where she is?"

"Only her brother, but I can't find him either."

"How old is this brother?"

"Ten."

"Great. And how old are you and Lisa?"

"Fifteen, almost sixteen."

"Bull."

"Okay, so we're almost thirteen, but who gives a shit? We've been taking care of ourselves for years. We earn a living and take care of our place. That counts for something, doesn't it?" She screwed her face into a pout, hands on her hips. She was a tough little bird.

"It counts for something." I struggled to maintain a neutral listening face, forcing back the urge to either smile or cry.

"Okay, dolls, here you go!" Dino brought everything at once, sparing us repeated interruptions. We ate in silence for a few minutes. She was obviously starving and devoured her entire plate before I picked up my second muffin.

"You want more? Go ahead if you're still hungry. Dino loves people who eat a lot."

"No, thanks." She smiled. "I need to use the bathroom. Where is it?"

I pointed. "Right behind the counter on the end. It's not the cleanest, but it works."

I watched her teeter off, wondering if she was going to bolt on me. She had left her coat. Anyway, why would she want to run? There was something furtive about her wish to use the bathroom. Drugs?

"Little early for Halloween, isn't it?"

Dino slid into the booth for one of our early morning heart-to-hearts. These chats took several forms depending on Dino's mood. He either flirted shamelessly or pretended he was my father, lecturing me on the hazards of my lifestyle. He has been at this since my days as a teacher in the South End, so it wasn't the PI work that he objected to. He just hated that I was alone. No husband, no kids, no anyone.

"Enough, Dino. And don't you dare say anything when she gets back. She's scared enough without you giving her the third degree."

"Hey, you know me, Rick. But I ask you, what's the world comin' to, kids runnin' around like that? What's the matter you anyway. You look like you've been up for five nights straight."

"Too much to drink last night. Dumb."

"Drunk? Better watch yourself, doll. 'Specially at your age."

"Our age, thank you. No lectures, okay? I've learned my lesson. Can I have another tea, please?"

"Sure. But, you betta come back at lunch and Lois will fix you a coffee cab. Stay away from that McDonald crap. All chemicals, no milk."

"We'll see." I smiled, thinking about Lois's coffee cabs, so creamy and delicious.

Lisa Brown, a routine missing persons case, probably a runaway, probably mixed up with drugs, prostitution, and who knows what else? The usual shit that neglected, abused city kids got into these days. I'd seen too many of them the past few years. Sometimes it appalled me, but none of it shocked me anymore. Maybe in my hungover state, the wall I'd erected was kicked away allowing me to feel. Whatever, my gut wrenched thinking about these two kids and I didn't even know them.

I polished off my second cup of tea. She still had not returned from the john. Out of the corner of my eye, I spied Dino headed my way. Here we go, I thought, bracing myself for further effusions.

"Hey, Rick," he said in a low voice. "I think there's something wrong with your friend. Sounds like she might be sick in there."

I followed him and we tried the bathroom door. It gave way, and I spied Natalie crouched near the toilet wiping her face with a paper towel. As the dry paper scraped across her cheeks like sandpaper, I shivered. "You okay? What happened?"

"It's nothing." Her face was pale and streaked with tears, eyes bloodshot and watery.

"Did you make yourself throw up?" I asked, trying not to sound accusatory, but probably failing miserably. My roommate in college spent four years doing this, so I was well acquainted with bulimic purging.

"No, it just happens sometimes after I eat a lot. I have kind of a funny stomach, you know?"

"Natalie, you need to see a doctor. This is nothing to fool around with, and you're pretty thin. I can take you to my doctor and he'll look you over." What was I saying? Too involved, Steele.

"No, I'm okay. If I rest, I'll feel better."

I lifted her up and half carried her out of the bathroom. Dino brought her coat and we wrestled her into it. After handing me my bag and Natalie's sack, he helped until we reached the door muttering about "kids today." He refused the money I dropped on the counter and since my hands were full, I let the bills stay in my jacket pocket where he stuffed them. I would settle with him later.

We staggered back toward the office. She collapsed on the sidewalk outside the building, so I heaved her over my shoulder and toted her up the stairs like a sack of potatoes. All three flights. Fortunately, my back is stronger than my stomach which was feeling queasier now. Any reference to vomiting sets it off, and my impaired health didn't improve the situation. I deposited her, none too gently, on the couch, and threw an old overcoat I keep in the office over her. As I paced around wondering what to do, she opened her eyes.

"Sorry about this. I've had the flu. I'll be okay. Can I sleep here? I'll feel great in a few minutes. You'll look for Lisa, won't you?" she rambled on, not waiting for my reply. "Her mom's address and phone number are on a paper in my bag. Maybe she's seen her. I doubt it, but it's worth a try. And there's Teddy, her brother. Please, I'll just crash here a while then take off. I can pay, no problem. I mean, I got money, you know. Not on me, but I can get it. I'll just take a nap. With those words she closed her eyes and drifted off, leaving me standing with my mouth open, stomach in knots.

I rifled through the psychedelic carpet bag she called a purse and unearthed a scrap of paper.

"Oh, for Christ's sake."

I grabbed my bag and headed out again, locking the door behind me.

Chapter 5

My car, an ancient jeep Grand Wagoneer with wooden sides, was parked in the lot behind the building in my spot. No one but a lunatic or insurance swindler would bother to park there. The chances of a car being intact or even around upon one's return were slim. My car was always there. Its paint, once a deep blue, is now faded to dull grayish mud. It's never locked and the windows are usually down. The radio has long since been ripped out, but I don't miss it. Too many headaches from the static generated by punctured speakers. Several bungled robbery attempts had pretty well trashed the quadraphonic sound.

The motor is fine and it's fairly reliable transportation. Doesn't like the heat, but it starts without hesitation even on the coldest days of winter. Has a tendency to stutter when starting up, particularly when I'm trying to make a getaway, but it's relatively sturdy. I don't do much high speed chasing. Couldn't if I wanted to!

Hopping in, I shoved a pile of laundry aside. It was in the driver's seat to remind me that the laundry was a top priority today.

I shook my head, trying to chase away the ringing in my ears and the incessant pounding in my head. "Get a grip, Steele. Do something for yourself before heading on a wild goose chase."

Striking a blow for domestication, I decided to swing by Little Pearl Laundry before heading out to begin my "new case." I left my clothes with Linn and felt comforted by her, "See you tomorrow!" At least she had faith that I would live through the day. Pond Street was closer than Bedford and the police station, so I headed to the address scrawled on Natalie's paper. I pulled out my cell and dialed the number on the paper. I listened to the phone ring and ring and ring. Just as I started to hang up, she picked up, "Yeah?" Her voice rasped like nails on an emery board. I gritted my teeth, willing my voice to be soft and pleasant.

"Mrs. Brown?"

"Who wants her?"

"Mrs. Brown, I'm a friend of Lisa's. Ricky Steele. Is she at home?"

"Never heard of you, and no friend of Lisa's talks like that. Who the hell are you?"

"Mrs. Brown, can I please speak to Lisa? It's important."

"The little bitch ain't home, so fuck off. And if you're one of the sluts she hangs with, don't call me again."

Slam.

What a nice friendly chat.

I got back into the jeep and headed toward Pond. At least I knew she was home. I'd have to try a different approach. When the semi-honest approach fails, I find it best to fall back on my arsenal of lies and fake personas. I've had some theatrical experience in a local "Little Theatre" group and I fancy myself to be quite an actress. One of my many delusions.

Number 263 was the upper half of the duplex. I parked next to a deli and walked a half a block. This was not my favorite part of the city. There was probably no danger mid-morning, but it was not the most scenic area in which to take a stroll. Row upon row of tenements lined the street. Most of this end of town was untouched by the rehab fever that had swept through many of the city's neighborhoods.

With the commuter rail, the old mill town was fast becoming another outpost for Boston commuters seeking affordable housing. An hour's commute was worth the low real estate prices and yuppies had snapped up the grand old Victorian homes. When the Highlands, the affluent part of the city, had been bought up, buyers branched out into other neighborhoods. This street was still an iffy place to settle, but the "up and comers" weren't far off. The far end of the street had several restoration projects in progress.

Down at this end of the street, the people living at number 263 seemed to have other things on their plate besides restoration. Things like staying alive or keeping ahead of the enormous pile of trash, household goods and litter piled on the sidewalk. I noticed hunks of old plaster lathe and scraps of lumber and wondered if the renovators down the way might be using this end as an interim dumping area. Nice.

Number 263 was flanked on both sides by abandoned tenements. To its left stood a boarded up behemoth, paint peeling, gutters falling off, its interiors most likely denuded off by an erstwhile salvage crew. Salvaging was big business in the city. Oak and maple floors, woodwork, fireplaces of Venetian marble and carved mahogany, marble mantels, banisters and stairways, and claw footed bathtubs were ripped out of abandoned homes and shipped everywhere. When a building finally fell to the wrecking ball, there was little left to knock over. The market for recycled building materials grew every year. Friends of mine had built a whole house with salvaged stuff. Except for the framing lumber and walls, their home came straight from the yard.

To the right of 263, was a partially burned out shell of a building that appeared to be resting on its neighbor. The latter resembled a lopsided Atlas with Hercules nowhere in sight. Walking up crumbling concrete steps, I approached the front entry and knocked on the door. Not surprisingly, there was no response. After a minute or two, I pushed open the outer door and entered a small vestibule.

Two metal boxes hung askew on the wall to my left. Below each was a call button. I pushed 263, expecting no response. After thirty seconds I was about to proceed up the stairs when a voice scratched over the intercom. "Yeah." At least she was consistent.

"Constance Peabody from *Young People's Assistance*, Mrs. Brown. Can I come up and talk? It'll only take a minute."

A grunt was the only response I received. No buzz, no "sure come right up," no "it'd be a pleasure."

I took the grunt to be an affirmative and proceeded up the stairs to knock on her door. No response. What a surprise.

"Mrs. Brown, hello."

Still no answer. I tried the door and it gave way so I walked in. "Hello, Mrs. Brown?"

"Well, you're in. What do ya want? Make it quick. I'm sick and shouldn't be up."

This friendly greeting sprang from the parched lips of a middle-aged woman; her skeletal body slumped against the doorframe leading to the kitchen. She was dressed in a flowered house dress that hung on her like a sack. Wispy brown hair was tied in a scraggly knot behind her head. Her feet were bare. It was cold in the apartment, and I wondered how she stood it with that thin dress and no shoes or sweater.

The living room was furnished in varying shades of dirty brown with a scatter rug, an old couch, a couple of tacky tables and lamps and, of course, a huge gleaming, new television set. From the look of things, she had been lying on the couch and had risen to answer the buzzer. Probably switched off the set to be hospitable. Why she was positioned in the doorway instead of back on the couch was unclear. Perhaps she wanted an escape route. More likely she desired a quick visit from yours truly and was unwilling to invite me to sit. I sat down on a straight backed chair by the door and tried to look relaxed.

"Look, Mrs. Brown. I'd like to talk to your daughter. I've just recently spoken with her friend, Natalie Remy. Are you familiar with the YPA?" Already abbreviating my phony organization.

"No."

"Well, we're a group that offers financial help to families with young children."

That got her attention.

"What for?"

"For the benefit of the children, of course. We particularly want to give young adolescents a chance."

"Yeah, so?"

"So, we offer a few hundred dollars a week in assistance. Would you be interested in learning more about our program?"

She was already calculating. "Maybe that'd be okay. When can I get the, I mean, when can you start helpin' the kids?"

"Well, first I need to talk with Lisa and Teddy. Will they be home soon?"

"Nope." Hope faded fast as her eyes clouded over.

"Do you expect them soon?"

"Forget it. Get the hell out."

"But?"

"I'm not interested, now get out."

"Mrs. Brown, if you'd just tell me where I can find the kids. I can talk with them whenever. Just a short interview then I'll bring you the money. Why, I could stop in later."

"Didn't you hear me, bitch? I said get out!"

"Mrs. Brown, about Teddy? Have you seen him? Perhaps we could work together?"

"Look, bitch, I don't what you're selling and I don't fuckin' care. My kids are my business and you got no right to be snooping around. I know the law. I know where my kids are and I don't need to tell you, so get the hell out before I call the cops."

My patience was gone and the nasally voice I'd affected as Constance Peabody was giving me a headache. Forgetting myself, I lashed out, in my own naturally melodious voice, "A regular PTA president, aren't you, Mrs. Brown? Judging by the track marks on your arms, you're in pretty deep. I don't think you have the slightest idea where either of your children are. I'll find them myself, with or without your help, so if I have to get the police involved, I will."

I slammed the door on my way out. Walking down the stairs, I felt like a total jerk. Here the poor woman was half dead, and I'm yelling at her. She could barely stand up, clearly needed medical attention. The thought of kids living in that hell hole depressed me and I didn't even know them. Perhaps if I'd been cagier, Mrs. Brown might have produced a photo of Lisa or the brother, if she had any. Fat chance. Anyway, it was too late now. A hangover certainly wreaked havoc with my interrogative style.

I stopped at the deli near the car and bought a coke. The guy behind the counter had never heard of Lisa Brown. He suggested I check with the owner who he expected would be back "later." Discouraged and nauseous, I slipped behind the wheel and headed downtown. I wasn't up to wrangling around the station house, but there was no escaping it. I had to file a missing persons report before I went any further. Maybe Lisa had a record, maybe a photograph or something,

I debated stopping back at the office to check on Natalie and get a little more info. I didn't even have a description of Lisa Brown. Gerry would probably laugh me right out of the station, but I was past caring, so I drove on.

Chapter 6

Did I happen to mention that I'd almost joined the force? The pursuance of that career caused the final break with my father. I love him, but we don't get along. He hit the roof when I quit law school. He complained bitterly when I took a job at the University of Massachusetts as a lowly research assistant. He shrugged and looked stricken when I set off to teach in the South End of the city, but the Police Academy was the straw that broke the camel's back.

Even after I explained my reasons, I had the idealistic notice that as a cop I might make a cent in the rampant crime destroying the lives of my young pupils, he stood firm. Since my mother's death, Dad's heart has hardened. His marriage to Rita, the bitch, hasn't helped either. He forbade me to join the Academy. When this had no effect, he warned that our relationship was in serious jeopardy, a topical piece of news. When warning and prohibitions failed to bring me back in line, he and Rita delivered what was meant to end my law enforcement aspirations. They cut off my inheritance. I think he was genuinely shocked, I know she was, when this drastic measure did nothing to stop me.

I've seen little of my father or the home I grew up in since then. We get together sporadically and I keep up with him through my younger sister, Annie, who is still tenuously in the fold. Rita brought a couple of spoiled, somewhat unlikeable children into the marriage, who are now adults. Annie lives in Laguna Beach, California and doesn't get home much.

Truth be told, I was a pretty bad police cadet, at least according to my superiors. I never kept up with the paperwork, never issued enough parking tickets, and never followed police procedures. Just a few of the criticisms. Sergeant Roberts, my supervisor, celebrated wildly when I quit, but I think he secretly misses me. I have kept in touch with Gerry Singleton, a fellow cadet and friend.

Gerry enjoyed my flakiness and laughed at my constant complaining. He was organized and a good honest cop with a spotless record. Not your run-of-the-mill Fall River cop. In a world of machismo, he was gay. If cops were sometimes hard on women, they were brutal to homosexuals, but the taunts and cruelty never seem to get to him. He is one of the friendliest, optimistic and kindest person I know. He's also a great listener, a quality I especially appreciate. Who else walks into a rat hole, taps gently on a door and calls out a friendly hello. With rapt attention, he listens to the most drug-crazed garble, then responds with genuine concern.

I needed Gerry today. Parking in a spot near the station house designated "for police officers only" I strolled in, hoping to find him free. He was out. Tim Cottrell was at the desk. He was sorting through a pile of stuff on the counter: clothes, wallet, beer cans encased in plastic bags, awaiting finger printing.

He looked up as I approached. "Hey, stranger, long time no see."

"Hey, Tim, I'm lookin' for Gerry. He around?"

"Sorry, Rick, he's on vacation. California, visiting family. I hear your sister is in California."

"Great, for how long?"

"Couple of weeks. Left yesterday, not due back till the 8th of May. Anything I can do for ya?"

I picked at the pink mohair sweater on the top of Tim's pile. It was a nice sweater, soft, good quality, except for the buttons which were imitation mother of pearl poodles. How to ruin a nice lookin' sweater.

"I have a missing person report to file but I don't have a description of the kids. There's two of 'em, a boy and girl, ages ten and thirteen Anyone turn up the past few days? They're from the South End, pretty much on their own. Mother is a serious user, usual depressing shit. I wondered if they have a record. Probably not, but you never know. Maybe vice has something? Last name is Brown, Lisa and Teddy."

"Look, I gotta get this stuff catalogued and over to the Lab, then I'll help you. Head down to the computer room and I'll be right back. If you find anything I can check with vice. Don't sweat it. Roberts is out cruising somewhere. Another John's turned up dead. Fill out this form about your MP's and you can complete the rest later, but with no description, they're just gonna throw 'em in a drawer.

I rolled my eyes and grabbed a pen from the can on the desk. "Johns?" I asked, filling in what I could. I left a lot of blanks.

"Some guy was shot in a warehouse down by the river. No leads yet except some drunk who may have been hanging around. Looks like another "John" hit. The fourth one this year. Could be a lady was involved, but who knows. Same old, same old. He threw all the stuff into the box. He looked older than the last time I'd seen him and it had only been a couple of months.

Tim was handsome, dirty blond hair, wide shoulders, tall, angular rugged face and deep, brown eyes. His face, always tan and healthy, had acquired several new lines around the forehead and eyes. Too many lines for a person in his mid-thirties.

"Think you'll stay at the job?"

"Who knows, Rick. It's a job. Wait here a sec while I run these over and I'll be back."

Still thinking about Tim's brown eyes and broad shoulders, I searched through the arrest records. After about fifteen minutes, I'd located three entries for a Lisa Brown. I had finished when he walked in.

"Vice gave me this. Remember, you didn't get these from me. You got five minutes. There's no record, no nothing about the brother, leastwise not in their files."

"Thanks, Tim. I'll be quick."

The file was a thin one, just a couple of sheets of notes and three photographs. A pathetic face stared out at me from the top snapshot. True to her name, Lisa

Brown had dark brown hair, lots of it, tied in a lopsided ponytail on top of her head, errant wisps and strands falling everywhere. Might be beautiful hair, but in this picture it looked like a rat's nest. The slender face beneath the mane was pale, cheeks sunken. Her huge brown eyes were ringed with black mascara, eye liner laid on thick. There was a large, black mark on her left cheek that I first took to be a bruise, but decided with closer inspection, was probably just a smudge of eye makeup. She looked defeated and sick.

Prostitution was the charge. She had been picked up walking Canal Street in the early hours of morning. The bust was in January of this year. Her age was listed as twelve, address, 263 Pond. As a minor she was referred to Juvenile Court and released with follow-up work to be undertaken by Child Welfare. I wondered whether Agnas Brown had ever been contacted. Probably not.

The file held two more photos, one taken the previous October, prostitution again the charge and one a year ago March, for shoplifting at WalMart. The October shot looked similar to the January one, lots of makeup, frizzy hair. The earlier shot however, was markedly different—face fuller, hair neatly combed, no makeup. Despite the gobs of makeup and hair styling in the other photos, she had looked young, but in this photo she looked like what she was, a baby. She had a trace of a smile, like being arrested was a new experience and she was enjoying it. What surprised and alarmed me was the complete absence of fear in her eyes. Here was a fifth grader, dragged into the police station, finger printed, photographed and probably locked up, and she looked like she was on a field trip.

"Seen enough, Rick?"

I jumped as Tim entered the room behind me.

"Yeah, do you remember her?"

"Sorry, you know how it is. We get so many. She's pretty young. Not my department. I probably wasn't even around those nights. 'Course she wouldn't be apt to hang around long. Ruth Channing would have scooped her up within an hour or two."

Ruth Channing was head of Child Services. She ran a halfway house for juvenile offenders, the city's latest attempt to make up for the critical shortage of foster homes. The number of child offenders was growing at an alarming rate and no one had been prepared. Because Lisa was not considered dangerous or violent, she was a low priority candidate for rehabilitative services. In the city today, unless a juvenile is a threat to society, she will bounce around from street to station with a little inconvenience, but no real attention. Nevertheless, I planned to check with Ruth next. She would remember if Lisa had passed through Belmont House. Maybe if we were lucky, Lisa was sleeping one off at this very minute under Ruth's watchful eye.

Tim walked out with me. I stopped at the front desk, now manned by a young officer I'd never met. I filled in a few more blanks on the missing persons form.

"Thanks, Tim, and good luck with the homicide. Let me know if you hear anything about either of the Brown kids, okay?"

"See ya, Ricky. Watch yourself."

It was now almost 2:00 p.m. and I was fading. There was no time to hang around at Dino's waiting for a coffee cab and a sandwich, so I swung by McDonald's drive-in window and ordered a coffee milkshake and a fish sandwich. A poor substitute for Lois's cooking, but it would have to do. I've been told in no uncertain terms by my doctor that both of these items were not to be part of my diet, but fat would have to win out today. The milkshake, in particular, was therapeutic and the fish my only protein of the day so far.

I devoured the sandwich in the parking lot and sipped the shake slowly as I drove up President Avenue, turned right onto Highland, and headed for Belmont House. The Highlands is the ritzy-titsy section of the city, but a few enterprising souls, Ruth Channing among them, had managed to convert some of the grandest residences into facilities to serve the community, despite the neighbors' objections. The huge, three-story Belmont House, once the showplace of a wealthy mill owner, now provided temporary refuge to hoods, punks and all manner of disturbed juveniles.

As I drove up and parked, I spied the lady herself sitting on the front porch in conversation with a sullen looking boy of fourteen or fifteen. As I approached, he rose and slammed into the house. Ruth turned away disappointed, but resigned.

"Why, my stars, Ricky Steele! What a lovely surprise! Come on up and sit down."

A dear family friend, Ruth had gone to grade school with my father and still kept in touch. Rita didn't care much for Ruth, so they didn't socialize anymore, but she and Dad were buddies and Ruth was probably the closest thing to a sister he had. His own sister, Julia, ten years older and now deceased, had been flighty and emotionally unstable. Growing up, she had tormented her timid younger brother. In contrast, Ruth was caring and steady. Never married, she had adopted the city's neediest children. And, she always kept a soft spot in her heart for the lonely, shy friend of her youth.

"How's your dad? You two seeing more of each other these days?"

"No, and I'm not here to talk about him, Ruthie. We saw each other a bit last year, but we're never gonna be bosom buddies."

"I heard all about your caper up in the Berkshires. You never cease to amaze me, my dear."

"Yes, well, that caper has given me yet another career. I'm sure Dad's told you I'm now a licensed private investigator?"

"Yes, he has. Are you here in that capacity or just stopping in for a friendly chat? Do you think you'll ever return to your true calling, teaching?"

"Probably not, Ruthie. Now that I've got my license, might as well use it. I'm looking for a kid, actually two kids. Last name is Brown. Girl is around thirteen, been arrested a few times, shoplifting and prostitution. Her brother is ten, no record that we could find. Ever seen 'em?"

Ruth encounters hundreds of kids a year, but without hesitation, she replied, "Lisa I know, the boy I've just heard about. Tim, Tom, something like that."

"Teddy."

She nodded. "Never met him. Lisa spent some time with us in January, I think it was, but I first met her last fall. She's a tough nut. Not in manner, in fact, considering her life, she's remarkably sweet and sensitive. But she's had to be tough 'cause she's in so deep. Home is a wreck. She and her friend Natalie something or other, have been living on their own for two or three years now. When she came here, the home address given to us was her mother's. I don't think she's lived there for years. Mother was never around when we tried to visit, but no one on the street had any recollections of children being around the apartment. When we finally located her, the mother claimed that the kids had gone to live with an uncle.

"I knew about Teddy, but she'd never say much about him. The first time we released her to an aunt. We subsequently learned Auntie was a fellow street walker, but by then she'd disappeared. Auntie, I mean. Then, after Lisa quit school last fall, there was no way to trace her. When she came in for the January bust, I thought finally, we've got her, now we can really get her some help.

"Unfortunately, it was not to be. The week she came in was bedlam around here. One of our frequent guests, Nicky Forno, was brought in crazed on drugs. He should have been hospitalized, but they brought him here and he immediately stabbed one of the workers with a kitchen knife.

"Lisa stayed two nights, but in the confusion of Nicky's arrival, she bolted and that's the last I've seen of her. We tried, with no success, to locate her. I heard from a couple of the kids that she and a friend lived in an abandoned building somewhere near the river. The address is in her file. When we checked it out, it was empty. I think they move around a fair bit and travel light. There was some talk about an older man, who they are sharing an apartment with, but we never got a name or an address. I figure sooner or later they'll bring her in again and maybe we can do something."

We traipsed into Ruth's office past the double parlors of the old house where a few guests were stretched out watching television. I read the bits and pieces in Lisa's file. Technically I wasn't supposed to see it. I wrote down the riverfront address without much enthusiasm, then thanked Ruth and promised to visit again soon.

It wasn't far so I cruised by the address in Ruth's file. The warehouse had been razed and a new office building was up, ready for occupancy.

My watch read 3:15 p.m. and I figured I'd better swing by the office and check on Natalie. Then, home, dinner, and bed. I could make a few more calls from the office on an insurance case I was finishing up, try to get information out of Natalie and be home by six. No more leg work today, I needed a rest.

Chapter 7

I swung by McDonald's again, this time picking up a Big Mac, some fries, a vanilla milkshake and one of those fried pies. If Natalie was awake and coherent, a little grease might be just the thing. Just the thing to induce more vomiting probably, but it was worth a try.

I pulled the jeep into a parking space and rummaged around in the back. I hauled out a small cooler, dirty, but serviceable, to store the hot food in. If Natalie was still sleeping, I could keep things semi-warm for a while. Nothing worse than cold, coagulated grease. The milkshake I would put in the fridge, or she could have a soda.

My rooting around called to attention my deplorable housekeeping on all fronts— car, home and office. Clothes in the back had been buried for months under old food bags, athletic equipment, garbage, a sleeping bag with feathers poofing out of several moth-eaten spots. Road maps, bags of potting soil and a dried up flat of broccoli that I had purchased three weeks ago and forgotten to plant in the garden were on the back seat. Eying a nearby dumpster, I considered chucking the whole lot and making a fresh start, but my pack rat tendencies won out. I hopped back into the driver's seat and carried on.

It was a five minute drive from McDonald's to my office and I used the time to mull over the situation with my new non-paying client. I didn't mind the money, much. Despite my disinheritance, I had a small trust fund left to me by my maternal grandmother. Not enough to live on, but good in a pinch as a fall back. I used it sparingly between jobs and lived modestly.

God only knew if Lisa would turn up and what condition she would be in. If I kept at this, I would certainly have to visit my new best friend, Agnas Brown, not a cheering prospect. Maybe I'd get some help from Natalie and we would track her down before nightfall. Fat chance.

The outlet parking lot was almost empty when I pulled in at 3:45p.m. Mondays were pretty slow, but this was unusual. Still, I was glad to be spared the aggravation of maneuvering the jeep around the shop-till-you-droppers. I trudged up the stairs and met Cal Bowen, the writer, coming down. We exchanged perfunctory greetings. We both appreciated solitude and privacy, two rare commodities in today's world. He was working late today.

I turned the key and opened my office door as quietly as possible to find the couch unoccupied. Natalie sat behind my desk, legs propped up, drinking a coke and talking on the phone. She had the good grace to look guilty when I entered. She ended her conversation, slid her legs to the floor, heels clattering on the linoleum.

"Hi! I'm feeling a lot better. I borrowed this from your fridge." She held up the soda. Borrowed, that was a good one. "Hope you don't mind."

"Sure, that's what they're for."

I was beginning to wonder if this was all a game and I was fool enough to have played along. If the next words out of her mouth were "Lisa's fine and dandy and just got back from the Mall," I would need to count to ten very slowly. My mouth was dry, my stomach was grinding again. I grabbed a soda. What the hell, a little more junk couldn't hurt, besides the caffeine and sugar might be just what I needed to get me home.

"I brought you something to eat." I plunked the cooler on the desk, opened it and handed her the McDonald's bag. I'd forgotten the milkshake in the car. "Hope you like Big Macs and fries."

I removed my camera from the desk where she had obviously been fiddling with it, and shoved it into the metal locker where I stored all my surveillance equipment.

I had a bunch of lenses for the big camera, as I like to call it, and a little "Canon Sure Shot." The cameras and a good pair of binoculars comprised the sum total of my surveillance arsenal. Photography was not my thing, but I had a steady hand and my pictures were usually adequate for the types of jobs I picked up.

"Great, thanks."

She picked out the lettuce and pickles, but ate the burger and fries.

"Slow down a little and maybe you won't get sick again."

"Oh, no sweat. I'm better now." I eyed her skeptically. "Really, I am."

"So what's new? Has she turned up?"

"No, I was talking to another friend. No one's seen her for days. Hatchet, the person on the phone, hasn't seen her, but Teddy was by this morning. Our roommate, well the guy we stay with, hasn't seen her either."

"Who's Hatchet?"

"She's a girl from our class. Lisa sometimes stays with her if she needs a break. I do, too. She hasn't seen her since we were both over there last week."

"You neglected to mention that you guys were hooking."

"You didn't ask. Besides, that's not all we do and we probably won't do it forever. Anyway, what's the big deal?"

"What's the big deal? You're not even thirteen years old for Christ's sake. Have you even gotten your period yet? Do you have any idea what you're doing to yourself and your body? When was the last time you saw a doctor or had a checkup? You're a mess and from the look of your friend's recent mug shot, so is she.

"What's the big deal? I'll tell you what's the big deal. I'm lookin' at one sick kid, searching for other two. I've got a hangover, no leads and a nagging voice that's telling me to turn you over to Child Services before you finish your fried pie. That's the big deal."

Tears trickled down her sallow cheeks.

"Look, I'm sorry. I know you're worried about your friend. I know you're scared. I know life's hell. I'm not feeling well, that's all."

She sniffed. "You don't understand. She is really missing. Lisa has never done anything like this before. Ever."

"Okay, okay. Give me a few minutes to finish some work. I'll drive you home and we can talk on the way. Lie down and rest. Have another coke."

She got another soda, and then spent several minutes rooting around in my sorry pile of magazines. After throwing aside several *New Yorkers*, *National Geographic*, and *Time*, she finally located one of Bud's old *People* with Lucille Ball on the cover.

With Natalie settled on the couch, I tried to take care of some work, the kind of stuff I usually dispatch during my morning routine. I had a number of bills, two of which I paid, the other three I tossed in the trash. I could wait till the second notice on those. I had a letter from an old client, thanking me for my surveillance and letting me know that she and hubby were in counseling and doing great. I probably should send her an email with congrats, but I didn't feel up to it.

I had a report to type on an insurance investigation. A warehouse fire, suspected arson. Arson seemed to be all the rage this year. In this case, arson had been ruled out. The police had been over everything with a fine-toothed comb. I had ruined several pairs of running shoes and tore my favorite jeans mucking about in the wreckage.

A malfunction in the electrical system appeared to be the culprit. I'd gone over blueprints of the electrical system, taken samples to be analyzed from all parts of the building and snapped photos galore. Apparently, the sprinklers, which were triggered electronically, had also malfunctioned. I finished typing my notes, attached the photos and would email everything to Bud.

I dialed Bud's office number. He seemed to be in no rush for the hard copy of the report and photos and declined my offer to deliver. He said he'd pick them up in a day or two. He likes to stop by the old building. I think he misses his old digs. Not nearly as much fun as his new concrete prefab on South Main. I dropped the envelope in my "out box." Bud had a key to my office and he knew where to look if I was "away from my desk."

"Okay, Natalie. What 'd ya say? We'll talk while we drive. Maybe we should check out your apartment before we go farther. Lisa might've turned up or left a message or something."

Chapter 8

Natalie did not seem eager about the plan to check out her apartment, but she acquiesced. On the drive to 37 Howard Ave, another not so great part of town, we chatted. I stopped several times along the way to jot down notes. My aging brain was so fuzzy. I'd never remember it tomorrow if I didn't take now. I'm almost obsessive about my notes. I jot 'em on post-its, sales slips, market lists, paperback books, any paper handy, then I transcribe them later. Transcribing helps me to organize my thoughts and make sense of things. Sometimes it works, sometimes it doesn't.

The two girls lived with an older guy, Carl. No last name. From what I could gather, he rented his extra room to them on the cheap and otherwise left them alone. There didn't appear to be anything illicit about their relationship unless you counted aiding and abetting minors in growing up too. According to Natalie, he was a bartender at a seedy bar on Front Street and he spent most of his time at the bar, whether working or not. I supposed I would have to stop in for a beer, another cheery prospect.

Natalie explained that they had met Carl through a friend of Lisa's, Billy Linden. She gave me Billy's address which was right around the corner from their apartment. Miraculously, they had been on their own for two years and survived. Natalie had been the first to leave home. Her father sounded like a child molester, no mother in the picture. She had bumped around in foster care since age six and had a couple of siblings she hadn't seen in years. As she talked, I thought about how much support and strength I got from Annie, and from my whole family as a child. Despite her inner demons, my mother had been loving to her daughters. She had kept us safe and secure. How did these shattered children hold it together?

Natalie's last foster home had been, in her words, "a hell hole." Seven foster kids, all screwed up, parents always fighting, kids on their own most of the time.

Lisa and Teddy had lived with Agnas all their lives. Agnas had been raped by an uncle at the age of twelve and became pregnant with Lisa as a result. My sympathy for Agnas rose a tad. Mentally I computed her age, twenty-four Agnas looked fifty. Teddy's father was apparently unknown to him or his mother. Teddy was the only offspring from her years of prostitution.

The kids had attended school until last year, even preschool at the settlement house day care. They had lived precariously on Agnas's wages, but at least they got a free, hot lunch during school. They'd been living in the tenement on Pond since Teddy's birth, locked in their room every night while Mama worked. There seemed to be no extended family in the picture except for Agnas's sister in Tiverton. Apparently she had taken Teddy four years ago, but refused to take Lisa who, in her words, "had already been ruined." By this time Agnas had put Lisa to work nights, right along with Mommy dearest. An-eight-year-old brought a substantial boost in revenue to support Agnas' heroin addiction.

Lisa still attended school. God knows what or how she learned, with only occasional absences for "illness" and her "modeling career." Agnas had been very enterprising in those earlier days and "kiddie porn" paid well. I could not believe what I was hearing. Eight years old? The days of *Mr. Popper's Penguins, Peter Pan* and *Charlotte's Web*. The wee bit of sympathy I'd mustered for Agnas Brown evaporated.

"Lisa's the strong one. When she got out of the house, she got us set up. I'm hopeless, you know? Always cryin' and moanin'. Not Lisa. She hooked up with Billy right away. Knew him through her mom. She got us a place. For a while we stayed with him, but he's got a lot of shit goin' on at his place, so he introduced us to Carl. It's been great. We're on our own, we're savin' a little and we're free from everyone who was hurting us, you know?

"We've got plans. We're gonna save up, get better jobs. We both want to be models, so we keep ourselves thin. Doesn't hurt business neither. Billy's always telling us to keep looking young, if we want to make money, you know? We're both lucky 'cause our boobs are small. We don't need bras yet. Guys pay extra for that. Bras put you in a whole different category. Different customers, different services. Our customers want kids and they pay plenty."

I shuddered and goose bumps ran up my arms. "So Lisa has no contact with her mother at all?"

"Yeah, she sees her. I don't know why, but Lisa feeds her. Brings her shit every week. Canned stuff, bread, milk, fruit. She even cooks her a meal sometimes and leaves it. She always goes when the old bitch is out. I go sometimes. Lots of weeks the food is hardly touched, but she keeps doing it. She won't buy her stuff, drugs I mean, but I think she leaves her money sometimes."

We pulled up to the Howard Avenue address and Natalie hopped out.

"Better let me check it out, see if anybody's home. Carl is kind of a private person."

I waited on the street leaning up against the jeep, trying to decide if I should liberate my .38 Smith and Wesson from the trunk. I bought it a few months earlier and have been religiously going to the range. I'd be better off with a little semi-automatic, but I'm too cheap to go through the rigmarole of acquiring another gun. Natalie reappeared while I was still in the throes of indecision. I decided to leave the gun in the trunk. Probably a dumb move.

Chapter 9

We proceeded into the building, a lovely shade of pink. Paint peeling, loose or missing shingles spotted exterior like an advanced care of leprosy. The foyer smelled of urine and smoke, my favorite sensory combination. There was a man sleeping at the base of the stairway and we stepped over him on our way up.

"That's Chuck. He's always there. Sometimes we feed him if he's conscious. Don't worry, he won't bother you."

"How often is he conscious? Would he have noticed anything funny going on? Do you suppose he's seen Lisa?"

"I already asked him. He's been in New Bedford the last five nights. Didn't get back till yesterday afternoon. He walks so it takes him a while."

We reached the third floor and Natalie jiggled a key in the door of apartment 3-B. There were two other apartments on the floor, 3-C and plain old 3. I could still see a faint shadow on the door where the A had been.

"Come in. It's kind of a mess."

"Don't worry about me. I'm pretty comfortable in messes."

She needn't have worried. The apartment was not ready for the cover of *House Beautiful*, but it looked pretty good. The living room had a sofa, a couple of chairs and a table in front of the sofa with an ashtray holding 3 or 4 butts and some newspapers stacked neatly on one side. The furniture was old and patched, mostly grayish brown tweeds, but it looked comfortable and relatively clean. There were three doors off the living room, one leading to the kitchen the bathroom off of it. I assumed the other two were bedrooms. Both doors were closed.

She pointed to the door on the left. "That's Carl's room. He's not here, but he doesn't like us messing around with his things."

"When will he be back?"

"Who knows, probably not till tonight."

I proceeded directly to the door on the left. Better search now while I had the chance. It was a small, square room with faded cabbage flower wallpaper peeling and patchy in spots. In addition to the bed, neatly made with threadbare blanket and yellowing sheets, there were three staked orange crates, serving as a dresser, a table beside the bed and a small string rug on the floor. The closet door was ajar. I peeked in and spied a couple of shirts, two flannel and one white oxford, several pairs of pants and an old robe hanging on a hook. There were several pairs of shoes on the floor of the closet, jumbled with clothes and other junk. He kept the room neater than the closet, but there wasn't much to keep neat. His few possessions were laid out on the small table or folded in the orange crates, clothes, comb and brush. He had a small notebook under the bed, which contained what looked like bills and other household paperwork, but that was it. Carl seemed to be a man who traveled light and lived simply.

"How about your room?"

"Sure, come on."

Natalie led the way into a small room with two mattresses on the floor. The wallpaper had brightly colored rocket ships, flaming across a darkened sky, perhaps attempting to avoid the water stains and gaping plaster holes that dotted the walls. I tried to picture the little boy who must have fallen asleep staring at these rockets twenty or thirty years ago.

Near the mattresses were two orange crates, same vintage as Carl's, that held the girls' clothes. In contrast to the other room's Spartan closet, this one bulged with clothes. Dresses, sweaters, blouses, hats and pants flew out as you opened the door. No shortage of cash here. I took a cursory look through the assortment of garments, a mixture of gaudy, tacky, and plain old kid clothes. Some sequined jobs in fluorescent colors hung alongside sweats, oversized tee shirts and jeans. The shoe assortment on the floor reflected the same variety. Spike heels were thrown helter skelter among sneakers and flip-flops. The jumble of shoes must present a challenge when one wanted to step out. No telling how long it would take to find a match. By then, your black net stockings would be hopelessly snagged and slumped down around your ankles.

As we went through the closet, Natalie pointed out Lisa's clothes, and we checked the pockets together. We threw whatever paper we found on the mattress to peruse later. Then, we followed the same procedure with the orange crates, which held mostly underwear, socks, and a few tee shirts.

"Aside from Billy Linden and your girlfriend, did Lisa hang around with anyone else?"

"Hmm."

"Do you want to find her or not?" Exasperation crept into my normally melodious voice and I sat down hard on one of the mattresses. "There's not much to go on here, so if you have any other ideas, you better lay 'em on me, now."

"Lisa's pretty secretive, you know? There are parts of her life she never lets me see. I think she sees a guy, or used to anyway, a rich kid, preppy type, that lives in the Highlands. Every time I've tried to ask about him, she tells me to go to hell and mind my own business. I'm not even sure how she met him. She'll sometimes go off for a day, or part of a night and not tell me where she's been."

"What else?"

"When she first met him, last summer, she was real up, you know? Mega happy. She wouldn't talk about him or tell me his name, but she'd say stuff like "we're getting outta here soon, Nat.

"By the end of summer, she'd come back from him bummed. I don't think she saw him at all till around Christmas. When I asked about him she told me to fuck off. That's not like her. I mean, Lisa didn't usually talk to me that way, except about him.

"A couple of months ago, she came home beat up and sick. Stayed in bed two days. I tried to get her to go to a doctor or to the clinic, but she wouldn't. Said it was nothing, but she had a lot of bruises and a black eye. She never said, but I think Mr. Slimeball kicked the shit outta her. She was seriously hurting. We've both been beat up a couple of times, but this was different. I knew it didn't come from no "John" and she knew I knew it was him. She was really down. Far as I know, that was the last she saw the prick. That's all I know. We came and went at different hours. I never saw him or nothin'."

"Did she ever mention where they went, what they did, if they saw anyone else?"

"Nope. I think one time they drove down to the Cape."

"How did she contact him?"

"I think she called him or sometimes they texted, or maybe sent notes? One day I saw her reading something and she crumbled it up when I came in. She always erased all her texts, too. He might've left messages at her mom's. For some reason I think Lisa's mother knew him."

"What about transportation? How do you guys get around? Did she meet him here?'

"Oh, he was older than us, lots older. He could drive and he had a car. I saw the car one day. Least I'm pretty sure it was his. Red sports car. I'm not positive it was him, but one day she got dropped off by a red sports car and she wouldn't say who it was. Only reason I saw it was I heard shouting on the street and I looked out the window. Whoever it was took off fast and burned rubber."

While she was talking, I'd been leafing through the paper scraps we'd found in Lisa's pockets. Most of it was gum wrappers and useless shit, but there were three slips with phone numbers on them, two had the same number with an S. beside it.

Natalie cleared her throat, like she was trying to decide whether to tell me something or not.

I turned and stared at her. "Natalie, if you know something, let's hear it."

"Well, Lisa would kill me if she knew, but she kept a little book. Kind of a diary, where she wrote shit down."

"Do you know where it is?"

"She keeps it under her mattress. She'd die if she thought I'd read it, never mind a stranger."

After a brief search, I located the diary under the mattress I'd been sitting on. It was one of those compact little thick ones with a lock.

"She keeps the key around her neck," Natalie added, assuming that that would thwart any further invasion into her friend's privacy. A part of Natalie seemed afraid of Lisa.

I grabbed a nail file off of the orange crate nearest me and popped the lock. The lines on the pages were small. Lisa used two for each line of her large print, writing with a childish hand, half print and half cursive. Her lettering was round and wobbly. Bud's second grader could do better than this, I thought, leafing through quickly. It appeared she wrote in her diary several times a week, but not daily. At the end there were a number of blank pages and a mini-address book section. She had no addresses listed, but a couple of phone numbers. The same number from the scraps appeared again and another number had been written under it and scratched out. There was a third number beside the word "friends" underlined in red marker.

"I'm beat, Natalie. I've got to get home to bed. Can I keep this for a day or so? I'll take good care and lock it up when I'm done."

"Well, I guess so."

"What are you gonna do? You want to go out for something to eat before I go?"

"No, I can fix something here. I'm pretty tired myself. I haven't slept much the past couple of days. I gotta rest and start workin' again tomorrow. Don't worry, I'll pay your fees. How much are they anyway? I forgot to ask."

"The only pay I want from you is a trip to the doctor's office, first thing tomorrow. Do you have one?"

"No, but I'm fine. I already told you."

"No bullshit, Natalie. That's my price. Take it or leave it. You don't see the doc tomorrow, I drop the case. Since you don't have a doctor, I'll get you in to see a friend of mine. If he can't see you tomorrow, he'll see you by the end of the week. And no working till you've seen him, understand?"

She pouted and shrugged, but agreed to go. I gave her my home phone and cell number and she gave me her cell and another number "over in Billy's building." When I reminded her that she had promised "no work," she said not to worry, that it was just a place to hang.

Part of me wanted to reach out and shake her; the other part wanted to hug her.

"Call me if you think of anything else. I'll be home all night, asleep I hope. You gonna be okay? You can come home with me if you want. I've got an extra bedroom."

"No, I'm good. 'Sides, I gotta be here if Lisa comes home."

I said my goodbyes, descended the stairs, hopped over the still motionless Chuck, and breathed a sigh of relief when I spied the jeep, still waiting loyally by the curb to transport me home.

In no time flat, I was sailing over the bridge. I considered stopping for a ready-made meal at Ally's Country Store, a euphemism if there ever was one. The place was about as close to a country store as the space shuttle, but the soups were great and oh, those pies. Truth was, I didn't have the energy to pull myself out of the car. Heaven forbid I should see someone I knew and be forced to carry on a conversation. I drove straight on by Ally's, figuring I could rustle something up from my meager store.

Chapter 10

I turned into the driveway and breathed a deep sigh. Home. I share a tiny, two-bedroom bungalow with a finicky, scruffy cat, Beakie, who only appears on rare occasions when I least expect her. The house is close to the river surrounded by similar dwellings, same style, same period, early forties prefab-tacky. Actually it wasn't so tacky anymore, with its weathered shingles and new roof. The outside of the house had asphalt shingles and an aluminum roof when I bought it. My sister Annie and I labored long and hard to put on new cedar shingles. The roof I did myself with help from Vinnie, my next door neighbor. Vinnie watched me rip off the old roof, but as I tacked down the tarpaper, he leapt into the fray. Several battles ensued as he attempted to take over as foreman of the job, but when the dust settled, we got the job done in three days, including the garage.

Vinnie's a mechanic, but he works odd hours, like me. Unlike me, he seems to have an unlimited supply of cash. I suspect some of his employment is not on the up and up, but I don't ask. Who cares how he makes a living. He listens to my ranting and raving, helps me at home when I need it, not often, and generally watches out for things around the neighborhood. We have dinner together about once a week. He cooks, I wash. Vinnie acquires a new girlfriend every month, none of whom I've gotten to know beyond a quick hello.

Maddie Stockman, my elderly neighbor to the left, waved from her front porch. She and her husband, Fulty, have lived here for sixty years. They moved in after their marriage at age eighteen Their home has been washed away twice by hurricanes, but they always rebuild and vow to stay until they die.

"Hi, dear, how about joinin' me and Fulty for a cocktail? Not summer yet, but it's pretty warm."

It had warmed up, but it was not warm enough to be sipping drinks on the porch. Maddie was bundled up in a coat, with a blanket over her knees.

"Thanks, Maddie," I shouted. "I'm beat so I'll have to pass for tonight. Tell Fulty hello!" As I headed toward my back door, I heard her call, "Fine, dear, I'll tell Fulty to mix one right up."

Did I happen to mention that Maddie and Fulty are hard of hearing? Deaf would be closer to the truth. They both have hearing aids, which they never wear. Doesn't seem to make little difference anyway. I'd forgotten to shake my head "no" while declining the drink; Maddie's eyesight is fine. I used my last bit of energy to sprint over and catch her before she rose. This time my shouting and "no thanks" delivered six inches from her ear, did the trick. She smiled and settled back in her rocker.

I beat a hasty retreat lest I get caught up in a lengthy, rambling conversation with Fulty. As his hearing diminishes, Fulty has perfected the art of the one-way conversation and happily chats for hours keeping up his end of the conversation while creatively filling in what he assumes your unheard responses would be.

Shutting the door behind me, I gave a cursory glance at the mail on the floor; the usual junk mail, no letters, a couple of bills. I sometimes let the mail go a few weeks before going through it. All those catalogues make my trash heavy. I hung up my jacket on a hook by the door and peeled off my jeans and tee shirt, then I tossed my jeans into my trusty Maytag in the laundry nook by the back door.

The house came with the washer and dryer. I run them about once a month. I've been dropping off my washing at the Little Pearl for years and I don't adjust to change easily. Maybe someday when I learn how to launder without turning everything gray or pink, I'll get some real use out of my laundry nook, for now it makes a handy storage spot. My sweatshirt, turtleneck and underpants followed their pals in the washer. Since my mastectomy and reconstruction, I no longer wear a bra, one of the few perks of breast cancer. I kept my socks on and grabbed a robe, tying it as I walked through the kitchen.

My kitchen is small and compact. It's more like a kitchenette, with all the appliances and cabinets are on one wall. The lovely fake wood grain cabinetry, that I unsuccessfully attempted to paint white, was now full of blisters that bubbled and flaked off a little more each day, giving the cabinetry a "Holstein cow look," all white with dark spots. A real country kitchen.

The sink has a tiny window over it looking out over my postage stamp front yard, with its grass weedy and unmowed. I had to get the push mower out soon or the task would be beyond my strength. I hoped Vinnie would take pity and mow it with his power mower next time he did his. Nine times out of ten, he did.

The opposite kitchen wall was bare except for a large piece of bulletin board. It was covered with notes, notices of upcoming road races that I usually forgot to sign up for or felt too tired to run when race day rolled around, coupons that I clipped and never used, phone numbers, photographs, my calendar and various other stuff I tacked up and promptly forgot about. The only part of the bulletin board kept up to date was the calendar, which I consulted every morning after my run. Next to the bulletin board is a small table, more of a tablette really, where I eat if I'm in hurry. I have a table in the living room in front of a large picture window where I prefer to sit if I'm not too rushed or too lazy to carry the food out of the kitchen.

The kitchen door leads to a hallway. The living room and both bedrooms open off the hallway. There's no upstairs, but I do have an attic. The realtor, Bunny, is also a friend and she gave me a big sales pitch about this hot property and how I could utilize the attic for all kinds of expansion, increasing the house's value. I guess she thought my imagination could conjure up second stories, raised ranches and whole bungalow remodeling. The attic is full of junk.

In fairness to Bunny, the surrounding neighborhood is looking up. Actually it's never been a slum, just a little beach front ricky-ticky. As water views become scarce, however, people are circling like vultures over this blue collar stronghold. I hope us carrion can keep 'em at bay.

My living room walls are pine installed by yours truly under Vinnie's supervision. The pine replaced the washable vinyl walls Bunny had touted so highly. I had a lot of cast-offs from my father's house, given to me during Rita's frequent remodeling frenzies, a couch, a couple of easy chairs and the table in front of the window, maple with turned legs. I've rounded out my furnishings with purchases from Keen Junk, a secondhand shop just down the street. I've picked up some treasures there including a couple of spindle tables, lamps, an old sewing machine in working order for five dollars and an assortment of small tables, picture frames, table linens, and pots and pans.

The only new thing in my living room is a thick, wool rug that I bought last year. It has a sort of Indian pattern of grays, browns and reds. It covers most of the floor and it's soft because I bought a thick pad to go under it. It's my most extravagant purchase. I spied it one day in a carpet store window, when I was in California visiting Annie. I had just finished a case, with paying clients, and had some cash, so I bought it. It reminds me of Annie and California and a sunnier, warmer life.

Two of my most prized possessions are also in my living room. A painting done by my mother, when she was young and a patchwork quilt, also her work. The picture window, in front of which I have my dining room table, is part of an alcove that juts out about two feet from the rest of the room. When I'm sitting at the table on a bright clear morning, I feel like I'm outside, but safe and warm, even in winter. Because it's my favorite place in the house, the picture had to hang there.

The painting is framed in a plain pine frame and shows a plump, tidy little woman carrying a tray. She wears a starched white cap on her head and a blue dress with a white apron. Her surroundings appear to be a Victorian pantry with crockery bowls and milk jugs lining the shelves behind her. She's bustling about her task with an aura of confidence, good cheer and efficiency. There is just the trace of a smile on her lips.

Why mother had chosen this subject, and whether she was someone she knew, I have never known, but I love it. Looking at that little lady makes me smile. It also gives me a sense of security and peace, as if her tidiness and efficiency could spill into my disorganized life. Like Janey Larkin and her blue willow plate and Ma Ingles and her china lady, my little lady goes up first thing when I move to a new home.

When I get disgusted with Dad, I think back to the days after mother's death. He had loved her desperately and his grief was terrible to see. I sometimes entertain the idea that he married Rita to punish himself for making mother's life boring and hellish all those years. By marrying someone dreadful, like Rita, he would somehow atone for some of the wrongs. The theory has a number of holes, but I sometimes cling to it when I need to feel compassion for Dad.

Beyond the living room a sun porch faces the water. Bunny extolled the virtues of this Florida room, prattling on and on about its potential when she first showed me the house. "Oh, Rick, you'll live in this room. So warm and sunny." It was July then. "And the solar heat, not to mention the water view!"

When the December winds blew, with no insulation, single glazed windows, no storm windows, the wind chill in the Florida room was thirty below zero. That first year, I shut it up and waited until the following summer when I replaced all the windows, insulated the walls, floor and ceiling and added a gas stove. Now it's my studio, I do leaded glass windows and lamps on the side.

I learned my craft during the two years I lived in California. Usually I pick up three or four commissions a year, enough to finance my infrequent vacations. I enjoy myself, but don't feel pressured to crank out dozens of windows, assembly line fashion. That's no fun, it's hard on the fingers too. I cut myself a lot.

Glancing wistfully at the work in progress, two side panels for Phil Rubin's front door, I closed the studio door. They were simple, uncomplicated windows, but I just didn't have time to get out to them. Fortunately, Phil was patient. I've already installed six windows in his old Victorian and fixed a bunch of beveled windows that were already in the house.

My bedroom is cozy, good mattress and box spring on a metal bed frame, no headboard, a bureau and bedside table, and a straight ladder backed chair with a broken rush seat. I bought the chair up at Keen Junk and intended to have the seat fixed. It's usually buried under a mountain of clothes, however, so why bother?

My guest room is a train wreck. Mattress on the floor, junk everywhere. This is the room where I throw everything and shut the door. When a guest comes I straighten up by throwing all the stuff into piles in the corners of the room and covering each pile with a sheet. Not the best arrangement for guests who believe in ghosts, but they make the best of it.

I started a bath, then wandered into the kitchen to put on the tea kettle. I decided on lemon tea, then rooted around in the fridge and cupboards and located some moldy cheese, peanut butter and a box of Triscuits. I cut the mold off the cheese and made peanut butter and cheese crackers, and poured a glass of almond milk from a carton I found in the cupboard. Full after nine or ten double crackers, I put the food away, grabbed a banana and my tea and headed back to the bathroom. The water was almost overflowing and too hot so I took out the plug and put on the cold water. I returned to the kitchen to peel a carrot, my daily vegetable, and retrieved Lisa's diary from my bag. Time to find out what she was up to with her mystery man.

Chapter 11

Water temperature perfect I sank blissfully into the tub, water up to my eyeballs. My muscles slowly stretched and relaxed. Eventually I reached for my tea, drying my hands, I grabbed Lisa's diary.

It was the usual kids stuff, with almost no indication of the life she led. If she related something about her day, shopping at the mall, hanging out in the park, whatever, she always left the nights blank. It looked like she'd been keeping the diary for about a year. There was little mention of her mother, except for an occasional—*"Took A. some food on our way to the movies"* or *"A's sick today. I didn't go in. Left stuff at the door."*

She mentioned Natalie, Hatchet, Billy once or twice, and Teddy lots of times, by name, but a few others were mentioned with initials only. "S" figured prominently in the entries and seemed to be the catalyst for most of her writing. The mystery boyfriend. The early entries went along with Natalie's description of her moods. She was wildly in love and assumed they'd be together forever. He was seventeen handsome and of course, perfect in her eyes. She had little written down about where they went. They seemed to spend a great deal of their time somewhere that she simply identified as "the B."

A drive to the Cape was described in more detail, perhaps because they were away from the city, and she felt safer in her descriptions. They'd gone as far a Hyannis, stopping to eat at a *real fancy restaurant.*

The waiters called me "Miss" and helped me pick the best thing to have. S. helped me too. God, I love him so much. On days like today, I know everything is gonna be fine. Like he'll marry me and things will be great. Not sure about Natalie, but she'll understand and after me and S. get settled, maybe she can stay with us. We were gonna go to a motel or back to the B. on our way home, but S. said his parents wanted him home for something. I asked him if I'd get to meet them sometime and he said, 'sure, babe, sure.' I know he loves me. I can't wait. They have a humongous house on Clifton. I had a taxi drive me by a couple of weeks ago. I'd never tell S., but I had to see it. It's beautiful, all those columns and glass.

Later, in bed now, I resumed my reading, becoming more frustrated with every page. "Come on Lisa, give me something." I tried to visualize the homes on Clifton, but columns were a dime a dozen in that neighborhood. What I needed were specifics on the manse.

Most of the later entries about S. were mournful in tone. He had become distant, verbally abusive and had eventually resorted to physical violence.

I don't get it, what's wrong? S. loved me last week and now he's shut me out. He calls me names, says I'm a slut. I can't change that yet, but he knew it when we met, that's how we met. That's the one thing I can thank A. for, the day I met my darling S. I'd die for him, doesn't he know that? I hope he hasn't found a new girl. One of those rich bitches he says he hates. Oh, God, what'll do if he leaves me?

There were a number of pages after this one where she had simply written, *saw S.* no elaboration. Then, an entry in February, *I'm sick, God, I think I'm gonna die. Wish Nat would leave me alone. All over between S. and me. Wish I'd been smarter, even Billy treats me nicer.*

I read through shorter entries about Teddy, Natalie and her other friends. More kids stuff.

After her first break with S., she wrote of feeling suicidal. *Billy can get me a gun, or enough downers to end it.* In March, *Maybe I'll jump off the Braga Bridge. At least my name would be in the paper and I'd be famous for a day. Maybe S. would even feel sorry.* Both accounts of her suicidal despair ended with, *called Friends and felt better.*

Who the hell were these Friends? I wondered, thinking back to the scraps of paper found at the apartment. Bleary-eyed, I had one more piece of business I had neglected in my haphazard investigation today. I dialed Natalie's number with a pad and pencil handy.

She answered on the third ring with a sleepy, "Hello."

"Sorry, Nat, I won't keep you. Just need a quick description of what Lisa was wearing last time you saw her. Oh, and how does she do her hair these days?"

"That's easy. She borrowed my new green stretch pants. They're wicked awesome, bright green, you know the kind you see a lot?" I knew. Fluorescent, glow in the dark. "Her jewel shirt, it's pink. She wasn't dressed for workin', so she didn't have much makeup. Probably had on her Reeboks, not sure. Want me to check the closet?"

"No, thanks, that's okay."

"That's about it. She probably had her hair in a braid, it's real long ya know. And 'cause she wasn't workin', she had on her favorite sweater. It's heavy, that's why she probably didn't need her jacket. Yeah, she always wears that sweater; it's kind of her good luck charm. She got it in Boston last year. We took the bus up for the day and went to all the stores. She bought it in Lord and Taylor for eight-five dollars. It's real soft.

"The color, Nat, the color."

"Oh, yeah, pink. But let me tell you the best part, about the buttons, 'cause it's typical Lisa. Changing things to make 'em special, make 'em hers. Unique, ya know?"

I'd almost drifted off listening to her ramble on, but her last words made me sit up. I knew what was coming.

"Yeah, she hated those dull, rich bitch buttons, you know? Cut 'em off and sewed on cool pearly dogs that she found in a shop downtown. They made the sweater so much more awesome. One of a kind, you know?"

It had to be the same sweater.

"Natalie, did Lisa have a gun?"

"No way. We had pepper spray and whistles. Plus, we knew where to hit someone. Billy taught us. No knives, no guns. Why?"

"No reason, just curious. Go back to bed. I'll call you in the morning about the doctor."

She said goodbye and I hung up the phone, threw my notebook on the floor and closed my eyes. I willed my brain to let go of the case till morning, but I drifted off with pearly poodles dancing in my head. The station house would be my first stop in the morning. I needed specifics on a certain homicide victim. I'd probably have to deal with Sergeant Roberts too. What a dismal prospect.

Chapter 12

The alarm didn't go off I just woke up. It was 5:00a.m. I usually sleep until 6:00a.m., but visions of pearl poodles had haunted my dreams and I was more than glad to bid sleep goodbye. My body felt a hundred percent better than yesterday morning and I went through my usual routine: yoga stretches, three mile walk on the beach and a hot shower. By the time I sat down with my tea and two oat bran muffins, I felt alert, alive and ready to go. My energy would be flagging by two, but I could catch a nap in the office or in my jeep somewhere. A fifteen minute power nap, mid-day, was one of the secrets of my boundless energy, even at this stage of life.

I checked the *Providence Journal*. No mention of a killing in the city. I'd have to wait for this afternoon's *Herald* to get a name for the homicide victim with the pink sweater among his effects. In the meantime, I would talk to the police. I needed details that only they could furnish, if they were inclined.

I prayed Sergeant Roberts would be in a good mood, but that was about as likely as pigs flying. I parked around the corner from the station. Blue-eyed Tim was not on duty this morning. A young woman officer manned the desk.

I bit my lip and said, "Is Sergeant Roberts in?"

"Yes, he's back in his office. Who's looking for him?"

"The name is Steele, Ricky Steele. He knows me and I know my way, thanks. I'll go on back."

She opened her mouth to protest, but then closed it and shrugged. I headed down the hall trying to conjure an approach that would avoid confrontation. Fat chance. Douglas Roberts was tall and slender, he was fifteen years my senior and way past retirement age. Since he refuses to retire, they've chained him to a desk. He has a short fuse, something we have in common. This sometimes makes discussions less than productive.

Peeking round the corner, I spied him, coffee in one hand, flipping through the sports page with the other.

"Sox are gonna be hot this year."

He looked over the wire rims of his glasses. "You're up early. Is this a social visit or have you come to tell me about your latest career? Getting a little long in the tooth for private eying, aren't you?"

The pot calling the kettle black came to mind, but I smiled my best smile. "If I had a dime for every time I've heard that in the past year, I'd be filthy rich. Good morning, Douglas, you're looking well."

"Bullshit."

"Do you have a few minutes?"

"Is this about your own charity case, runnin' after missing kids? Thought you were the darling of the Newport set these days?"

"Look, can we please just talk? I have a license. I'm just trying to do my job. I'm not asking for much, just a little information. Please, I could really use your help."

"Here we go, what is it this time? Access to all our records for the past eighty years? Download every missing person's file from the system? The entire force at your disposal for the day, what'll it be?"

Ignoring his sarcasm, I sat down. "I need information on the dead "John" they brought in yesterday morning. You know, the guy they found shot in the warehouse down by the river."

"Whoa, Steele. You been reading too many detective novels. You know I can't give information to you during an active homicide investigation. What is your interest anyway?"

"I may be able to help you." His eyes registered a tiny flicker of interest so I decided the best course was to tell him most of what I had. I went through the basics of what I knew about Lisa, leaving out the preppy boyfriend part, but mentioning the sweater that tied the two together.

"I know it's the same sweater, Douglas. There can't be two like it. Somehow my missing kid is linked to your homicide. Maybe she was there? She might've seen something, gotten scared and gone into hiding. She's only twelve years old for Christ sake. She's got a ten-year-old brother who might be in danger too. I'm not asking for much, just a name and a few specifics about the scene."

He took five minutes to rifle through papers, open and close file drawers, clean his glasses and even type on the computer. Finally, he grew still and stared at the wall. He was trying to drive me crazy, so I began counting one, two, three, four, five in my head.

"Name's Phillips, Peter Phillips, a legal assistant or somethin'. No record. Not the type to be cruising Summer Street looking for fun, but then, they seldom are. One shot, at close range. Gun's a 45, same gun that's killed three other "Johns" this year. He died sometime Friday night. We'll know the time more precisely after Ernie gets through with the autopsy. No leads, but we're questioning hookers in the area. If your kid is on the streets, we'll pick her up. What's the name?"

"Lisa Brown, but I don't think you'll find her on the streets. She's disappeared. No contact with friends. Nothing. I have a boyfriend to check out, but that's it. Where did Phillips live anyway?"

"Somerset, has a wife and three kids. Wife's a basket case and knows nothing. She swears he was a devoted family man, usual unsuspecting wife crap. Always the last to know. Maybe there was a dark side to old Pete that she never knew about."

"Mind if I talk to her?"

"I guess not, but keep it short, the lady's been through hell and I want to know everything you find out. Get a hold of Cottrell if you get into trouble. It's his baby and I don't want him mopping up another one of your messes. Don't think I won't throw you in a cell to cool off for a day or two, if you rub me the wrong way."

I wrote down Phillips' address and hopped up.

"Great to see you, Douglas."

He grunted and returned to his newspaper.

Chapter 13

I was in the office by 8:15 a.m I made a second cup of tea, then settled at the desk with a note pad and phone numbers. My first call was to Phil Rubin. I caught him at home, miracles of miracles, one of those rare mornings when he wasn't out running a twenty mile loop before sunrise.

"Hey, Rick. Long time no see. Where you been keeping yourself lately? We waited for your last Saturday, three quarters of an hour, Mary, Chris and I did the hills course. You were supposed to meet us, remember?"

"Sorry, Phil. Maybe next week, if my body cooperates. I've been feeling kind of tired."

"No excuses."

"Phil, I've got a favor."

"Oh, no, you don't. I love ya, Rick, but I'm not taking over the membership job. That's your baby."

"Relax, I'm not calling about the club."

Phil and I belong to the Spindle City A.C. (Athletic Club), actually we founded it, a loose bunch of runners who get together to run for fun and to socialize. We train together, put on two or three runs a year for charity and hold meetings once a month that hardly anyone goes to except Phil, yours truly and a few loyal diehards. I'm not a clubby sort of person, but the SCAC suits my style. Low dues, loose structure and good people. Most Saturdays we get together for a long run and Wednesday nights we do track work at the high school before jogging a few easy miles through the Highlands.

"My windows ready?"

"Dream on."

"Aw, Rick, my mom's coming to town next week."

"It'll be soon, Phil, I promise. Listen, what's your day like?"

"Crazy, booked solid. Why?"

"I've got this sick kid. A case I'm working on. She needs someone to check her over."

"I'm a dermatologist, Rick! I can't be fooling around with a sick kid. What's the matter with her anyway?"

"She's a street kid, a hooker actually. Hasn't been takin' good care of herself. Poor diet, undernourished, you know, the usual."

"No, I don't know the usual. I don't know diddly squat about street kids and their ailments."

"Phil, you're selling yourself short. Why, you graduated top in your class."

"Stop right there. I definitely don't have time for your bullshit flattery. Oh, what the hell, bring her around noon. I'll take her on rounds with me. Maybe someone at the hospital will look her over."

"Thanks, Phil."

"You owe me, girl. I'm dragging your ass 12-15 next Saturday and we're running the Hilltopper course, and, those windows had better be ready when I—"

"Bye, Phil, you're a sweetheart." I hung up before he could elaborate on my future in "jogger hell!"

My next call was the S. number. I held my breath, dreaming up a good line of bullshit to reel out when the upper-cruster or one of their underlings answered the phone. I was totally unprepared for the deep, friendly voice that answered, "Pro Shop, this is Don."

"Uh," I sputtered. "Is there a tournament this morning? I'm thinking of playing a quick nine."

"Well, the ladies will be out till noon. Are you part of the ladies day group? Who's calling please?"

Ignoring both his questions, I altered my voice slightly, replying nasally, "Thank you, dear, I'll hold off for today." I didn't want him to recognize my voice later on when I went out to make inquires in person.

I grabbed the Fall River yellow pages under the phone. Looking under "Golf Clubs," I matched the number I'd reached at the Pro Shop. It belonged to the Aquinessett Country Club, the area's most exclusive golf and tennis club.

Built nearly a half a century ago in the rolling farmland and woods of Aquinessett, just north of the city, it was the verdant paradise of city executives at the end of a long hard day at the office, or perhaps any time of the day. Anyone with the right connections and the fifty grand initiation fee, not to mention the ten thousand a year in dues, was free to frolic on the emerald green lawns to his or her heart's content. The indoor pool complex, new several years ago was reputed to be a "one of a kind," visited by club representatives from all over the country. Paradise in humble Spindle city. Due to its exclusive clients, security was tight. I might have to have help on this particular foray, and I knew just the man for the job.

I've known Mark Fallon for about a year. We met when I was interning as a PI. Still slightly green around the edges, I had taken a job trailing a friend of his, Russ Palmer, hired by Russ' live-in girlfriend. Tara suspected he was seeing someone else and she was right, but Russ didn't stop at one someone, I counted six different ladies in the course of my investigation. He kept me busy. However, my harried surveillance of Russ' peccadilloes came to an abrupt halt one morning three weeks into the job.

When I arrived at the office, at my usual time, I discovered a large manila envelope pushed under the door. It was too early for mail delivery so I assumed that it had been hand-delivered, probably Bud leaving work for me. I headed to the phone, intending to phone him, but as I tore open the envelope, I stopped in my tracks. I was looking at an 8 x 10 glossy of yours truly! The envelope dropped to the floor just short of my desk. Stunned, I read through an incredibly detailed investigative report, complete with clear, professional quality pictures. It took me a minute to place where I was in the several dozen photographs, but then I realized I was looking at an almost complete history of my last three weeks.

There I was, photographing Russ Palmer peeking through the plate glass window of a restaurant where he was dining with one of his many ladies, taking a break for a McDonald's fish sandwich. Lovely shot of me chewing. "Yum-yum" was written across that one in red marker. There was even a shot of me going into my house after a run. I had on shorts and a singlet. "Great legs" was scrawled across the back of that one. Who was this person who knew where I live? What the hell did he want?

Five minutes later, I had my answer. The phone rang, the voice deep, sensual and unfamiliar. "What did ya think? Have I got a future as a PI?"

I slammed down the phone.

Mark Fallon, best friend to the zealously unfaithful, Russ Palmer, didn't stop at that phone call, but made several more over the next few weeks. Curious, I finally agreed to meet him for lunch. He was good looking, intelligent and fun to be with, and has a warped, but wonderful sense of humor. It didn't hurt his case either when he told me over and over that he couldn't resist following me 'cause I was so gorgeous and interesting. Lies, of course, but I'm a sucker for flattery.

A self-employed woodworker by trade, his cabinetry, most bureaus and reproduction desks and secretaries, is exquisite and commands a high price. He's s terrible flirt and miles too young for me so we haven't taken things to the next level, and probably never will. Who knows though. Maybe, someday?

Mark leads a Spartan existence, except for golf. Once a golf pro, he's still a familiar sight on the links and picks up games whenever he can. He has lots of connections with the golfing set and I was sure he'd know this Don, whatever his name, out at Aquinessett. I was also sure he'd jump at the chance to help.

I'd have to go over to see him. He didn't have a phone in his workshop and I knew if I left a message on his machine, he wouldn't get it until late tonight, if at all. With any luck he'd agree to spend the afternoon on the links. I'd have to catch him early.

My next call was to Nat to tell her about the doctor's appointment. She hadn't heard from Lisa. I decided not to tell her about the sweater.

"Thanks, Ms. Steele, I mean Ricky. Don't worry, I can get there on my own, no problem."

"I'll pick you up at quarter to twelve, Nat."

"Well, okay. What do ya think it'll cost?"

"Nothing. Dr. Rubin is a friend and we have an arrangement. He owes me."

"Thanks." Her voice sounded soft and fragile, like she was about to cry.

"Take care," I added, my own voice slightly gruff, to hide the fact that I, too, was choking up. "Eat a good breakfast and I'll see you in awhile."

Before we rang off I asked her the name of Lisa and Teddy's aunt. She gave it to me, but said, "Won't do no good."

Apparently Teddy had stayed with them up until a couple of months ago but had run off 'cause Uncle Ralph was "fooling around with him." Aunt Peggy, no last name, had done nothing to intervene. Natalie found a phone number and read it to me. I rang off trying the other number, next to "Friends" in the diary.

On the first ring, a voice came on. "Friends On The Line. I'm here to help. My name is Karen."

I'd reached the local suicide hotline. "Friends" had been around a long time, probably ten years, but it had just recently caught my attention because an old schoolmate of mine, notice I didn't say friend, had taken over as head. Her name is Lola Richards.

Thinking quickly, I said, "Hi, this is a friend of Ms. Richards, is there a number I could call to make an appointment with her?"

Reluctantly Karen gave me the number, which I dialed, reaching Lola's secretary. She wanted to know the nature of my business. Was I a fundraiser, or what? I told her the nature of my business was personal and that Lola would know and understand. I stated emphatically that I needed to see her today. I was praying Lola was a late riser and was not in the background ready to contradict my assertion of close personal relationship. She finally penciled me in for two o'clock.

I looked up Peter Phillips' phone number in Somerset, but decided I would be better off popping in on Rachel Phillips unannounced.

Chapter 14

As I stuffed notebooks and papers into my purse, Bud Dixon tapped on the door.

"Hey, Rick, where ya been? Haven't seen you in a week or so. Gets dull downtown without one of your frenetic visits to break the monotony."

"Believe it or not, Mr. Main Street, some people have work to do. Do I get any cash for all this?"

I handed him the report I'd completed the previous day. He smiled and gave me a pile of folders in return.

"Check is buried in that pile somewhere. Use some of it to take out a few magazine subscriptions will you? And, call an upholsterer, this place looks like shit."

"No, siree, this money is for me. Maybe I'll take a nice vacation. I'll need one. How urgent is this batch?"

"Not very, but if I tell you that, you won't drag your heels too much, will you?"

"Me, drag my heels?"

He laughed. "We've already decided to pay. We just need the paperwork for the files. Pretty routine, so I won't waste your time goin' over 'em unless you want to go to breakfast with me?"

"Bud, my dear, some of the world is almost ready for lunch, but thanks. Another day.Gotta run. Say hi to Mary and the kids for me. Am I gonna get a dinner invite soon?"

"Mary will call you. Take it easy and be careful. At least my jobs keep you out of trouble."

I left Bud chatting with the real estate appraiser down the hall. As I headed out I was nearly sideswiped by an early morning bargain hunter turning into the parking lot doing at least 30 mph. It was only 9:30 a.m., the outlets didn't open until ten a.m. Maybe she needed the half hour to sit in her car and plot her attack strategy? I gave her a glare, which she most likely did not notice, then made an exaggerated swerve out of her way.

Mark's workshop is an old, converted mill building located in Battleship Cove. At the edge of the Taunton River, the Battleship Massachusetts, Big Mamie as the natives call her, sits proudly, flags flying, along side a World War II submarine, a destroyer, PT boat and a bunch of other stuff. War memorabilia has never been one of my "passions."

Near the docks was a new building, headquarters of the Heritage Association, a group designed to promote civic pride in the city's textile, capital of the world past and its outlet capital of New England present. It was a beautiful building with lots of interesting stuff about the old mills.

People were always dumping on the old mill city, calling it somewhere to get in and out of fast, a wasteland of empty factories and unemployed laborers, outlet central, the list went on and on. But I love the city of my birth with its patchwork of ethnic neighborhoods and hundreds of historic buildings from triple decker row houses to three-story mansions on the hill, their widow's walks peeking up above the treetops to gaze down at the waterfront below. I hated that the city's biggest claim to fame and infamy was Lizzie Borden's ax murder. Not as bad as New Bedford's reputation after the Big Dan rape trial, but a raw deal nonetheless. What about the Rolling Rock, the Flat Iron Building, the Historical Society, and of course, Battleship Cove and the Heritage Museum? Forty whacks indeed!

Farther down along the street was the Marine Museum. It housed a small, but impressive collection of maritime relics, most notably a large collection of artifacts from the steamship company that operated out of the city during the gilded age, before mass transportation and automobiles came into full swing. Ships from the line carried passengers on luxury cruises back and forth from New York, via Long Island Sound. My grandmother often talked about the cruise she had taken as a young bride, when she returned home covered with bed bug bites. They don't dwell much on that kind of stuff at the museum. No bed bugs encased in glass on display, but the collection is interesting all the same. The building also houses a growing collection of "Titanic" memorabilia which draws limited interest from people not raised in the area. Alas, none of the steamships ever hit an iceberg and sunk two miles beneath Long Island Sound taking Clifton Webb along with them.

Mark's workshop was in the old mill building adjacent to the museum. It was owned by the Museum Foundation. Someday they hoped to extend their collection into this building. At present, they rented the cavernous space to several local artists and crafts people.

Parking the jeep, I felt my heart race. He might be young enough to be my son, but Mark Fallow never falls to bring color to my cheeks.

Chapter 15

I surveyed my reflection in the plate glass window on the side door. A disaster as usual, jeans worn, but clean and as always too tight, too many coffee cabs and Big Macs. Ratty hair and ragged sweater, jacket, everything a mess. I always hope people will focus on my steely blue eyes and ignore the rest, not to mention the wrinkles and sagging chin.

A sander hummed as I walked into the shop. He was bent over a piece of pine, sawdust flying. As I approached, he straightened up and he wiped clean the spot he had been sanding.

"Take a little too much off did ya?"

I kept my voice light and breezy He looked great in sawdust, face tan from working outdoors, blue eyes the same faded blue shade as the carpenter's apron he wore. With great self-control, I resisted the urge to throw myself at him.

"Hey, Rick, where ya been? Been tryin' to reach you for days."

"Oh?"

He smiled, a killer smile and moved forward to hug me.

"Hey, you'll get me covered with sawdust and I'll itch all day!"

He ignored me, advancing to within inches.

I put out my arm." Halt, big guy. That's close enough. You're way too young, as I've told you a million times."

"Bull."

"Please?"

He backed off and sat on a stool. "What's up? Actually, before you start, I really was trying to get you. There's a party at the museum a week from Friday, the 6th. Some kind of fundraiser slides and shit. John needs help setting up. Wanna come? Probably won't last long then we can go out to dinner afterwards to celebrate your birthday."

"My birthday will be long past by then." Shocked that he knew my birthday, I then remembered that he had an entire dossier on me. "Sounds okay, but can I let you know Friday?"

He nodded, smiling at my flustered state.

"I've got a favor to ask you."

"Gonna cost you. And I don't want your money."

"Very funny. This is important." I quickly related the information about the case, filling him in on most of the particulars. I trust Mark, maybe not with my nonexistent love life, but he's discreet. He sometimes helps me sort things out. As I suspected, he knew Don Heckman at the Pro Shop.

"Always up for a round at Aquinessett, but I've got a shitload of work. Does it have to be today?"

My look told him it did. I started relating the sad saga of the kids, and he raised his hand. "Okay, okay, Steele, I'm in. Sucked into another one of your cases. At least this time there is a round of golf in it. What do you get out of it? Sounds like another charity case. Hey, here's an idea. Why don't you take the afternoon off and we'll both play? We could work as a team; I could give you private lessons. You'll probably want some hip work, I'm guessing? You could bring me up to date on all your cases. I like to keep abreast of things you know."

He moved closer.

"Aquinessett has some nice, secluded spots, perfect for the kind of lessons you need, and the course will be empty on a Tuesday afternoon. What do you say?"

I declined his invitation and said goodbye, asking him to call that evening with whatever he learned from Don. Walking backwards, I watched his every move. Another grab and I was his, there's only so much resistance in one sex-starved body.

Chapter 16

Back in the jeep, I was planning a trip to Somerset to visit Peter Phillips's widow when I realized how close I was to Natalie's apartment. On the off chance she might be ready to go, I decided to swing by. She was.

"Where are we going?"

"Thought we'd pay a call on your friend Billy Linden."

"Geez. I don't know. Billy don't get up all that early, and he's kind of a grouch in the morning, you know?"

"I like to catch people off guard. You wanna come or not?"

"Well, sure, okay."

As we pulled up in front of the building, she pulled at her jersey, yanking it down to reveal a nonexistent cleavage. The v-neck was practically at her waist by the time I'd shut off the engine.

"Get that shirt up where it belongs, young lady! You're not working now and we're not paying a social call on Mr. Linden."

"But—"

"Pull up the shirt or sit in the car."

"Okay." She was pouting, but the shirt slowly crept back into place. "Don't never call me young lady again. That's bullshit."

"Point taken. Let's go."

Number 151 was another candidate for "Tenement of the Month." Gray with black trim, desperately in need of a paint job and unlikely to get one in the near future. Unless this neighborhood fell prey to yuppie expansionism and went condo, there wasn't much hope for this dilapidated bohemian. The front door stood ajar, the glass panels of the door frame long since broken and boarded up with moldy particle board. So much for security.

"Come on," she called already ahead of me. "It's back here."

Billy's apartment was on the first floor. There appeared to be three apartments on each of the three floors of the building. I knocked and held my breath.

A few minutes passed and I raised my hand for a louder knock, when we heard scuffling sounds from within. I lowered my arm and waited. After a series of metallic clicks, a deadbolt collector no doubt, the door opened. Before us stood a startling vision in a beige terry robe, black slippers and a hair net, drawn over a pointy head of limp, thinning, greasy hair. His face was pockmarked and pinched like a wedge of swiss cheese. I stared at the extraordinary visage, squinting back at me, half-asleep and none too happy. Why would anyone open the door in such a ridiculous get-up?

"So?" As he spoke, I was reminded of a character from the old *Laverne and Shirley* television show, although Squiggy was better looking and way more affable, not to mention dignified.

"Hi, Billy!"

"What the fuck, Remy? Do you know what fucking time it is? Haven't I told you to stay the fuck away from me before fucking noon?"

He was definitely experiencing word retrieval problems, no doubt substituting fuck for all those pesky little words that refused to kick in when he needed them."

"Billy, come on."

Nat was cringing, recoiling perhaps fearing retribution. Billy grabbed her bony little arm and twisted it back in a most unnatural position, at the same time he attempted to shut the door.

I stuck my foot in the door jamb.

"Let her go, asshole."

I grabbed ahold of the slimy lapels of his robe and prayed that he didn't have a .45 in his pocket since he still had one hand free.

"What the fuck?" he squeaked and released Natalie, who fell backwards.

"We need a few minutes of your precious time, Mr. Linden. Thanks so much for asking us in." I pushed past him, keeping Nat behind me.

"Who the fuck are you?"

"I'm a private investigator. I'm looking for Lisa Brown."

"So what the fuck you want from me, a fuckin' medal or somethin'?"

"Have you seen her?"

"No and the bitch owes me money so I won't fuckin' see her sorry ass till she fuckin' poor again. Now get the hell out. I ain't talkin' to no fuckin' middle-aged cop."

"Look, wedgeface, I'm not a cop and I'm not interested in spoiling your thriving business (another lie, I actually felt like strangling him with the belt of his robe). I just need information."

"I don't hafta tell you a fuckin' thing, bitch."

He stepped farther back into a room furnished in naugahyde and fake fur. As he noticed his reflection in a long, dusty mirror, he yanked off the hair net and stuffed it in his robe pocket. His black hair, that little there was, lay flat and lifeless, his skin gray. If I had to guess, I'd say he was in his late thirties.

He flopped down on a sofa and glared at us. I settled gingerly into an easy chair covered with zebra stripes. Nat sat on his left, her body tense.

"Mr. Linden, how long have you known Lisa Brown?"

"What's this fuckin' Mr. Linden shit?"

"Billy, how long have you known Lisa?"

"Couple of years. She and Remy came around lookin' for work after they split from home. They always do, these kids. 'Course I knew Lisa from her old lady. Aggie and I go way back. Her kid was a popular piece few years ago, long braids, freckles. Some guys'll pay plenty for that."

Fighting a wave of nausea, I stepped forward. "That's enough. I'm not interested in your filthy business."

"Look, bitch. I don't need to fucking be talkin' to you. I'm doin' you a big fuckin' favor just lettin' you in. Why don't you ask your little friend. She's the one who knows where to find the Brown bitch, not fuckin' me. Those two fuckin' bitches are thick as fuckin' thieves."

"But, I don't know, Billy! That's the problem! I hired Miss Steele 'cause Lisa's gone. She disappeared and I'm scared."

"Well, good thing that ain't my fuckin' problem, now ain't it?"

"Could we just stick to the point? What can you tell me about Lisa? Any new customers lately? Any regulars givin' her trouble? Have you seen her this week?"

"No, to all your questions. I don't know nothin'."

"Where'd she go when she was workin'? I mean, she didn't take tricks to her apartment."

"Ask this little cunt. She knows. There're rooms upstairs, but she ain't in any of 'em. I check 'em myself each night and lock 'em up. Believe me, she ain't here. Sometimes they go to motels in the area, too. Route 6 has a couple."

"We haven't been usin' motels for a while, Billy. You know that."

"Don't fucking yank me around, Remy. I know you two been skimming off the fuckin' top. I'm missin' out on half your action these days and don't fuckin' think I don't know it."

"I'd like to see the rooms upstairs."

"No fuckin' way!"

"It'll only take a minute, I'm in a hurry." I rose and walked toward him, Nat still cowering behind me.

"Okay, okay, but make it quick."

He led the way up. We checked each room, including the closets and bathrooms. Twice I heard scurrying and recognized the sound. Rats, and by the sound of it, big ones.

There wasn't much to see. Each room had a bed or mattress on the floor and a couple had small bedside tables with lamps. Two of the rooms on the third floor were lit by bare light bulbs, dangling from the ceiling on frayed wires. Depressing. When most twelve and thirteen year-olds were at soccer practice and having slumber parties, Lisa and Natalie spent their days and nights in this hell hole, enduring unspeakable horrors.

As we descended, I asked, "Where else mighta she gone?"

"Nowhere I fuckin' know about. I'm not her fuckin' mother. Maybe she skipped town. It's been known to happen."

"Don't you think it's odd that she didn't tell Nat, if she was skipping town?"

"Don't know, don't fuckin' care. These cunts ain't got no fuckin' loyalty. No sense of right and wrong neither."

"Oh, and I suppose you do?"

"Look, lady. You've had your five minutes. Now get the fuck outta my house. I got other girls to worry about."

As I pushed Nat out in front of me, she called out, "Bye, Billy."

"Remy. I need you tonight. Six sharp. I got a bunch of guys comin' in, some convention or something."

I shoved Natalie out the door in front of me. "Sorry, Billy. Nat's on vacation. Don't call us, we'll call you."

"What the fuck? He followed us into the street, shaking his scrawny white fists.

I turned back and gave him a glare. "Look, asshole. I just told you, Nat's on vacation. She's seeing a doctor and she's gonna rest and recuperate. I don't want you near her. If I find out you're harassing her, I'll come back and shove your hair net down your throat."

"You and who else? You fuckin' think I'm intimidated by a fuckin' grandmother?"

"This grandmother has friends. Now stay away from Nat, or you'll be more than sorry. Do I make myself clear?"

"Yea, fuck you too. Who the fuck do you think you are?" He whipped me the finger, before retreating into his rat infested lair.

Chapter 17

I delivered Nat into Phil's capable hands. In his own, bespectacled way Phil's very cute and I could see she was interested. As we stood chatting, she made several attempts at lowering her jersey, but icy glares from yours truly kept the cleavage under wraps. As soon as I was out of sight, I figured the v-neck would be down around her navel, but Phil could handle it. I watched them walk away and my heart constricted, thinking about the childhood of which she had been robbed.

Phil was giving Nat a ride home so I decided to swing over and pop in on Rachel Phillips before my two o'clock appointment with Lola Richards. The breeze felt great as I cruised over the Brightman Street Bridge into the burbs. Peter Phillips's widow lived in a subdivision known as River Glade, about a mile from the bridge, and the river too. The gate house was shaped like a gazebo and a fake wishing well stood on a tiny mound, or "the Knoll," as the sign read, right inside the gate. Maybe the homeowners throw pennies in the well and wish their houses were closer to the river.

I pulled up to the guardhouse and gave the attendant my brightest smile. "I'm here to see Rachel Phillips. I have authorization from the police department—just a slight exaggeration—to go in." He let me pass and picked up the phone as I departed, presumably to warn Mrs. Phillips.

The house was at the end of the street, its side yard bordered by a tall, chain link fence that ringed the perimeter of the subdivision. The Phillips lived in a raised ranch, distinguishable from its neighbors in color only, dark blue on the top half, the lower half brick. The garage was painted white, the trim and the garage doors the same blue as the house. Daffodils bloomed in neat bunches in front of the shrubbery and beds of impatiens surrounded a small dogwood tree on the front lawn. The lawn was pristine, loaded with chemicals no doubt. My lawn might not have a blade of real grass, but at least the weeds are chem-free.

I parked on the street and strolled up the brick walkway to the front door. As I reached over to ring the bell, a woman early sixties opened the door.

"Hello, can I help you?"

Her hair was neatly coiffed, and she wore a flowered golf skirt with a matching green top and green espadrilles. The mother or mother-in-law?

"Hi, I'm Ricky Steele, a private investigator working with the police department on a case related to Peter Phillips's death. I wonder if I might have a few words with his wife, Rachel? Is she at home and able to talk? I won't take long, I promise."

"I'm Rachel's mother, Emma Whiting. Rachel is not feeling well as you can imagine. Perhaps in a few weeks she'll be up to your questions, but I am sorry I really must protect her right now. She's already spoken to the police several times and told them everything she knows. I can't imagine there's anything new to be gained from your questioning her, except heartache and upset. Now, if you'll excuse me, I have grandchildren who need me."

"Please, Mrs. Whiting, I am so sorry for your daughter's loss, I really am, and I wouldn't dream of disturbing her if this were not so important. What I have to ask can't wait several weeks. There's a young girl's life at stake. She may be involved, a witness to your son-in-law's murder. She may know who killed him. I need help. I'll be brief, just give me five minutes, please."

"Listen here, my daughter is not up to any questions." Shaking now, her eyes rimmed with tears, she glared at me. I was beginning to feel like shit, wondering if maybe I could do without Rachel Phillips's two cents, after all when a voice called from within.

"Mother, that's enough. This is ridiculous. Let Miss Steele in like I asked you to."

Reluctantly, Emma Whiting allowed me to enter the living room where her daughter lay on a couch. She started to sit down beside her daughter, but before she landed, Rachel said, "Mother, Bobby's been calling you for ten minutes. Do you suppose you could go out and see what he wants? He's around back. Please don't let him climb on the fence. Go on, please. We'll only be a few minutes and then I'll be out."

Her mother cast a look of concern at her daughter, then retreated. Rachel rose to a sitting position as I approached and patted the seat beside her. A thin, fragile looking woman, she had fine, straw-colored hair, shoulder length. Her natural color, I guessed. Her skin was fair and unblemished, except for blotches around her eyes and a red nose from crying. She wore a light, pink sweat suit with a white turtle neck under it. The armholes hung down, miles too big for her thin, pale arms. Probably lost ten pounds in the last two days. Grief does that.

"I'm sorry to barge in."

"It's okay. Don't mind mother. She's a trifle overprotective." She gave me a wan smile.

I went through the case to date and explained about Lisa's disappearance. I ended with the discovery of her sweater among Peter's things the night of the murder. This last part elicited a fresh spate of tears and shaking of the head.

"I don't understand it. Everyone's been asking me if I knew. They keep asking how often and for how long Peter has been seeing prostitutes. How would I know such a thing? I'm sorry, Miss Steele, but I still can't believe it. Peter was the most caring, sensitive loving husband. He seemed content and happy with me and the kids. I just can't imagine him with a prostitute. My God, he was petrified of AIDS and scared the kids would come into contact with the virus through school or sports. I can't imagine that he'd take the risk himself. It just doesn't make any sense."

"I don't know what to tell you, but there could be another explanation. At the moment I'm not sure what it might be, but maybe my investigation will turn up something. Outside of his job, how else did Peter spend his time? Did he have hobbies, play any sports?"

"He has a buddy he plays… played tennis with once or twice a week. At the Somerset Racket Club in the winter, summer on the courts here in the Glade. There are six courts up the street around the corner. "She gave me the friend's name and I dutifully wrote it down. "And, just recently, he took up golf."

"Where did he play?"

"He usually played at Touisset, the public course, but honestly I didn't pay much attention. Golf is not my thing."

Rolling my eyes and shaking my head in agreement, I asked, "What was your husband's job like? Anything unusual goin' on there?"

"He was an assistant in the District Attorney's office. He worked at the Courthouse most of the time, but you probably know that. This was his second year. We moved in here right after he passed the bar. We, well I, wanted to be near family and friends.

"Peter worked on all kinds of cases. He didn't talk too much about work, but lately he seemed really preoccupied with something. Sometimes cases came up that got under his skin. He was working a lot of nights lately, but that's not unusual when he's behind. Now the police are telling me he wasn't working, but that he was with a prostitute." She broke off and sobbed, bony shoulders trembling.

"First off, don't believe everything the police tell you. They're just fishing. They didn't know your husband. Do you know what he was working on? Anything about it?"

"No, I asked him last week and he just said, "Don't worry, hon." Said it was something big that would shake up a lot of people if his hunch was correct.

"He promised he'd get to the bottom of it before Disney. We were going to take the kids out of school the last two weeks and go to Florida. Peter always said they never learn anything from May on. The teacher in me wanted to protest, but I bit my tongue."

"Did he say anything, do anything differently when he cam home lately?"

"Not really. He was pretty tired, but spent a fair amount of time writing in his diary. He keeps it on and off, but he's been pretty religious about it lately. That was funny too. He always leaves his diary at home, in his desk, but lately he's been keeping it in his briefcase and taking it to the office.

"Is it there? Do you have it now?"

"No. That was the first thing I looked for when I found out about the prostitutes. I thought the diary might explain, but the most recent one is missing and all the previous diaries have no mention of anything like that. He often wrote about his cases. As I said, they unsettled him sometimes, and he loved playing amateur detective. All the diaries are in his desk except the latest one. In fact, his briefcase is missing. I called the office today and asked. Jeanie, the secretary, looked everywhere and couldn't find it. Tomorrow I'm going in to collect his personal things. I'll check again."

Begging her to call if the diary turned up or if she remembered anything else, I gave Rachel Phillips my card and scribbled my home and cell numbers on the back. I expressed my sympathies again, and thanked her, promising to let her know if I found out anything related to her husband. I liked her and I hoped the investigation would clear away the cloud hanging over her husband's memory. Unlikely there was another explanation for his whereabouts that night, but who knew?

It was nearly 11:00 a.m. and I hadn't gotten any closer to Lisa. I pulled out my notebook and looked up the phone number for Lisa's aunt and uncle. My cell phone was dead, as usual, and there was no phone booth visible within the confines of the "Glade," so I pulled out and drove along Route 138 until I came to a gas station with two phone booths at the edge of the lot. I dialed the number and waited. Natalie had not given me a last name for these people, just Peggy and Ralph. I'd have to ad-lib, the familiar, old friends routine, if anyone answered.

A voice snarled. "What 'd ya want?" Definitely not Mr. Rogers.

"Hello, may I speak to Peggy please?"

"Ain't here, who's lookin' fer her?"

Just the kind of man I admire, gets straight to the point, no bullshitting. I wished I knew his last name; I didn't feel we were on intimate enough terms for me to address him as Ralph. "I'm a friend of hers. Any idea when she'll be home?"

"Any friend of Peg's would know she works till five, now who the hell is this?"

I put down the receiver at this juncture. Old Ralph had been more helpful than he knew. I would call back after five and pray that Peggy answered.

Chapter 18

It had been a while since my muffins so I headed back into the city and swung by the Little Pearl to pick up my laundry, then decided upon lunch at Bella's downtown. No telling who I might run into there, I might find someone I knew from the courthouse to ask about Peter Phillips.

Discouragement was settling in. I was getting nowhere and Lisa Brown had been missing too long to be healthy. Maybe a civilized lunch, minus the grease, would cheer me up. I parked in the lot to the right of the restaurant and sauntered in. Bud eats at Bella's a couple of times a week, but I didn't see him. Due to the early hour, there were few people seated in the dark, mahogany interior. I asked for a table near the back. I like to sit back in the dark and watch people come in.

The hostess seated me and took my drink order. I was tempted to order a beer, but ordered an iced tea instead. Drinking at mid-day makes me sleepy, especially in my less than tip-top condition, and I had a busy afternoon ahead. Five minutes later a waitress appeared with my tea and took my order, half a tuna salad sandwich and a cup of lentil soup.

I had my notebook out, sifting through my jottings, a pretty dismal sift, I can tell you, when I was interrupted. "Well, well, this is a pleasant surprise. What brings you out of the low rent district?"

It was Bob, nickname, "Robbo" Carlson, an attorney in the city's biggest law firm, Cain, Hawks, and Grossman. An old family friend, we'd gone through school together and enjoyed a brief uninspired affair after college and a five second marriage.

"Hello, Bob."

"It's good to see you, Rick. May I join you?"

I gestured, halfheartedly, to the empty chair opposite.

"Thought you usually lunched at the Q-Club. Why are you slumming today?"

Bella's was hardly slumming, but Robbo took great pride in his membership in the Quequehassett Club, formerly an exclusive, all men's club, now the private club for anyone who was anyone in the city. Business was often transacted in the dark, lush interior, over all day poker games and other shadowy doings. The ladies played bridge upstairs in the parlor. Even Bud felt it necessary to join, for business sake, of course. Mary refused to have anything to do with it and insisted he use up his meal assessment at lunch.

"I'm meeting a client, but I don't see him yet. I have just enough time for one drink."

My lucky day, I thought and resolved to be pleasant. Searching for a non-irritating conversation topic, I suddenly remembered Phillips.

I beamed across at him. "Bob, do you know Peter Phillips? He's an assistant D.A.?"

Clearly unnerved by my hundred kilowatt smile, he sat back in his seat. "Whoops, hold on now, babe. Didn't I hear you're a P.I.? What kind of work is that at your age?"

"Our age, ya mean?"

"You're bright and talented. You could have a stellar career instead of wallowing in the mud. If you'd get rid of all the lowlife nail bangers and find a good, caring man, you'd be a heck of a lot better off. Matter of fact, you don't look well. Have you lost weight? Pale, too. You getting any regular exercise?"

"Can we skip the Neanderthal lecture? I like what I'm doing. Now, do you or do you not know anything about Peter Phillips? If the answer is "no," can you move to another table and insult someone else?"

To tell the truth, Bob's words had found their mark. Much as I didn't like to admit it, it stung me to look disheveled in Bob's presence. Our break up had been mutual, but a part of me felt like such a failure that I couldn't make things work.

"Rick, hold on a second. Okay, okay, Phillips? Lemme see, he's the guy they found shot down on Summer Street the other night, right?"

I nodded.

"Rough stuff, Rick. You'd better watch yourself. Why are you messing around with that anyway?"

Quietly I told him about Lisa' sweater. "For the tenth time, what about Phillips?"

"Well, I didn't know him well. He's been at the Courthouse a couple of years. We didn't run in the same circles."

My bite of tuna stuck in my throat and I slurped up a mouthful of lentil soup to help it along.

I ordered a coke to settle my stomach, and Bob, his second martini. I pitied his afternoon clients, but maybe he was finished for the day, being so important and all. "Please, Bob? Peter Phillips, what do you know about him?"

"Well, I can't tell you much. He was quiet, minded his own business and no one ever complained about him. He worked for all the top guys. I know Richards used him a lot. Did a good job. Thorough and conscientious. He was pretty friendly, well liked by the office staff. There was a lot of sniffling when I was down there this morning."

"Speaking of Richards," I asked remembering that Bob and Lola had a fling in high school. "Do you see much of Lola nowadays? Does she stop in much at City Hall to see the hubby? Livens up the office parties, I'll wager."

"We've lost touch."

"As it happens, I've got an appointment to see her highness this very afternoon. Can't wait to hear about her new life with old Tone. Don't imagine he has much time for Lola's shenanigans?"

"That was a long time ago, Rick. Now, we're in different social circles. Tony Richards is older than we are and they seem to go around with his friends more than Lola's."

"You mean, they haven't got time for drug-crazed social climbers and alcoholic barflies? Probably not with him being the D.A. and all."

"Now that's unkind, Rick. Lola's come a long way and from what I hear, she's kicked her drinking problem. Besides, everyone says the rumors about her drinking and taking drugs were greatly exaggerated, perhaps even untrue. I'm surprised, you of all people, would listen to such malicious gossip about an old school chum."

"Bob, who've you been listening to? The lady's a lush and I've heard it from reliable sources that she's far from walking the straight and narrow."

He shrugged. "Suit yourself."

Bob was clearly looking around for someone more important to talk to. Embarrassed by my comments, I asked, "Anymore you can tell me about Phillips?"

"Nope. I didn't know him well. You might check with Richards though. You didn't tell me much about your end of the case."

"That's okay. Gotta go. Sorry." I grabbed the check and paid the waitress for his drinks along with my lunch.

"Expense account, don't sweat it. If you hear any dirt on Phillips, I'd love to know about it. You know where to find me. Say hi to Sheila and the kids." Plunking down the tip, I exited quickly, leaving Bob visibly miffed at not having the last word and no sign of the client he was supposedly meeting.

Chapter 19

It was 12:45 p.m. now and I figured I'd snoop around the Courthouse and see what I could learn about Peter Phillips before meeting with Lola. I parked on Bank Street and walked up the hill turning the corner at Rock. The proud old Courthouse sat, squished between two shoebox brick office buildings, the kind that got up overnight. The tired jewel was in need of a cleaning and facelift, but it didn't deserve the indignity of rubbing shoulders with such uninspired neighbors. As I trudged up the steps I realized it was time for my afternoon nap. After this visit, I'd catch forty winks in the car before my two o'clock with Lola.

The first floor held offices. Upstairs was the courtroom itself, the various consulting rooms and the offices of the more prominent attorneys. The third floor, more offices, storage rooms, and the library. Richards' office was on the second floor. I sidled up to Reception, where I found Sissy Mello.

Sissy is a fellow Rainbow regular. In fact, she and her husband, Eddie, live right down the street from me. She happily buzzed Richards' office and was told by his secretary that he was out for the afternoon on business and wouldn't be in until the following morning. Sissy hung up the phone, gave me the news, then leaned forward to whisper.

"Translation, he's on the golf course. Let me check here. Yep, it's Tuesday. Always plays golf on Tuesday from March to November."

"Think I could take a look at Peter Phillips' office?"

"You can try, Rick. It's down the hall, last office on the right. I'm heading to lunch now, but will we see you at the Rainbow any time soon?"

"Sure hope so, but only for one beer. I'm cut off."

She laughed. "Vinnie told us. We're getting too old for this shit, Rick. You should know that."

I waved and headed down the hall. Phillips' office was next door to the ladies room, a prime location. The door was open so I walked right in. A plump, middle-aged woman in double knit and low white heels was tidying up, putting things in boxes. I thought I detected a sniffle as I stepped in.

"Hello." I spoke softly, trying not to startle her.

She jumped. "Oh, my, you scared me. Can I help you?" Her eyes were red-rimmed, cheeks puffy.

"I'm interrupting, I'm sorry."

"No, no, come in. I'm just sorting through poor Peter's things. I'd be glad to take a break."

"My name is Ricky Steele. I'm a private investigator assisting the police with their investigation into Peter Phillips's murder and his wife suggested I check in here."

"I'm not sure I can help you, Miss Steele. I'm just part of the office staff. I've been asked to straighten up the office. The police have already been through the place. I don't think they found much. Did they?"

"Not much I'm afraid. That's why I wanted to chat with you, Ms?"

"Oster, Carol Oster." She smoothed back a lock of gray hair that had fallen over her forehead.

"Did you know Peter well?"

"Well, yes, he was a dear, Miss Steele. I can't for pity's sake imagine why anyone would want to harm that poor sweet man. And those horrible things they've been saying about him! I can't imagine Peter being involved with a prostitute. He was devoted to his family and he worked so hard. I can't understand how he came to be in that part of town."

"As I told Mrs. Phillips, there may be a very different explanation. Perhaps we'll uncover a completely plausible reason, maybe related to his work here. Rachel mentioned that he kept a diary. Is it with his things?"

"The police asked the same thing. No, his briefcase and all the notes from the trial he's been working on are gone. His notebook is missing also. He wouldn't like that. He took great pride in that notebook, kept everything in it. I don't know where it could be. Besides home and here I can't think where, except maybe the Racket Club, in his locker? I doubt it, though. I think he would have had it with him."

"What was the case he was working on?"

"Oh, just a routine breaking and entering, but the boy was a multiple offender and the judge was ready to put him away for a good long time. Peter was trying to get some background on the boy, to help out. That's the way he was, especially if the case involved kids. Always trying to see the good in people, always trying to help."

"Do you think that case is the one that's been keeping him working nights?"

"I doubt it. In fact, Rachel asked me about that, and I lied a little bit. I said, I wasn't sure when he left work, stuff like that. I didn't want to add to her hurt, you see. He hasn't been keeping late hours here. In fact, he usually left before me. You could check with the night watchman, but I don't believe Pete was spending his evenings here. I have no idea where he's been going, but the past few weeks, he's spent a lot of time on the phone and a lot of time scribbling in his notebook. He's had his door closed a lot too. That's not like him."

"Is there anyone else who might know about Peter's current caseload? Someone here at the Courthouse? A friend?"

"The closest associate he had would probably be Ron Cathers. He's a clerk, works here in the building. They go to lunch together pretty regularly and have drinks after work, that sort of thing."

"Where might I find Mr. Cathers?"

"Montana, I'm afraid. His father is quite ill. Ron took an indefinite leave of absence two weeks ago to be with him. I'm not sure when he'll be back. You can check in the clerk's office. It's just down the hall. Ask for Kate Myers, she'll know."

I thanked her, inquired briefly about Anthony Richards. He had his own private office staff, so she didn't know much about him. I gave her my card and asked her to be in touch if she thought of anything, then headed down the hallway.

Kate Myers was on the phone. I strolled in the direction of her cubicle, nodding thanks to the woman who had pointed her out. As I reached the back of her chair, Ms. Myers hung up.

"Hi, Ms. Myers?"

"Yes?" She smiled. Hers was an open friendly face, a mass of freckles splayed across the bridge of her nose. "You look familiar. Do I know you?"

People are always saying that to me. They're certainly not mistaking me for Susan Sarandon or Jane Fonda. Maybe I put them in mind of Edith Bunker?

I returned her smile. "I don't think so. My name's Ricky Steele. I'm a private investigator assisting the police with the Peter Phillips case and need to get in touch with Ron Cathers. Have you heard from him?"

"Yeah, his dad just died. Funeral is tomorrow. Ronnie and Peter were tight. Ronnie, I mean, Mr. Cathers, is a basket case, what with his dad passing right after Mr. Phillips. Bummer."

I nodded. "Did he give you any idea when he'd be back to Fall River?"

"End of the week, he thought, but he was really down when I talked to him, so I'm not sure. Cops contacted him the day his father died, asking all kinds of questions about Mr. Phillips."

"He won't want to hear from me either, but it's really important. Do you have a cell number? I'll be brief, promise."

"I guess it'd be okay." She scribbled the number on a tiny piece of pink note paper and I thanked her and left.

I was disheartened; I seemed to be getting nowhere. I plodded out to the jeep, reclined the seat, and closed my eyes.

Chapter 20

I must've conked out because the next thing I heard was a wailing baby passing by in a stroller. When I looked at my watch it was 1:45p.m. Oops, a little longer than my usual fifteen minute siesta. Groggy, I raised the seat and hopped out.

The office of "Friends On The Line" was in the Haywood Building, only three blocks away so it was easier to walk. Once in the lobby, I found a ladies room and went in to pee, comb out the snarls in my wild hairdo, wash my hands and face, brush my teeth and apply lipstick. A nap and a little cleaning up and I felt like a new woman. I took the elevator to the fourth floor. "Friends" occupied three adjoining office suites, 403, 405 and 407. I entered 403 at 1:55p.m., on time for once.

The receptionist, a flaming redhead dressed casually in beige slacks and soft blue sweater, with matching scarf, smiled up at me. "Hello, welcome, can I help?"

"Hi, I'm Ricky Steele. I have an appointment with Ms. Richards."

"Of course, hello. Mrs. Richards is on the phone right now, but if you'll take a seat, I'll buzz her when she's free. She's expecting you. She has a rather busy schedule this afternoon, but she very kindly squeezed you in."

"Thank you."

I smiled, then moved to sit on one of the three matching sofas in pale gray ultra suede. I picked up a copy of *Town and Country*, and began flipping pages. The subscription label was Lola's home address. Perhaps she imagined Siematic kitchens and terraced spas would help take one's mind off suicide and self-destruction. After a minute or two, I flung down the magazine and pulled out my notebook. Why was I so grouchy? I decided I desperately needed a vacation.

I had just started jotting notes from my visit to the Courthouse when a familiar voice interrupted me.

"Why, Ricky, what a wonderful surprise! I was so glad when Martha told me you'd made an appointment. I hope you're here for a friendly call. You're not in trouble or anything?"

Don't you wish. "Lola, good to see you." I smiled through gritted teeth. "This is a friendly visit. I just have a couple of questions about a case I'm involved in."

"Come in, come in."

She waved me into her office, recently redecorated by the look of things. The walls were white, the moldings polished mahogany. The walls held several steamship prints with frames much classier than mine, and a large oil painting of her husband. I had only met him once and it had been a while ago, but the portrait appeared to be a good likeness, judging from the recent photographs I'd seen in the newspaper. The carpet was a pale mauve, wool and expensive. Her desk dominated the far wall and in front of it were several, small, boudoir-type chairs, covered in floral chintz that picked up the mauve in the rug. The effect was elegant, impressive and, in my opinion, totally out of keeping with the image of "Friends On The Line" but what do I know?

"Can I get you anything? Coffee, a soda, whatever?"

"Thanks, a soda would be great."

She rose. "Be right back."

I watched her go, then gazed down at my jeans and the rest of my ratty apparel, feeling frumpy and wanting to crawl under the desk. I had known Lola since grade school. She has always been drop dead gorgeous. Unlike most mortals, she never went through an ugly stage. She grew up dirt poor, but that didn't stop every boy from swooning over her and every girl envying her long, thick, brown hair, luminous brown eyes and hourglass figure.

After elementary school, we'd gone separate ways. She went to modeling school, then on to win the title of Miss Spindle City, a dubious honor. After that I'd lost touch with her. While I didn't envy her or her life, I've always felt like a slob in her presence. Today, she was wearing a two-piece, soft wool sweater outfit; just the thought of it made me itch, but the soft grayish green brought out the hazel in her dark eyes. Her hair fell loose over her shoulders, the perfect adornment. Her figure, slim, but full where it mattered, was perfect as ever. She wore black Italian leather heels, probably at least a five hundred bucks.

As I waited, I tried to recall what I had heard about her in recent years. Her stint as a news reporter had flopped big time, amidst rumors of drinking and drugging. No official proof ever surfaced so perhaps they were just ugly rumors. A couple of my running buddies, who belonged to her health club knew her. According to them, Lola had missed a couple of important fundraisers, due to illness. Translation, she was probably too soused to stand up long enough to get dressed. Who knew, maybe the lady, and I use the name loosely, had a drinking problem, maybe she didn't? That was not my concern at present.

She swished into the room smiling, as she handed me a Diet Coke. She had one, too. Apparently she'd assessed my figure and decided diet soda was the wisest choice. She settled herself, catlike, into the chintz chair opposite the one I had already taken.

As she sipped her soda, she fiddled with her sweater's turtleneck, a nervous gesture as the collar looked fine. "How have you been, Ricky? Still a P.I. or are you back teaching? I couldn't believe it when I heard you were sleuthing, at your age. If you'd stayed with the schools, you'd have been at full pension by now, right? The city sure needs good teachers. Why I was just saying to Tony the other night, where are we going to get teachers? It's really becoming critical."

The last thing I wanted to do was discuss my life choices with Lola Richards. "Lola, I know you're busy, so I'll come right to the point. I'm here about one of your call-ins. I need some information and I thought maybe you could help me."

"I'm sorry, Ricky. All our records are confidential. I really can't tell you anything."

"All I need are a few yes or nos. Does the name Lisa Brown mean anything to you?" For just an instant, I thought I saw recognition, but then it was gone.

"Doesn't ring a bell. Sorry, should it? Is it important?"

"She's turned up missing and I'm trying to locate her. We found the "Friends" number in her things and I thought she might have called in for help. I'm not asking for confidential information, necessarily, just something to go on. She's only thirteen, Lola, just a kid. She's led a real rough life and she may be in some deep shit." She blanched at my use of profanity. Who was she kidding? In grade school Lola's mouth kept right up with the longshoremen.

"Well, we keep records of all our call-ins, if they give us their names and numbers. Sometimes we just get a name, but we still keep them, for three years at least. Then we update the files. It's all on discs. Martha or one of the volunteers take care of this every morning. It's against policy, but if you're working with the police I guess it'd be okay if we looked her up. All our files are strictly confidential, you understand, Ricky?"

"Of course," I said, following her. "None of this will go any farther than me." Martha, who looked to be in her early twenties, was at the computer when we returned to the vestibule. She rose and said she would try to locate the discs Lola requested, indicating that it might take a few minutes to call up the information. We strolled down the hallway and sipped our sodas, chatting about nothing in particular.

She asked if I still see any of the old crowd. That was a laugh. We'd never had an old crowd, but I played along telling her how just today Bob Carlson had been asking for her.

"Oh, how is Robbo? Such a dear. Why, Tony and I saw him and that gorgeous wife of his somewhere this winter. I can't think what the function was. Maybe the Hospital Ball or was it the Holly Hop?"

The remark about Sheila's appearance was a not-so subtle dig at me. Sheila was far from gorgeous, despite frequent trips to the tanning salon and several rounds of cosmetic surgery. Unless she was going blind, Lola, of all people, would never describe Sheila as "gorgeous." Well-heeled maybe, but gorgeous? No Way.

"How's your mom?" I asked, deciding a change of subject was in order. Mrs. Petty had been a rude, vindictive sort of person, who, in my opinion, had ruined her daughter's life with all her pretentious social climbing.

"Oh, she's great, just great. She's eighty-eight still on her own. Lives in a condo in Florida, at Amelia Island. Do you know it? Very private and exclusive. She feels right at home there."

I'll bet she does. "That's terrific."

Martha called us at this juncture. "I think I have something. I thought Lola looked less than enthusiastic, but she ushered me into Martha's office and peered over the desk, oozing concern.

A girl, by the name of Lisa called in twice in the past year, once in late October, the 21st and again on the 17th of March. The March date seemed to coincide with the diary entry I had noted. Two different volunteers, Ethel in October and Jeremy in March noted that Lisa had been suicidal on both occasions due to troubles with a boyfriend. Jeremy had tried to get her in for help. He offered to pick her up, give her a place to stay, had even given her his home phone number, but there was nothing further in the records about any follow-up.

"That's Jeremy all over, always putting himself out. We don't encourage that kind of involvement in our volunteers, you understand, but that's the way he is."

"Is he around today? Can I talk to him?"

"Sorry, he doesn't work for us anymore and I'm not sure where he is now." Lola did not look the least bit sorry.

"I know where he is," Martha said, earning her a scowl from the boss. "He has a girlfriend in Boston. He moved in with her. I have his address, you want it?"

I thanked Martha profusely and decided to wind up my visit with Lola. "She didn't call more recently I suppose? Like maybe this week?" I aimed my question in Martha's direction.

"Afraid not, those calls haven't been entered on the computer yet, but I checked everyone's handwritten logs, no Lisa, sorry. No unidentified callers either, at least that fit your description. I mean, they often don't like to give their names, but the notes log in all the no names as well."

I edged toward the door, certain there was more that Martha wasn't saying. "Please let me know if you hear from her. She's got some pretty worried friends who want to be sure she's okay." I passed out my business cards to both Lola and Martha.

On impulse, I turned at the door and asked, "Lola, did you know Peter Phillips?"

She paled. "Yes, of course. Peter was a lovely man. So tragic. Tony was terribly upset of course. Peter was his most valuable assistant and of course, a friend too. Why do you ask? You're not mixed up in that investigation are you?"

"Nope, just curious. Thanks, Lola, this was really helpful."

"Wonderful to see you, dear. We have to have lunch soon, okay?"

"Sure, see ya."

Time to head back to the office to check in and make a few calls.

Chapter 21

My building parking lot was hopping, but I wended my way past the bargain hunters without incident and headed upstairs. The first call I made was to Natalie, no answer, out on the grand tour with Phil no doubt. I dialed his cell, which went right to voicemail. I then dialed the number Rachel Phillips had given me for Steve White, Peter Phillips's tennis buddy. It turned out to be his office number. The receptionist said he was gone for the day, but that I might catch him at the Racket Club.

Too soon for another call to Ralph and Aunt Peggy so I decided to call it quits and head home. On the way I stopped at Stop and Shop for a few things then decided to take a chance and swing by the Somerset Racket Club. My lucky day. Steve White was there and in the shower. I hung around scrutinizing tennis balls and ladies court apparel until he appeared.

"There he is now, Miss."

Nancy, the healthy gal behind the counter pointed as a typical tennis type, tanned legs of iron, crossed the lobby.

"Hi, Steve," I called, extending my hand.

Clearly startled by this visage out of nowhere, White nonetheless stepped forward and gave me a firm handshake. "Do I know you?"

"Ricky Steele, I'm a private investigator looking into the circumstances of Peter Phillips's death."

"Not a cop?"

"No, but I've been consulting with Sgt. Roberts. Perhaps you've spoken to him? Actually the case I'm working on is indirectly related to Peter's. Rachel gave me your name."

"God, how is she? I haven't gotten over to see her yet. I should, but I know her mother's kind of protective."

I nodded. "I bet Rachel would appreciate a visit, if you could manage the end run around Mrs. Whiting."

He smiled and led the way to a bench. "How can I help you, Miss Steele?"

"Anything you can tell me about Peter, what his last few weeks have been like."

"Well, we'd both taken up golf, Rachel probably told you. Truth be told, we'd kinda gone crazy over it. Stupid really. We both stunk. Don't know why we bothered."

"Could that account for Peter's late nights? I mean, did you guys play then go out or anything?"

"No, only on weekends. I heard Peter had played once during the week, but that was during the day. He played with some guy out at Aquinessett. Probably weaseled his way in by begging and pleading, but he said it was the other guy's invite."

"Do you remember who it was?"

"He didn't say. Why?"

"No reason. Anything else? Did he seem to have anything on his mind the past few weeks?"

"Not that I know of, but we mostly play tennis without a lot of chit chat. He did say he was working on something important that might shake things up in the city. He even canceled a couple of our tennis games to work on it. That was Peter all over. If it was something he really cared about, he gave it his all."

I nodded.

"And, Miss Steele, I don't believe for a second the crap they've been saying about him. No way in hell Peter Phillips was involved with a prostitute. He lusted after his own wife that's for sure, and he adored her, but I never heard him say anything about any other woman. They've got the wrong theory there. I haven't a clue what he was doing that night, but he wasn't cruising for a hooker."

"Did he have a locker here? Some of his things are missing and it was suggested they might be here in his locker."

"Yeah, I can get you in. Come on."

He led me back to the men's locker room, shouting as we entered to make certain the coast was clear. I waited while he went to get the master key from someone named Al.

He reappeared, key in hand, and led me to locker 65. It held a heap of smelly tennis togs and little else. No briefcase, no notebook, just several pairs of rancid socks, a white polo shirt, worn recently during a sweaty workout, and a pair of tennis shorts. All the clothes were flung on the floor of the locker. Above, on the shelf, was an assortment of the usual male toiletries, razor, shaving cream, hairbrush, some after shave and a comb. Inserted into the teeth of the comb was a small piece of paper.

The locker's contents were pretty gamey and I was having difficulty breathing. In my rush to complete my investigation and seal up the odor, I almost missed the paper. Pulling it out, I opened and read among the folded creases. "Summer- 8:30." The warehouse where Peter Phillips's body was found was 101 Summer Street. Did Peter know his killer and had arranged to meet him? And what, in God's name did it have to do with Lisa Brown?

Steve peered over my shoulder. "Did you find an important clue?"

"Maybe, don't know. I'll let you know when I find out more." I gave him my card and thanked him. After he returned the master key to Al, we walked out to the parking lot together.

"You know," he said, leaning on the jeep's door as I got in. "Peter Phillips was one of the nicest guys I know. Whoever killed him should burn for it. Sorry, that sounds cruel, I know, but I sure miss him."

I couldn't think of anything to say, so I just nodded and waved goodbye.

Chapter 22

By the time I turned into my driveway, it was 6:45p.m., and my stomach was growling. Luckily I'd picked up some Lean Cuisine at the market. I popped two pouches holding red Thai curry into a pan of water and switched the burner on high. As I headed for my bedroom, Beaky streaked by, a flash of gray, so I went back and filled her food and water dishes.

I peeled off my clothes and donned my robe, ready to settle in. Business first, I told myself and sat down with the phone. Still no answer at Natalie's, but Phil was home. He had friends at the hospital do a complete physical, including a gynecological exam. Results of the lab work wouldn't be back for a couple of days. Yes, they'd tested her for HIV and every conceivable STD.

"Rick, she's been around. A kid maybe, but her insides are hurting. Ed Coleman did the vaginal and found a lot of wear and tear. No visible disease, but who knows. We're talking seriously messed up. She's anemic, probably from a lousy diet, which has stunted her growth. There's some bone and tissue damage. I'm not sure how she'd respond if fed well, but it can't hurt. Definitely bulimic. Throat cut-up, teeth a mess, probably from the vomiting. Damage could be from other things as well."

I swallowed hard, shutting out the images Phil's report called to mind. "Have you got any good news?"

"More tests, more blood and tissue analysis and a hospital stay of a month. That would be my recommendation. I'll know more when the rest of the tests come in, but you're not gonna cure what ails this kid overnight."

"Thanks, Phil. Can we just put this on my tab?"

"You owe me, Rick. I'll get it back one way or the other. And if you're gonna keep up with Mary and me Saturday; you'd better cut down on the boozin'."

"Where'd you run into Bud?"

"Never mind. Listen my friend; you're not thirty anymore you know."

"If I had a dime for every time someone feels compelled to tell me this, I'd be living in Bora Bora."

"Not a bad idea."

"Ha, ha."

"Look, babe, I'm a happy, middle-aged Jewish dermatologist, minding his own business, and suddenly I'm asked to be a gynecologist, internist, pathologist, and babysitter. Besides, you ask for it, Rick, all the shit we give you. If Vinnie wasn't there to feed you one decent meal a week, I'd be really concerned. Shots of tequila, and God knows what else you put in your system."

"Enough, Daddy dearest. And you and Bud can rest easy; I learned my lesson the other night. Seltzer water and one beer a day is my new limit."

"What happened to Gatorade and protein shakes? Fruit smoothies and power bars?"

"You know I hate Gatorade and I often drink smoothies."

"At MacDonald's?"

"Maybe once in a while. I drink nice pretty green smoothies too."

"When hell freezes over."

"Give me a break, Phil. See ya Saturday, and thanks. I'll work on the month long hospital thing. Maybe I can get Child Services involved."

I hung up and decided I would not speak to Bud ever again. Did I have no privacy?

My next call was to Peggy Stanley. A quick online search and I had good old Ralph's last name. This time, a woman answered.

"Hello." Much less hostile than her hubby.

"Mrs. Stanley?"

"Yes?"

"My name is Ricky Steele. I'm a private investigator and I'm trying to locate your niece, Lisa Brown. Would you have any idea how I could reach her?"

"Who hired you? Aggie?"

"No, not Mrs. Brown, although I'm sure she's concerned. No, her friend, Natalie Remy hired me. She's very worried."

"Yeah, right. She's a no-good, just like Lisa."

"Mrs. Stanley, I'm just trying to find Lisa. She is only thirteen years old, you know."

"Thirteen goin' on fuckin' forty, if you ask me, and a little bitch to boot. I ain't seen her in a couple of months. That trashy friend of hers neither. Ralph don't let 'em in the house, no way."

"What about her brother Teddy. I was told he was living with you? Is he there now?"

"Nope. Ran off, probably to join his no-good sister. He's ruined now. I'm through with 'em both."

"From what I hear, your husband didn't help matters any. Sexual abuse of a minor is a felony."

"Look, bitch, I don't have to listen to this shit. Maybe I'll call the cops."

"Why don't you do that, Mrs. Stanley. We can all have a nice little chat. Ask for Sergeant Roberts. He's familiar with the case."

"Look, what do ya want? I told ya all I know. He run off and I ain't seen him in months. I ain't seen either of 'em. Ralph'd kill me for even talking to you."

I gave her my phone numbers and then asked if she had any photographs of the kids. She thought maybe she had one of Teddy, but didn't know about Lisa.

"It'd be a young one if I did. Like I said, it's been a while, plus we don't own a camera." She took my address and promised to call if she heard from one of the kids. Fat chance.

My pouches were ready, so I ran my bath while I ate, savoring every mouthful. After dinner, I soaked in the bath for a good long time, then climbed into bed. Too tired to go over my notes, I decided to put work off until morning. I tried Natalie again. Still no answer. I made a mental note to visit Carl some time tomorrow, turned off the light and was just drifting off when the phone rang.

"Hey, Sheriff Taylor, it's me, Barney, checkin' in."

"Who's this?" I mumbled, recognizing Mark's voice through the fog.

"Rick, come on, what civilized person goes to sleep at 9:00 p.m.?"

"A hardworking, middle-aged person, that's who. I'm awake now, what did you find out? Did you play golf?"

"I thought I might come over and tell you in person. It's very confidential."

"Tempting, but I'll pass. Now, please, speak freely, my phone is not tapped. What did you find out?"

"The guy you're looking for is probably Sandy Wilkerson. A college kid, or will be in the fall. Was supposed to work as a caddy out at Aquinessett this summer, but had a sudden change of plans. Don seems to think there was parental pressure and that he might've been in some kind of trouble. Anyway, they shipped him out to some resort in the Adirondacks for the summer. Don wasn't sure of the details and didn't know the name. That's all I got.

"Don's never seen him with a girl around the club. Says he's kind of a loner, did his job and then took off. Although his folks are members, he didn't seem to socialize with other kids or the country club set. Sure you wouldn't like a back rub?"

"Thanks, I'll take a rain check. Mark, thanks for the help. Hope the golf wasn't too strenuous for you."

"Oh, no you don't. You owe me and I have just the ticket."

"Mark, we've been through this a million times."

"Hold your horses, sweet cakes, nothing like that. I've got a fundraiser at the Marine Museum. Come with me. No strings, just drinks. What do you say?"

I agreed and hung up before he could begin outlining other possibilities for the evening.

Chapter 23

I felt great. Going to bed early always makes a new woman out of me, I felt better than I had in weeks. I hopped into my running stuff and headed out for a three mile run. The air was crisp and the slight breeze off the water made me feel tingly all over. The beach was quiet. Usually, I pass neighbors, or they pass me, since truth be told, I walk–run. Sometimes, my new neighbor, Gary, a techie recently transplanted from Albany, New York, slows down and runs— walks beside me, but today no one was in sight. I liked having the beach to myself. It is peaceful, egrets wading near the shoreline, terns skittering at the water's edge. The birds ignored me as I loped past them.

After the run, I showered and headed to the city, stopping at Grove Corner Café for coffee, tea and muffins. The station house was my first stop. I wanted to bring Douglas up to date, even if all I knew was zip. I thought he might be interested in the slip of paper in Peter Phillips's locker.

Tim was at the desk when I arrived, and he smiled giving me a wave. He was pretty cute. I wondered if he had a girlfriend gazing into those gorgeous baby blues, emphasis on "baby." I really did need to get a life.

Sergeant Roberts's eyes were mud brown and he was in a foul mood. "I don't have time to play cops and robbers this morning, Steele. Sorry, but I got City Hall breathing down my throat about these homicides. I'll have to pass right now on one of our little heart-to-hearts."

I plunked down the coffee, two creams and five sugars. "Douglas, please, I'll only be a minute. I've got blueberry, bran and cranberry-orange, what'll you have?"

"Now it's bribery, is it? Well, I'm not telling you shit so you wasted your money." As he spoke, he reached into the bag and grabbed a cranberry-orange muffin.

"I just wanted to let you know what I've learned about Phillips. I won't even ask about the missing kids, since City Hall isn't interested in them."

"Out with it and make it snappy."

He rumpled his thinning hair until it stuck out all over, giving him a half-crazed appearance. I fought to keep a straight face.

I told him about my visit with Rachel Phillips, my trip to the Courthouse and my discovery in the locker room at the Racket Club. It was old news to him except the Racket Club business and he thanked me. Encouraged, I asked him how he was doing.

"Shitty. We've had every hooker in the city hauled in for questioning and have turned up jack shit. Only thing we've established is Phillips's trips to Summer Street have been very regular the past month or two. His car was sighted cruising the street by a number of our young ladies, but they never saw him pick anyone up. How do you figure it? Guy's driving around, just looking. What do ya think, one of them voyeurs?"

"I don't think he was looking for a good time, if that's what you mean. Doesn't fit anything I've heard about him. I gotta go, but I'll let you know if I hear anything else."

On my way out I asked Tim for a description of Phillips's car.

"Dark green Subaru Outback, roof rack, license plate number PVP-3."

I jotted the plate number in my notebook and thanked blue-eyed, gorgeous Tim.

Chapter 24

I was in the office at 8:15a.m., a record for me. After making tea and eating both muffins and a banana, I settled down to wrestle my notes into order. Loading the disc, I accessed the file, "L.Brown" and spent several hours creating an organized, cross reference, web of the case. After saving the file, I printed out two copies, one for the desk drawer, the other folded in my notebook for quick reference. No major breakthroughs came to me as I pecked away, but at least I felt up-to-date, a satisfying feeling in the midst of chaos.

By the time I finished pecking away it was after ten. As I straightened up and contemplated my next move, Nat walked in.

"Hey, Nat, lookin' good. Going to the doctor's must've agreed with you."

"He's okay."

"How'd ya make out?"

She shrugged. "He married?"

"No, but he's kind of old for you, don't you think?"

She shrugged. "I've been with older. Most of our steady customers are in their fifties."

"Where'd you go after the clinic?"

"Around. Saw some people. Hung out, shit like that, you know."

"You weren't working were you?"

"No way. I gave my word, didn't I? I'm not a fuckin' jerk off."

"Watch your mouth."

"Look who's talkin'. Besides, Phil told me not to work for a while, so I won't."

"Oh, well, if Phil told you then it's gospel, right? What had happened to Dr. Rubin? Phil, indeed.

"Billy's pissed at you. Well, at both of us, but mostly you. You better watch out, Miss Steele. He can be a real prick when he's pissed off, and he's got some evil friends."

"What is he gonna do, strangle me with his hair net?"

She laughed, and then turned serious, "No, I mean it. He can make people disappear."

Natalie looked twelve a sad, vulnerable twelve. "Don't worry about me, Nat, I can take care of myself. Just make sure he doesn't take it out on you. Listen, I want to talk to Carl today."

"What do ya want him for? He don't know nothing."

"Maybe, maybe not. He might've seen something you didn't. Don't sweat it, I'll be cool. Where's the best place to find him?"

"He usually eats lunch at the Blue Collar round the corner from the house. You know, the diner on Durfee Street under the 195 over pass? Then he spends the afternoon at the bar even if he's not working."

"What're your plans for the day?"

"Not sure."

"Want to come along? I'm running around this morning, but we can swing by the Blue Collar around noon."

"Sure, okay."

I asked her about Peter Phillips. She had never heard of him. "But Lisa and me ain't been on the streets lately. Billy's had a lot of work for us and we got some jobs by word of mouth. It sucks down on Summer. I've only been out there once, for an hour or two with Lisa. I like it better at Billy's. I feel safer, you know? Lisa don't get along with Billy, like I do. She's been busted on Summer a couple of times. That freaks me out, you know?" Lisa's braver. Loves the danger, you know? Says workin' Summer's like the Cork Screw at Rocky Point."

I hate roller coasters. Even discussing them makes me sick, so I changed the subject. After a few minutes spent tidying things up, I slung everything back into my bag and we headed out. I wanted to get away before the mail came. Too early in the day to get depressed. Tomorrow, I would get busy on Bud's jobs so I could pay the bills. I would take the photographs and do the interviews. I didn't like to start something until I could give it my all, but finding Lisa Brown could take months at the rate I was going and I needed to eat.

I stopped at the ladies room at the end of the hall and stared at my reflection. Faded blue jeans, a turtle neck sweater with no elasticity left in the neck and a pullover cotton sweater that appeared to have been knitted for a sloth. Dumpster woman came to mind. But, it was my lucky sweater so tough shit.

Chapter 25

In addition to the rest of my slovenly outfit, I wore a particularly grungy pair of running shoes. Thus, I was not expecting an effusive welcome at the front door in the Highlands. In fact, it would no doubt be slammed in my face, guard dogs released for good measure, all before I could say "Howdy-doo." Nat would be staying in the car. I might look seedy, but with her neon lycra two-piece stretch suit, and big hair, she would scare the living daylights out of the snooty set.

I turned onto Clifton, we began looking for the Wilkerson's house, Number 33. Finally, we spied it, just as Lisa described it. "Humongous," it was, with four white columns that framed the front portico of the massive colonial, white clapboards with black shutters. A brick circular driveway, veered off to the right toward the back of the house where I spied a six car garage. I parked on the street, certain there was an ordinance forbidding it. I would not be staying long.

Nat's hand was already on the door handle. "Geez, these guys live in a fucking palace. Must be awesome inside."

"Oh, no, you don't. You're staying right here."

"Come on! Give me a break. I've never been in a palace."

"And, you're not going in one today. Close the door and sit tight. I mean it now. This is a one-woman job, trust me."

"But I could help you."

"Do you want to find Lisa?" Silence. "I won't be long. Just stay put and keep watch. Okay?"

She gave me a sullen nod and I hopped out. I wended my way up the winding front walk and rang the doorbell. Chimes echoed within. Almost immediately, a short woman, in an apron, carrying a dust mop, opened the door.

"Is Mrs. Wilkerson at home?"

"Who ese call?"

I smiled sweetly, remembering not to shout, my culturally insensitive, knee jerk response when I know the person to whom I am speaking cannot understand me. "She won't know the name, but it's Ricky Steele."

The mop lady disappeared and reappeared, a minute later, "Mrs. Wilkerson say, you no buy here. We no sell."

"Good, I no buy. I come to talk about Sandy." What was I saying? Our conversation was beginning to sound like a scene from *Faulty Towers* with Basil and Manuel going head to head.

She disappeared again and this time returned to say, "Mrs. Wilkie say, no. Goodbye."

I was getting tired of this and I wasn't leaving until the lady of the house asked me to herself. With a smile, I brushed past, and opened the door to which the mop lady had been running in and out of. I stepped into what the landed gentry would call a morning room and spied a woman I assumed to be Mrs. Wilkerson in the small conservatory at the south end. She was pretending to fool around with some plants, but did not appear to be absorbed in the work. She had probably been too busy running back and forth listening to our conversation through the key hole. I looked down for telltale signs of sprinkled potting soil on the Persian rug before gazing up to meet her eyes.

"Mrs. Wilkerson, I'm sorry to barge in, but it's very important. I'll only take a few minutes of your time."

"I'm not in the habit of talking to strangers, Miss, whoever you are, particularly about my son. Now, would you please leave immediately or I will phone the police."

"Please do. You'll then discover that I am working with them. We can all sit down and have a nice chat about your boy. I haven't discussed Sandy's extracurricular activities with them yet, but I'm sure they'll be all ears. Assault is a felony in Massachusetts, as I'm sure you're aware."

That got her attention. She stopped what she was doing and turned to face me. Almost a clone of Emma Whiting. She wore the same kind of golf skirt with matching top and shoes and her hair was silver white, neatly coiffed in a page boy. She looked to be my age, late fifties, maybe early sixties.

"That'll be all, Consuela, thank you."

Consuela hesitated, obviously not getting the message so Mrs. Wilkerson repeated herself adding a shooing gesture and she retreated, closing the door behind her.

Mrs. Wilkerson advanced a few steps and motioned for me to take a seat. I sat in an upholstered chair, worn and tired, the slipcover slightly askew, cushions a little lopsided. Although worn, fabric was exquisite, small flowers with a cream colored background. It felt like silk. She sat down on the edge of a matching chair about five feet away from mine. Her hands shook as she fussed, finally settling the unruly digits into her lap.

"I have absolutely no idea what you want. Now, how can I help you?"

"I'm looking into the disappearance of a friend of your son's. Her name is Lisa Brown. Do you know her?"

"The name doesn't sound familiar. Was she a schoolmate of Sanderson's?"

"No, I'm not sure how they met. There is quite a difference in their ages so I expect they did not meet in school."

"How old is this Lisa person?"

"She's thirteen, Mrs. Wilkerson. I have reason to believe that she and your son were on very intimate terms."

"That couldn't be, Miss er?"

"Steele."

"What possible reason could Sanderson have to be involved with a child like that? I'm certain there must be some mistake. Now if you'll please leave my house, I have a great deal of work to do."

"She was a hooker, Mrs. Wilkerson, and your son was one of her steady customers for a good part of this past year. Does that clear things up?"

"Look, I'm afraid I cannot help you. I'll be forced to call my husband, if you do not leave my home this instant!"

"Fine, let's call your husband and ask him to hurry home. Then I can describe to you both in full detail the battering your darling Sanderson gave to a twelve-year-old kid. Used her for sex all year, led her on with promises of love, and a life together, then he beat her up and dumped her like a piece of trash when he'd had enough. It's all well-documented."

Her face crumbled at my blatant lie.

"Look, Mrs. Wilkerson, I don't mean to hurt you, but I need to talk to Sandy and I'm not leaving this house until you tell me how to get in touch with him."

She was crying now and dabbing her eyes. "Sandy's a good boy, really he is. He's just going through a difficult stage. All children do. He's away this summer in a healthy environment where I'm sure he'll grow out of it. We don't want him disturbed."

"Mrs. Wilkerson, your son is a grown man and needs a lot more help than a summer in a healthy environment. He needs counseling and perhaps other stuff as well, but that's not my business. A child's life is at stake and your son may be able to help us find her. I only want to talk to him. I promise. I'll take him aside, I won't make a scene. I'm not looking to report him or anything; I just want to talk to him."

"My husband would be very upset if he knew about this. If I tell you, will you go easy on Sanderson? He's so fragile and he's a good boy. Really, he is."

She rose and went to her desk, pulled out a sheet of note paper and jotted down a name and address—Sunrise Lakes Resort.

"It's just east of Albany."

I gazed down at the engraved notepaper. It would be a long trip. "Do you have a phone number?"

She shook her head. "He doesn't have his cell phone with him. The service is poor there anyway. There's a camp number, but my husband has that."

I thanked her and let myself out. No sign of Consuela and the mop.

Chapter 26

I cut across the manicured, chemical-green lawn and waved to Natalie, who was slumped down in her seat, half asleep. Muffy Wilkerson had given me a headache and I was tempted to join her, but instead turned the car around and headed back to the office, where I could make a few calls before my lunch at the Blue Collar. We didn't have much time, so I took the stairs two at a time with Nat trailing along behind.

I knew something was wrong the minute I reached the landing. It was too quiet. The sinister quiet when someone's waiting in the shadows. My office door was ajar, not unusual as Bud often drops in and forgets to shut it, but coupled with the oppressive silence, I didn't like the feel of it.

Turning to Nat, who had just reached the landing, I whispered, "Go down to the outlets and find the security guard. He's usually in the coffee shop or the men's room. Hurry up, and don't come back up here without him. Now hurry."

"But?"

"Do it, Nat, now!"

She retreated and I pulled out my Smith and Wesson, inching slowly down the hall. No one else on the floor seemed to be in. Perfect. When I reached my office, I kicked the door open. Nothing appeared to be disturbed in the outer office, and I was beginning to chide myself for an over-active imagination when

I spied my inner sanctum. The desk was littered, papers thrown everywhere, the whole room in shambles.

"Oh, for Christ's sake," I said aloud, as I stepped in to survey the damage.

They waited behind the door. One knocked me down, the other one kicked me in the ribs. He was wearing shiny cock-roach-in-the-corner kickers and they stabbed like dull knives.

"Not in here, you morons." The voice was vaguely familiar, but I couldn't place it before I blacked out.

Next thing I knew I was upside down, my face underwater, spluttering for air. My face was hitting something hard and white. Porcelain, God, they had my head in a toilet. I hoped it was the ladies room, I had swished out this very bowl only last week. What a way to go!

"Bring her up, she's awake."

They threw me on the tiled floor of the ladies room. As my head cleared, I wiped my eyes to find Rollo Duffy's ugly puss five inches from my face. Duffy was a major sleaze, a middle level player in the city's drug trade. Grotesquely obese, Rollo was definitely one of the ugliest people in the world, which is probably why he's always grouchy. His fat face was pockmarked and his bulbous nose was red and pimply. He was a lousy dresser too.

"Well, if it isn't little Miss Dick."

"That's clever, Rollo. Who'd you expect to find in my office, Cinder-fucking-rella?"

"Shut up, bitch. You're a fucking waste of time, you know it?"

"You tell your goons to get back in my office and clean up every goddam scrape of paper."

He slapped me sideways. "I said, shut your fucking mouth."

He pulled his huge bulk to a standing position and one of his goons kicked my thigh for good measure. I shut up.

"You listen to me and you listen good. Stay the fuck out of the Peter Phillips case, comprende?"

"Your sources must be slipping. I'm not on the Peter Phillips case." Another slap, another kick. I saw stars.

"Look, you stupid cunt. I'm only warning you once. Stay the fuck outta this or next time won't be nearly as much fun."

I started to protest, but then decided I had had enough. They kicked me a few more times, dumped me headfirst into the toilet and wedged the stall door closed from the outside.

"Get a fucking life, Steele. You're too fucking old for this shit."

"Fuck you too," I sputtered, slumping down beside the toilet, miserable, wet and cold and spitting blood.

Chapter 27

I must have passed out because the next thing I remember was lying on the couch in my office, the security guard, old Speedy Gonzales, Natalie, Phil, and Sergeant Roberts standing over me.

"Hey, guys, you shouldn't have. Not my birthday yet, is it?"

"Are you nuts?"

"Not my fault, Doug. Ask Nat. I was mindin' my own business. Duffy's gonna hear from my lawyer too!"

"You go near that horror show and I'll lock you up for a month. What did he want?"

"Wants me to stay out of the Peter Phillips case. I tried to tell him I wasn't in it, but he wasn't listening. What does he have to do with it anyway?"

"That's none of your business, and I want you out of it too. No more dicking around, pretending you're workin' with the cops. You hear me?"

"Look, I have a client, Doug."

"Geez, Ricky, when we dragged you out of that bathroom…" He stopped, his eyes almost misty.

"What time is it?"

"Two-thirty, why?"

"Shit, Nat, we missed our lunch date at the Blue Collar."

Phil stepped forward. "You're not going anywhere except home to bed or I'll put your ass in the hospital so fast it'll make your head spin."

"Where'd you come from?"

"I called him." Nat held her head high, grinning.

I started to protest, but every movement sent my head to pounding. I decided to follow the good doctor's advice and call it a day. Phil drove me home. The rest of the day and night was a blur, thanks to Phil's uber pain pills.

Chapter 28

It took me most of the next morning to clean up the mess Rollo's goons had made of the office. My head pounded ferociously. If Rollo Duffy was responsible for Lisa's disappearance, the chances of finding her alive were zero to none. By eleven things were back to normal and I was at my desk. Nat and I arranged to meet at the Blue Collar around noon, so I decided to make a few phone calls before heading out.

I located the number of the Sunrise Lakes Resort and Spa, wrote it in my notebook, then dialed. A cheerful voice answered on the fourth ring.

"Sunrise Camp and Resort, Cindy speaking, how may I help you?"

"I'm trying to reach Sandy Wilkerson. Is he available to come to the phone?"

"The name doesn't sound familiar. Do you know whether he's with the camp or the health club?"

"I'm not sure. Can you check, please?"

"You know our season hasn't opened yet. Perhaps he isn't with us yet?"

"He is there. Don't you have a list of your employees handy or maybe a directory?"

"Hold a minute. I just started this morning and I don't know everyone yet."

She put me on hold and some easy listening, dentist office music kicked in. I held the receiver away from my ear, close enough to hear when she clicked back on, but far enough away to avoid Wayne Newton's vocal assault.

"Hi, me again." Did she think I was expecting Mario Lanza? "Sandy Wilkerson works at the camp, but I'm afraid he's not available right now."

"When can I reach him?"

"He's on a camp-out. It's part of our counselor training. He won't be back till late tomorrow afternoon, no cell phones allowed. Would you like me to leave a message for him?"

"No, thanks, I'll try back later. Where does he live at camp?"

"I didn't notice, but if he's with the camp, rather than the resort, he's probably in one of their cabins. Want me to check?"

"No, thanks, you have been a great help." I spent a few more minutes getting directions from Albany to the camp, pretending that I was an old friend that might be up to a visit later on in the summer. She was very accommodating. After she learns the ropes, she'll no doubt become boringly discreet, but as a neophyte she proved quite helpful. I told her I would call next month and rang off. She asked for my name, but I pretended not to hear, and hung up with a cheerful, "bye-bye!"

I then called my friend Bunny, a travel agent as well as my realtor, and asked her to book me on a flight to Albany. She found one due to arrive at 2:30 Thursday afternoon. That would give me plenty of time to rent a car and drive up to the resort. According to Cindy's directions, they were a half an hour from the airport. This plan would give me time to orient myself before Sandy's return. I wanted to be sure and catch him before he was warned off by Mommy, who I was certain had already left several urgent messages.

Flying was an extravagance I could ill afford, but it couldn't be helped. I had to talk to Sandy Wilkerson and I was not about to drive six hours to northern New York. The jeep probably wouldn't make it anyway. I'd rather beg meals for a few weeks than make that drive. Bud owed me some money and my window for the church would be finished soon. I wouldn't starve.

Bunny rang off, assuring me that she would arrange the car rental and bring the ticket by on her way home.

There had been no return flight until the following evening and nothing that even remotely connected Thursday night, so Bunny booked me on an 8:20 a.m. flight changing in Newark and getting me back to Providence at noon. It was either that or wait until 7:00 Friday evening, which I was loath to do. This meant an overnight in the Adirondacks, but I wasn't too concerned. I've slept in cars on many occasions and if that didn't work out, I would probably find budget accommodations somewhere in the area.

With that settled, I threw myself together and headed out. It was 11:50 a.m. and I was going to have to hustle my buns if I wanted to be at the Blue Collar by noon.

Chapter 29

A couple of minutes after twelve, I pulled into the Blue Collar's lot. The diner's parking lot was wide and deep to accommodate the semis that parked here at all hours of the day and night. There were three big rigs parked along the perimeter and a number of smaller vehicles.

As I got out, I spotted Natalie sitting on the curb by the front entrance. She was dressed like a kid for once, jeans, baggy shirt and one of those oversized jackets with rips slashed here and there revealing a colorful calico lining. No makeup, no frizzy hair, no flashy jewelry. She was a pretty kid, albeit kind of scrawny. The baggy clothes extenuated her emaciated frame.

Someone sat beside her, a young boy, slim and sandy-haired. I guessed him to be about nine or ten He bore a faint resemblance to someone. It only took a few seconds before it dawned on me that I was looking at Teddy Brown. His resemblance to his dark-haired sister was striking in every way except the hair. Clearly uncomfortable, I wondered if he had come along willingly.

"Hi, Miss Steele, I mean, Ricky. Here I, we are. This is Teddy, Lisa's brother. He's been at a friend's house. I found him this morning and dragged him along. He knows something, but he's not sayin'."

I extended my hand, which he ignored. "Hey, Teddy."

"What happened to you?" My thick layer of pancake makeup had apparently failed to conceal the bruises.

"It's nothing."

"Carl's not here yet, but he'll probably be in soon," Nat said. "What do ya wanna do?"

"Let's go in and have lunch, if we can find a table. Looks packed." Noticing their expressions, I added, "My treat."

We snagged a booth in the rear next to the men's room, just vacated by two burly looking fellows and the waitress appeared within a minute. Short bleached hair, the color of Bozo's on top and dark brown underneath, she wore a skin tight uniform, in varying shades of puke yellow. Her full breasts strained at the bodice and a plunging v-neck revealed ample cleavage.

"Hi, guys, I'm Lois, what can I getcha?"

Teddy and Natalie ordered burgers, fries and milkshakes. I was tempted to do the same, but uncertain of my evening plans, I decided I'd be good. I ordered a bowl of Portuguese kale soup, one of my favorites, a salad and iced tea. As we waited for our food I told Natalie and Teddy, who tried hard to pretend he wasn't listening, while not missing a word, about my upcoming trip.

"Please let me come," Natalie whined.

"Thanks, but I prefer to go alone. Besides, you have to be around in case Lisa calls or comes home."

"Please, I ain't never been on a plane and I can't just sit around and do nothin'. 'Sides, Teddy's gonna stay in the apartment, Carl don't mind. He'll be there if Lisa calls."

Teddy should be turned over to Child Welfare, I thought, but replied, "I don't know, Nat. I know you'd be a help and all, but—"

"Please, I won't be no trouble, honest. I can pay my own way!"

"Okay, I'll get another ticket, but don't say I didn't warn you."

She flashed me a beautiful innocent smile.

Our silent companion said, "Doesn't look like you've gotten very far, 'cept get yer face kicked in."

I was about to respond when Lois bustled up with our orders. For several minutes, we ate in silence. The kale soup was delicious, lots of vegetables, a flavorful broth and big hunks of chourico. The salad, a standard iceberg affair, supplied my daily fiber.

Halfway through my lunch, I glanced over to discover that both kids had finished their burgers and fries and were nursing their shakes. Teddy had devoured his burger in two or three gulps. I asked him if he wanted another. He shrugged which I took to be a yes, hailed Lois and ordered for him.

After she left I picked up the conversation from where it'd been before the food arrived, trying to respond to Teddy's remark, "I understand how you must be feeling, I really do, but there are so many tips to check out, so many possible connections. For all we know your sister may be shacked up having a grand old time."

"Lisa didn't run off."

"No, I don't believe that either. If we only knew why she or at least her sweater ended up in Peter Phillips's car the night he died, we might have somewhere to go. Maybe Sandy Wilkerson will have an idea about where she might be. She worked pretty hard to keep him a secret, huh?

"To be honest though, you're right, Teddy. I don't have much. If you know something that might help, it would be great to hear about it. Do you know where Lisa is? I'm assuming if you don't that you're as worried as Nat. We could sure use your help. Lisa may be in danger and we want to help."

He looked around, perhaps hoping his burger would arrive to forestall further interrogation. When it didn't materialize, he stared down at his empty plate.

"There he is. Just walkin' in," Nat whispered.

I glanced up in time to spy a shabby-looking guy, medium height and good sized paunch, headed for the far end of the lunch counter. He pulled himself onto a stool and looked straight ahead, greeting the woman behind the counter with a cursory nod. He knew what he wanted and she jotted it down and disappeared. No chit chat.

His hair was medium brown with a sizable bald spot at the back of his skull. He had a bushy mustache, but was otherwise clean shaven. He was dressed in baggy chinos and a flannel shirt, which I recognized from my foray through his closet. His face was jowly and bloated, too many late nights and way too many beers. He continued to stare straight ahead.

Teddy stayed put as Natalie and I slid out of the booth.

"I seen her, she told me about it." His voice was gruff and he was fighting tears.

I slid back into the booth and spoke softly. "When did you see her?"

"Saturday morning. She'd been over at our old lady's. Slept there. Don't suppose Mom even knew she was there. She was scared. I've been stayin' at my friend's house and I seen her comin' up his street, lookin for me. She knew to check with Ronny at his mother's if she was looking for me. We talked awhile, then she split."

"Who's the "he" you're referring to, Peter Phillips? Had she seen him? Did something happen?"

"She seen somebody named Peter, somethin' went down, but she wasn't sure what. Ronny and I read about the guy Phillips in the paper and figured, like, he hadda be the guy. She's been pretty bummed out lately, probably 'cause of that Sandy creep, but she never talked about him to me. She was on Summer Street Friday night. Not many of the girls was around, but she didn't care. Lisa don't care about herself or whether she gets hurt or nothin', does she, Nat?"

Natalie nodded. "Remember I told you the same thing." I kept my eyes on Teddy, afraid he'd clam up.

"She was there 'bout an hour when this guy drives up. Real nice guy, she said. Respectable lookin', polite. She figured him for a John and got in. She was happy 'cause he didn't look like an asshole. She figured it was easy money."

What was I listening to and out of the mouth of a ten-year-old?

"Right after she gets in she realizes he's no John, but a do-gooder. She tried to jump out, but he wouldn't let her. Said he wouldn't preach to her, just wanted to spend time with her and he'd pay too. They just drove around talking for a long time, maybe an hour or two. He was okay she said. Told her he'd help her if he could. He asked bunch of questions, about her life, 'bout the guys she went with and the other girls. She didn't tell him much.

"He offered to buy her dinner, but said he had to make a stop. He drove back to Summer Street and pulled up to a warehouse near the end, then rolled up the windows and told Lisa to lock the doors. He was afraid it wouldn't be safe for her. She waited around in the car for awhile. It was hot so she took off her sweater. She leaned back in the seat and had half closed her eyes, that's probably why the guy didn't see her."

"What guy?"

"A guy, with a long coat and hat come out of the warehouse about fifteen minutes later and walks off down the street, not Phillips, some other guy. His collar was pulled up and it was dark so she didn't get a good look.

She waited a little while longer, then got outta the car. It was real dark in the warehouse so she went back to the car and found a flashlight in the glove compartment then went back into the building and called, but no one answered. She was gonna leave, but then she thought she heard something. Probably rats, 'cause it sure weren't him. He was dead. Shot in the head. So she took off. Threw the flashlight in the river and ran like hell. Stayed the night on the couch at the old lady's. She was pretty freaked out. I mean, the guy was dead."

"Where was she going when she left you? Had she told anyone else about this?"

"Not yet, sure wasn't gonna tell the cops. She said she knew someone who'd listen and wouldn't bug her."

"Did she give you any idea who that someone was, a name, anything?"

"Nope, just told me it was someone who'd listen, but wouldn't hassle her. She said she'd meet me the next day at her apartment. I think that's where she was headed when she left Ronny's."

I looked at Natalie and she shrugged. "I dunno, I was gone all Saturday till about 10:30 a.m. on and I waited around all day for her. Carl mighta seen her that afternoon, but I doubt it. Never comes home in the afternoon."

"Maybe we should ask Carl, Nat, how 'bout introducing me?"

We left Teddy sitting alone. His second burger and fries in front of him. His confession must have whetted his appetite. I heard him ordering a Coke and onion rings as we made our way toward the counter.

Carl had already wolfed down his meal and was paying the check. He spied Nat and looked neither glad nor sorry to see her. Her "Hi, Carl," elicited a nod, her introduction of yours truly, a grunt.

Since Nat had introduced him simply as Carl, I avoided names completely, not wanting to seem too familiar. "Mind if I sit down?"

He shrugged.

"If I could have just five minutes, it's about Lisa. We're tryin' to find her."

He stood. "Why ask me?"

"Well, you live in the same house and I wondered if you knew anything about her whereabouts this past weekend, Saturday in particular."

"Nope."

"You mean you didn't see her at all."

"Nope, 'cept fer the time around two."

"And…?"

"Went home fer a nap, she was yappin' on the phone when I came in. Only time I seen her."

"Could you tell who she was talking to?"

"Nope."

Such a stimulating conversation. "Did you hear anything she said?"

"Sounded like she was meetin' someone, someone she'd never met em."

"Oh? Why do you say that?"

"Said somethin' like, 'how will I know ya?' Look, lady, that's all I know. I gotta go."

"Did she get a description, do you think?"

"Who the hell knows. I was takin' a nap by then."

With those words he was out the door, presumably off to another nap. An elusive character, perhaps, but he didn't give off sinister or dangerous vibes. I believed him.

As we watched Carl exit the diner, Nat shook her head. "Ain't never heard Carl talk that much. Ever."

I smiled at her. "Must be my womanly charm. Come on, we gotta get moving."

We collected Teddy and I paid the tab. They declined my offer of a lift, and we parted company in the parking lot. They were headed for the apartment and I was headed downtown.

Chapter 30

I went back to the Courthouse to make another attempt to see Anthony Richards. Once again, he was unavailable. This time I made an appointment with his secretary for 11:00, the following morning. She assured me Mr. Richards would be available then "unless he has an emergency." I thanked her and left wondering if a quick nine at Aquinessett constituted an emergency for my elusive Mr. Richards. The last time I'd seen Anthony Richards was in a photo splashed across the front page of the *Spindle City Herald*. Poor old Tone was dragging a dazed, half naked, Lola from a seedy motel. The story from the Richards's camp was that Lola had been drugged and taken there against her will, but I didn't know a soul who believed that.

This incident occurred years before she became director of "Friends On The Line." For a while, she simply disappeared from the social scene. Dried out, cleaned up and sanitized, she reappeared as Mrs. Do-Gooder. Rumor had it Tony had checked her into a suite at Ravenhill, Newport, a rehab establishment for the rich. When she reappeared, glittering and gorgeous as ever, draped on her husband's arm at the city's flashiest social events, her fall off the wagon was all but forgotten.

The strain had to be tough on Richards. Older than his wife, he had worked long and hard to reach his present status. He changed his name from Riccio to Richards and spent decades burying the skeletons in his own past so Lola's escapades must have driven him to distraction.

I poked around and asked a few people about Phillips. I learned nothing new or particularly relevant. Borden Middle School was just a short distance up the hill so I figured what the heck, I'd make a trip to the last school Lisa had attended. A brief chat with her guidance counselor afforded no new information, just the same depressing crap I'd been hearing for three days now.

It was after five, so I headed home. After a hot bath and a cold beer, I'd make my phone calls in bed, and then call it a day.

The sky was all pinks and oranges as I drove over the bridge and the breeze felt warm on my face. A beautiful spring evening; I hoped Lisa Brown was somewhere safe, right now, enjoying it.

Chapter 31

Home. I was so glad it hurt, ten minutes later, I was stripped and stretched out in a hot tub. After a good long soak and a cold Dos Equis, I roused myself. The world looked so much rosier now. My growling stomach sent me to the kitchen, where I opened the fridge to find moldy cheese, half a carton of skim milk and an assortment of crusty condiments. Grocery shopping, tomorrow, but tonight it would have to be the Rainbow. I could almost taste the chourico on a warm soggy roll, feel the grease slithering down my arm. Yum.

Pulling on a clean pair of jeans, I selected a dark green turtle neck with holes in the elbows and a gray sweat shirt, to hide the elbow holes, with "Friend's Academy" emblazoned on the front with navy lettering. Not my alma mater, but a cast-off I picked up sometime during high school. It was thick, warm and still like new. Tying on a beat up pair of running shoes, I grabbed my notebook and sat down to check my cell. Business before cholesterol.

There were two messages, one from Phil, the other from Jay Harp. I dialed Phil first, hoping he'd have some good news about Nat's tests. Miracles of miracles, he was home.

"Hi, Phil Rubin."

"Hey, doc."

"Ricky, for God's sake. I've been tryin' to reach you for hours."

"What's up?"

"I got some news for you about your young friend. She's clean, no HIV virus, nothing infectious, but she's pretty messed up all the same. Her stomach lining is ulcerated, bulimia definitely at a stage where she can't control the vomiting. Been going on for a while now. She should be hospitalized."

"I'll talk to her. Anything else?"

"Well, like I told you the other day, she's anemic. She has a number of vitamin deficiencies and almost no potassium in her body which is really dangerous. We should do something about that right away. I gave her an injection of vitamins and iron the other day, but, as I said, she should be hospitalized. These are prime growth years."

"I'll talk to her, but in the meantime, can you give me some stopgap measures to tide her over? She'll never agree to hospitalization while her friend is missing, but maybe after the case is settled. Besides, what hospital is gonna take her? There's a limit to my financial resources, you know."

"If she'll go, I'll get her in, you know that. Best thing now is to keep her eating good food. No junk. Goes for you too, my friend. Hopefully she'll keep some of it down. She should also be taking a good multi-vitamin every day and try to get her to eat one or two bananas every day to build up her potassium levels. She really should come in for a few weeks for heavy duty vitamin injections. If you can get her to the office, I'll fit her in."

"Thanks, Phil."

"See you Saturday?"

"Maybe, but don't wait for me."

"You're slipping, Steele. What are you gonna do when the Hilltoppers rolls around and you can't make it past the two mile mark?" He was referring to the ten mile, very hilly race we always do together.

"I've gotten really good at jog-walking. Much kinder to my joints."

"Sissy."

"Bye, Phil."

My next call was to Jeremy Bryson, whom I had located earlier. He lived on Huntington Avenue in Boston since his abrupt departure from "Friends on the Line." A sleepy voice answered on the sixth ring.

"Hi, could I speak with Jeremy?"

"Speaking." He sounded like he was nodding off.

"Jeremy, my name is Ricky Steele and I'm investigating the disappearance of a girl named Lisa Brown. I spoke to Martha at "Friends On The Line" in Fall River and she said the records showed that you spoke to Lisa a couple of times."

"Sorry, I'm in a fog. Worked the night shift at the call-in line here and I've missed way too much sleep lately." I could almost see him shaking himself awake as he talked. "Yeah, I remember Lisa. She was kinda the final straw between me and the new boss lady. She told me I wasn't going by the book and shouldn't give out my cell number to a troubled suicidal kid 'cause she might phone me at home when I wasn't "officially on duty." Big deal, you know?"

Ignoring his reference to Lola, for the moment, I asked, "Do you remember what you and Lisa talked about?"

"Vaguely, she was pretty messed up. Her life was in the toilet because of her relationship with an abusive asshole. He was always dumping on her, treating her like shit. She talked about him a lot and how she couldn't live without him. Didn't seem to be able to live with him either. One of the last times I talked to her, he'd beat her up, pretty bad from the sound of it. When we were talking it sounded like her lips were swollen shut. She was crying, sobbing the whole time."

"Did she mention his name?"

"No, but I got the feeling he was a preppy. You know the type. Spoiled, bored, rich kid, slumming for a thrill. Was getting his kicks stringing a poor little kid along, getting her hopes up, dangling marriage and all kinds of other crap in front of her. She never said how they met, but I bet he was cruising Summer Street. She told me she sometimes worked down there."

"When was the last time you talked to her?"

"Let's see. I think it was the night she got beat up. She was suicidal and thinking about using drugs to do the job. That's when I gave her my cell. She called me a couple of weeks later. It was late at night and she'd called "Friends." A lady had answered and she hung up without talking. She was just calling to say she was okay, starting a new life, rid of the creep for good. Her friends and she were gonna make it big. She had all kinds of hair brained plans, the kind you'd expect a twelve-year-old to cook up, but she was happy or least she sounded so.

"I tried to meet up with her. Said I'd help her get back into school and find a place to stay. I don't usually do that for call-ins. It's against the rules, but there was something about her, you know?"

"Yup."

"She got to me, poor kid. Most of the people who call in at night are real desperados, the kind that saw their last ray of hope extinguished a decade ago. Here was this kid, with dreams. She wasn't stupid either. From what she said, she and her close friends weren't into drugs. That's a minor miracle in itself. I saw a chance to help and I wanted to make all her kid dreams come true or at least prevent her from getting slapped down anymore. But, that's the last I heard from her. After I left "Friends" and moved, I thought about Lisa a lot but I haven't heard a word. How's Martha holding up anyway?"

"She seems fine to me."

"You know there are some people who are totally wrong for certain kinds of work. You take Nancy Raphael, the founder of "Friends." She had more humanity in her little finger than the current management could dredge up in a lifetime. That's politics for you. Too bad, I feel bad for Martha."

"Lisa ever say where the boyfriend took her?"

"No, he was keen on keeping their relationship hush, hush. Even the night she called all beat up, she said zip about what she'd been doing. I tried to get a line on the guy. Not that I could've done anything if I had, but she gave nothing away. I think she was scared. It's amazing the power he had over her. He was older, eighteen at least. He had her pegged perfectly. Before the beatings he was as affectionate as a puppy dog. Happens every day. We get a lot of battered wives calling in. You probably run into his type in your line of work?"

"Unfortunately, yes."

"They're the scum of the earth as far as I'm concerned. You know, one of the things he kept dangling in front of her was meeting the folks. What a pile of horseshit. I mean, get real. Can you imagine Mommy Nose-in-the-Clouds servin' tea to his Summer Street whore? That'd be somethin' to see. Poor kid used to walk by the mansion sometimes and dream of the day."

I conjured up a vision of Muffy Wilkerson and the scenario he described. "I hear you. Very depressing. Sounds like the game got a little out of hand and when he wanted out, Mommy's nice wide skirt was there to hide behind. Thanks, Jeremy, you've been a help."

I gave him my number and asked him to call if Lisa got in touch.

"Let me know when you find her. I'd like to meet that kid someday." He rang off, returning to his slumber.

Before phoning Jay, I called Bunny and asked her to book two more round trip tickets to Albany. I told her I'd pick them up the following afternoon, thanked her and rang off.

Despite my solemn vow never to speak to him again, I dialed Jay's number. He answered on the third ring with, "Hi, this is Jay."

"It's me, what's up?"

"Angelina, is that you?"

"Very funny, it's been a long day. You know very well who this is. What's up?" "Day that bad, huh?"

"It's been better. Did you have something to tell me?"

"Not particularly."

Against my better judgment and because I love hearing his voice, I gave him a brief update.

"Sounds like junior might be your guy. How's that tie into Phillips and all? I don't think you should go to New York alone. After that beating you took yesterday."

"Who told you about that?"

"Phil was concerned."

"So much for patient-doctor confidentiality."

"You should have protection, Rick."

"I don't need protection and I don't need you and Phil mother-henning me."

"Someone has to."

"Oh, and what would Mary say about that?"

"We broke up again."

"Ah, now I see why I'm hearing from you."

"That's not fair, Rick. I'm concerned about you."

The conversation was starting to give me a migraine.

"I'm fine, Jay, really. What's he gonna do, take me out in front of all the campers? I'm just going up for a friendly little chat. Besides, Nat and Teddy are comin' along to keep me company."

"The kids? Are you crazy?"

"They've never been on a plane."

"Seriously, Rick. Do you think that's a good idea?"

"Probably not, but they're coming."

My voice was starting to lose its last vestiges of patience.

"Okay, fine. That's not why I called. Listen, Rick, the firm has an agency that provides muscle for us when we receive threats. I have someone in mind who I think would work well with you."

"You're joking, right?"

"Rollo Duffy and his goons could have killed you."

"But, they didn't and I'm fine. Listen, I've gotta go, I'm starving."

"You okay? You sound kind of down."

"No, just hungry and I want to get to the Rainbow before Phil sells out of chourico rolls. I'll talk to you when I get back, okay?"

"Want some company?"

"No."

"Take care and don't drink too much."

"Humph."

I grabbed my jacket and headed out. The Rainbow is only a couple of blocks up and around the corner from my house. The night was warm, the sky clear and full of stars. I enjoyed every minute of the walk, my mind clearing as I tried to shake away the sadness. How could a man undo me like this, again and again?

The Rainbow smelled of stale cigarette smoke, beer and grease. Fluffo, the bartender, had Wednesday off so Jack, the owner, was behind the dark, mahogany bar that ran the length of the north wall. He waved as I came in. I sat near the door, enjoying the sea breezes. Most of the regulars were there. Jeanie was at her stool at the bar, already half swimming in her 16oz draft. Jack and Eddy were shooting dice at the bar and a group of guys were playing cards at another table. There weren't any kids tonight, this being Wednesday. Weekends and summers, a lot of college kids hung out at the Rainbow.

Jack brought me a Dos Equis. He orders them especially for me as most of the regulars prefer Bud or Miller on draft.

"How's the lady PI tonight?" He paused and studied me closer. "Geez, Rick, what happened to you?"

"Bad week, let's leave it at that, okay? Got any chourico rolls left?" He nodded. "Great, then two, heated."

"Sure thing, comin' up."

I had just taken the first luscious bite of my second roll, when Vinnie, my neighbor walked in.

"Hey, beautiful, long time no see. Where ya been? Christ Almighty, what ran over you?"

"Two assholes, whom I'd rather not discuss."

"Rick, you need a new job. Sure don't need to end the day lookin' like that. Fuckin' A."

"No mother-henning tonight, Vin, okay? Sit down. Have a beer. Talk to me, but no lecture, please."

He called over to Jack for a beer and plopped down. Jack doesn't like to serve men, except at the bar. He usually expects them to come get their own, but he likes Vinnie.

"Want another one of those?" He pointed to my half empty beer. I shook my head. I planned to order a seltzer and lime when Jack returned.

"What ya been doin'? Maddie, Fulty, and me been worried 'bout you. Haven't had one of our dinners in what, three weeks? We're all starved for neighborhood gossip."

"Well, you won't get any outta me. I've been home to eat and sleep, and that's it. This past week's been a killer."

"Better watch yourself, babe. Maddie's lying in wait. Wants you on that porch, drink in hand, it being mid-summer already. If you don't get over there pretty soon, you'll be on her shit list for sure."

I smiled thinking about Maddie bundled up against the April chill, waiting for her gin and tonic. "Soon as I get rid of the case I'm working on."

He kept me company drinking a couple of beers, yours truly seltzer, while we chatted about nothing in particular. When I looked up at the clock above the bar and read 10:00 p.m., I rose. Vinnie got up too, and was fixing to pay, but I wouldn't let him. He threw some money at Jack and I said, "Put it all on my tab, will ya, Jack? I didn't bring any money. See ya."

Jack shrugged and pocketed the money. Who knows how he calculates, but it all evens out in the end. Vinnie and I walked home in silence. I was glad he was there, a warm body beside me. As we came into my yard he said, "So you gonna tell me about your face?"

"Nope."

"Look, Rick, I know some people."

"Vinnie, I've already had this talk from Jay Harp."

"Good, listen to him, even if he is a first class weasel."

"I can take care of myself. I'll tell you about the face at dinner next week, okay?"

"I'll cook."

"Counting on it. Night, Vin."

He walked me to my door and stayed until I was safely inside.

Bed, oh you sweet thing. I stripped off my clothes, eyes closed before my head hit the pillow.

Chapter 32

When I woke at 6:15 a.m., the sky was dark. Looked like rain. Maybe the sun was out in the Adirondacks. I felt rested, but my stomach churned from last night's dinner. I was moving slowly, but I felt better and the bruises were fading. A hint of pancake and a dusting of powder and no one would be the wiser.

I wished I could stay home and forget Lisa Brown and this whole mess for one day. I love to straighten bookshelves, clean out closets, the kind of satisfying domestic chores that create the illusion of an orderly life. What a laugh.

There was one bit domesticity that I had to take care of. Grocery shopping. I threw on clothes, got a pad of paper and started a list.

A quick ten minute sweep through the frozen food and dairy section for some Lean Cuisines and cartons of milk and juice would be sufficient to tide me over for a few days, but I decided as long as I was going, I might as well do it right. I always shop at the same market, Stop and Shop, not because it's necessarily better than any other, but because it's the closet to home and I know the aisles.

My list complete, I banged out the back door and headed for the beach. A concrete sea wall runs along the edge of my back yard and the back yards of my neighbors, for several miles to the east and a shorter distance westward around the point. In front of the wall, boulders had been dumped as a makeshift hurricane barrier. I doubted either the boulders or wall would offer much protection in the event of a major hurricane. Most days the water fell ten to twelve feet short of the boulders even at high tide, so there was always room to run. If I had better coordination, I could probably run along the sea wall, but a mountain goat I am not. The lower the tide, the easier the run.

It was slack tide this morning so I had a small swath of sand on which to run. The air was cool and heavy although it looked like rain at any minute. Thankfully, the clouds didn't look like thunder clouds. I'm petrified of lightening. I always run east, usually for one1 and a half or two miles, then turn around. I usually see an older woman, who appears to be in her seventies, jogging along with her dog. She gives me inspiration. No sign of her today.

I returned home, cheeks ping, skin tingling, blood flowing. I ate a quick breakfast of muffins, juice and a brown banana, showered, deftly applied my concealer, and was off to the supermarket. At 10:00 a.m., I was back home, laden with bags. After shoving my provisions in cupboards and fridge, I packed a small overnight bag for my trip to Albany, including some bananas and Unicap vitamins for teens. I scribbled a note to Vinnie asking him to watch over Beaky, my cat. He had agreed last night, but the reminder never hurt. Beaky was in hiding at the moment, but I was confident Vinnie would flush her out.

I had on my uniform, jeans and turtleneck, and was just walking out when I remembered my appointment with Richards. Reluctantly, I returned to my room and changed into a skirt, cream-colored blouse and brown leather boots. I wouldn't give Lola any serious competition, but I looked a trifle more presentable. I suspected that was important when dealing with Anthony Richards. I stuffed my original outfit into my bag for a quick change at the airport.

After circling the Courthouse for fifteen minutes, I landed a parking space on Davol. It was a three block walk, but I had time. I arrived at his office at exactly 11:00 a.m. and, of course, was informed that the great and powerful one was tied up. Forty-five minutes later he became untied and appeared to escort me into his lair. Profuse apologies lingered on his lips for approximately five seconds then, he got down to business.

He waved me toward one of the huge leather armchairs in front of his enormous desk, then sat in its mate, straightened his shiny, dark suit, and looked me straight in the eye.

"Ms. Steele, to what do I owe the pleasure of this visit? My wife tells me you were in to see her yesterday? So nice for Lola to see old school friends."

"Did Lola tell you why I went to see her?"

"Something about a missing girl, wasn't it? Is that why you wish to see me?"

"Well, sort of. I'm working with the police on a related case." By now I'd gotten very comfortable with this line, although Richards would not be fooled or impressed by it. "It appears that my missing person, a girl named Lisa Brown, was on the scene when Peter Phillips was murdered. You know him well I'm told."

"Do you think this Brown girl could be Peter's murderer?"

"No, I don't, but anything's possible. I believe Lisa may be in danger. Whoever killed Phillips may think she can identify him. She did see someone leaving the scene."

"How do you know that if you can't find her?"

"She talked to her brother before she disappeared and described what happened that night." I went into a mini version of Teddy's story and watched his reactions.

"She got a pretty good look at the guy. The murderer, that is."

"And, you believe a ten year-old? These street kids'll say anything. Sounds like a load of crap."

"Maybe. Of course, you knew Peter Phillips? Do you have any theories about his murder?"

Richards was short, or least two inches shorter than his wife in her spike heels. Why would he want Peter Phillips dead? I was way off the point when I was supposed to be finding Lisa Brown.

"It's my job to know about such things. Of course I've been keeping close tabs on the police investigation into Peter's death. By the way, no one involved in that investigation has mentioned you. And Lola, of course, told me something about the girl yesterday. She didn't mention the brother. I believe I heard about him from Sergeant Roberts. As I said, my dear, I wouldn't put all that much stock in a street kid's story."

"I'm not sure I get your drift. Why would she make up a story like that?"

"No disrespect, Ms. Steele, but I spend my day with these punks. Don't let their age fool you. These kids are hard as nails and not fussy with petty details like the truth."

"Of course, you're entitled to your opinion, Mr. Richards."

"Tony, please. Any friend of Lola's is a friend of mine."

"Tony, these are not hardened criminals, no matter what anyone says. They're not angels, but they're not murderers."

"They've been walking the streets for four or five years. What do you think that does to them? They're not girl scouts workin' on their merit badges."

"They have no choice, but, we are getting a bit off track. Neither of us has a whole lot of time. I've got a plane to catch and your secretary said you have a lunch appointment. I want to ask you about Peter Phillips, okay?"

"I'm not sure how I can help you there."

"I'm told that he worked for you?"

"I used Peter's help on a number of cases, yes. He was a meticulous researcher and submitted work on time. Great guy, took his job seriously."

"What kinds of cases was he working on?"

"Routine stuff, research for upcoming trials."

"I'm not familiar with routine. Can you enlighten me? What kinds of cases they were?"

"Right now, I have a homicide. Husband killed his wife. A couple of armed robberies. Some routine felonies, breaking and entering, the usual day to day stuff, but Peter wasn't working on any of these. I've got a couple of land disputes in the North end that Peter was working on. I've been going crazy trying to find someone to replace him. Pain in the ass. All his notes were lost. Briefcase stolen."

"Could any of those cases have given him a reason to be down on Summer? Did any of them involve prostitution, drugs, or other kinds of activities associated with the Summer Street crowd?"

"Not unless he made a connection he hadn't told me about."

"What about Rollo Duffy? Was Peter working on a case that involved him?"

His eyes flickered, with surprise and something else I couldn't quite interpret. "Yes, as a matter of fact. Why?"

"Duffy and two of his henchmen paid me a visit the other day."

"That where you got the shiners? You need a few lessons in makeup application, Miss Steele. Perhaps Lola could help."

"What do you have on Duffy? Drugs?"

"Confidential, sorry. Peter was handling the whole thing. He hadn't briefed me in a few weeks. It's been crazy around here lately."

Sensing I'd get nowhere asking about Duffy, I changed the subject. "His wife seems to think he was conducting some research on his own that might've taken him down to Summer. What do you think?"

I thought I detected a slight tic. "I really couldn't say, sorry. Now, I hate to cut this short, Miss Steele, but I really do have to run."

He rose, smooth as silk. His suit had clearly been tailored by a master to fit his broad, barrel-chested frame. He smoothed back his hair, a completely unnecessary gesture as it was already slicked down with gobs of Vitalis. In his seventies, he still had a full, sleek head of dark hair, the lack of gray was no doubt due to regular trips to his stylist. His face had had work, the surgical lines not quite invisible. Botox was probably part of his regular regimen as well.

"Thanks, Tony. I'll let myself out. If you think of anything Phillips could have been doing that's relevant to my finding the girl, I'd appreciate you letting me know, particularly if it pertains to Rollo Duffy."

"Sure will." Already halfway out the door, he was barking orders to his secretary to have the car brought around and hold all his calls. Then, off he went to his very important lunch.

Chapter 33

We would have to hustle our buns to make the flight. I swung by, grabbed the kids, and sped over the Brightman Street Bridge into Somerset. Town Travel was a block from the bridge. I prayed Bunny had gotten my message about the extra tickets.

Nat had a load of cash which she shoved at me as we raced along. It was way more than necessary to cover the cost of the tickets. I started to protest, but the wounded look on her face silenced me.

"You guys wait here."

I grabbed the money and hopped out of the car. Bunny had the tickets waiting. I plunked down a signed, but blank personal check.

"Here, Bun, please fill it in, and leave the amount on my voicemail, okay? We're really late."

"I'll say. You'll never make it to Greene in time!"

"Watch us."

"And when did you ever balance your checking account?" she yelled to my retreating form. "Be careful, Rick!"

After a hair raising drive, I parked in the airport lot, and we raced into the terminal only to be informed that our flight was delayed half an hour. I hoped the problem was not major, like an engine falling out. Flying always made me nervous, especially now with my new "family" along. While we waited, I checked the ticket price then returned most of Nat's money. Bunny had gotten us bargain Summerblast tickets, seventy-five dollars each. I pocketed Nat's cash, intending to give it back to her when this was all over.

After an uneventful flight, I secured a "rent-a-wreck." The girl at the rental desk gave me a map and fairly coherent directions and we were on the road to "Sunrise Lake Resort" by 3:15 p.m. No GPS, but I gave Nat my phone so she could navigate with my maps program. It was a forty-five minute drive from the airport. The ancient Subaru sputtered along, bravely sallying forth onto the interstate.

The highway soon gave way to winding country roads, deep woods and green mountains on either side of us. Animated and excited on the plane, Natalie and Teddy had not spoken a word since we left the airport.

"Pretty up here."

Silence.

Nat cleared her throat, "Did you go to school for a long time? I mean high school and college and all?"

I nodded. "Went as far as my dad would pay for. Why?"

"Was it hard?"

"Sometimes."

"I think I'd like to go back to school, but I ain't very smart and it was real hard for me. Kids laughed at me and called me stupid and dummy. I hadda stay back twice. If I tried to go back now, they'd probably put me in the fourth grade. I can't hardly read either.

"First time I stayed back was kindergarten. It weren't bad 'cause I was little and didn't know better, but last year, to hafta stay back when all my friends were goin' on to middle school, no way, I just dropped out. Lisa got to go on, but not me. Too stupid, that's all."

"You're far from stupid, Nat. Nobody's stupid for that matter, just different wiring. People learn in lots of different ways. Maybe your school wasn't teaching you right?"

"Sounds like a lot of crap. Just another way of saying I'm stupid."

"Like hell it is. Look at yourself. Stupid people don't take care of themselves the way you do. Stupid people don't care about their friends the way you do. Stupid people wouldn't know how to get help. Would you've found me if you were stupid?"

I smiled, she didn't.

"You're just teasin' me. 'Sides, it's different, the stupid you feel in school. For me, I really feel dumb in math."

"That was my worst subject. My brain shuts down when someone starts talkin' numbers. I nearly flunked algebra and statistics. Had to have a tutor to get me through both."

"Really?" she looked over skeptically, wondering if I was joking.

"Really. Sometimes in class, my mind would shut down and I'd either break down in tears or explode, depending how the day was going."

"Did you get sent to the office?"

"Yup, and you're looking at a veteran or detention and Saturday night study hall."

"Saturday night? How'd they do that?"

"Because I was doing so poorly in middle school, my dad sent me to a boarding school, or prison, as we liked to call it."

"What about your mom?"

Now we were treading in dangerous territory.

"She died when I was in middle school. Nat, I wasn't teasing you before. I used to be a teacher, fifth and sixth grade. I know a smart kid when I see one. Besides, most of what constitutes intelligence isn't learned in school. You could go back, you know, if you found a good place to live, folks to take care of you and help you."

"No way. Forget it. I've already tried that and it don't work. All the foster homes I been in sucked. I ain't never doin' that again."

"Hey, not all foster parents are bad."

"Forget it, okay? Believe me, they suck."

I almost missed the sign at the fork in the road. It was a small, handwritten job, which surprised me until I spied the empty space between two white posts beside it. The real sign must be at the paint shop getting fresh coat, or maybe they take it in for the winter.

"You guys ready?"

"Yup," they replied in unison.

I followed a smooth gravel road several miles into the woods until we reached a clearing. Straight ahead was a huge, white rambling structure, surrounded on three sides by wide, white-railed porches. The porches were empty, save for a chair or two; the requisite white rockers no doubt still hibernating in winter storage. Beyond the building, to its left, stretched the lake with two or three docks visible at various points, reaching out into crystal clear waters.

"Awesome," Nat cried, upon spying El Resorte Grande.

"Cool," he echoed. "I'm going swimming."

"Oh, no, you're not! You two are to stay in this car. I mean it."

Ignoring the chorus of "no fairs," I pondered the best way to make my approach. There were several roads branching off of the circular drive, one of them marked "Camp Sunrise." The other three were unmarked. A small white sign, with black lettering hung near the front entrance to the main building was marked "Office."

I pulled up and killed the engine. The Subaru coughed and sputtered and I prayed it hadn't died. No one seemed to be about. Stillness settled over us like a warm blanket.

"Stay here. If anyone asks, you're waiting for your mother and you can't speak to strangers. Got it?"

I hopped out, and shut the door quietly behind me.

"Anything you say, Mommy Dearest," Nat said, her expression half pout, half wistful. Teddy shrugged and stared straight ahead at the lake.

Chapter 34

Bounding up the steps, I swung open the front door, not bothering to knock. I heard voices as I stepped inside. There was a sitting room to my left and on the right, closed French doors that led to a large dining room. The voices came from an open door at the end the hall so I proceeded down and peeked in. A girl, in her early twenties sat behind the desk. She wore a perky little outfit consisting of dressy pink sweats with a jaunty floral scarf at her neck. She was chatting with a man in a similar get-up, only his outfit was powder blue.

The monogram, S.L., was embroidered in curlicue lettering above the left breast of both sweat suit tops. I wondered why they needed to be in uniform during the off-season, but maybe this was part of the training regimen.

I took a wild guess. "Cindy?"

"Yes, hi. Do I know you?"

"Not really. My name is Ricky Steele. We spoke on the phone the other day. I called looking for Sandy Wilkerson."

"Oh yes, I remember you. I didn't expect you, I mean. They're not back from the overnight yet. I'm not sure when they're expected. Mr. Walker, he's the owner of Sunrise Lakes, he was wondering why you wanted to talk to Sandy."

I'll just bet he did. Probably a college friend of dear old Daddy.

"I'm in the area on business and thought I'd stop in and say hi. Won't keep him more than a few minutes."

"I'm pretty sure Mr. Walker would want to talk to you first. He's in town right now."

"No problem, if it's okay I'll just wander around. It's so beautiful here; I'll take a walk and check back with Mr. Walker later. Where will they be landing, when they get back? The camping party I mean."

"I'm not sure, but Mr. Walker will be able to direct you."

"Great, thanks."

I backed out, already plotting how to best avoid Mr. Walker, who obviously had no intention of allowing me to see Junior. Muffy must've told Sanderson Senior about my visit. I'd be dammed if after flying all the way up here, I was going to be diverted from my purpose.

The kids and I roamed around for almost an hour. We stayed around the main building, but out of sight, so that we could watch the comings and goings, while remaining inconspicuous. Two extra people make skulking difficult and we had to monitor Teddy closely as he was drawn to the lake like a magnet. I consulted my watch and found it was nearly five. I sent the kids back to the car and asked them to keep watch.

"Remember, no talking to anyone. Okay?"

"Whatever," he said with a scowl.

"Don't worry," Nat said, dragging him off. "I'll watch him."

I crept behind a storage shed, where I was startled with, "Hey, you, what're you doin'?"

"Oh, hi. I'm waiting for a friend."

"Funny kinda waitin', sneakin' around corners and peepin' down the drive. Sure your friend wants to see you?"

Just what I needed, Mr. Fixit ruining all my plans. Skinny and weather worn, he was about my height, probably in his early sixties. His clothes, olive khaki pants and shirt were dirty, but I noticed the same S.L. monogram on the shirt. A behind the scenes kind of a guy, grounds crew maybe? Definitely not one of the leisure suit legions.

"Well, you caught me," I grinned sheepishly. It's my son. It's his first time away and his birthday's tomorrow. I wanted to drop off a little present."

"Can't cut the cord, huh?"

He was leering now, but I swallowed hard, batted my eyelashes and stepped closer. "Do you have kids? He's comin' back from that canoe trip. I asked in the office and they said I couldn't see him till after I meet with Mr. Walker. Sounded to me like Mr. Walker wouldn't exactly be cooperative, camp rules and all. Please, I've come all this way."

I started to sniffle. I should have been an actress, really I should have.

"Listen here, don't you go blubbering now. Old Kip'll sneak you in. Come on, that's a good girl. I saw the canoes comin' upstream about a half hour ago. They'll be at the lake, unloading, or maybe still headin' for the docks. Uh, oh, better git. Here comes the boss now."

Turning, I spied an old woody station wagon rumbling up the drive.

"Just follow that road there. It's not far. They'll be pullin' up soon. Hurry up, if old man Walker knows you're here he'll be tearing down after ya. I'll wait till he comes out of the office and see if I can stall him a few minutes. He usually meets the kids when they get back from a trip though, so you better hurry."

"Thanks, Kip. I owe you." I would have hugged him, but I had to hurry.

I started down the path, running full on, careful to stay out of view of the main drive.

Chapter 35

They were just tying up as I reached the dock. I walked slowly toward the group. There were three canoes with four people in each, two women, the rest men. As I was trying to decide which young man might be Sandy Wilkerson, a very accommodating young lady helped me out as she spoke to one of the guys. "Sandy, see you later. Gotta run up to the lodge."

I had my opening.

"Sandy!"

I rushed toward a short, well-built guy heaving a large duffle onto the dock. He waved absently at the retreating woman, then looked up, dark eyes clearly registering dismay at the lunatic bearing down on him. His longish hair, appropriately sandy, stuck out from under a Red Sox cap. He wore a red flannel shirt and jeans, pretty cute actually, if you didn't know his history as a kid beater.

"Oh, Sandy, I'm so glad to see you! Can we go somewhere alone and talk?" I was counting on throwing him off balance for a minute or two, long enough for me to lead him away from the herd.

As we strolled down the path, farther into the woods, he finally woke from his trance. "Lady, do I know you?"

"No, but we have a mutual friend, Lisa Brown."

I'd barely gotten the name out before he bolted, running straight for the woods. He was young and quick, but my running shoes gave me a slight advantage over his new heavy-duty, Adirondack hikers. After several minutes, he was huffing and puffing and I gained on him. While running, I tried to mentally calculate the best way to tackle this young teenager without risking serious bodily harm, to my much older person. My calculations proved unnecessary as he suddenly stopped and waited for me to catch up.

Almost smiling as I reached him, I had visions of murder in the woods. My gun was in the car. I have rudimentary martial arts training but it's not particularly skilled or reliable.

"What do ya want?"

"Help. Information about Lisa."

"I could say I don't know her. You got no link between Lisa and me."

"Then why run?"

"Felt like a jog after my long, boring boat ride."

"Looks like Mommy and Daddy got you all fixed up for the summer, huh?"

"It's not bad."

"What about Lisa? Please, we haven't much time. Your boss will be here any minute to boot me off the premises."

"That's why I ran. He's a college friend of the old man's. He probably wouldn't let you come within ten miles of me. I wanted to ask about Lisa. Is she okay?"

"She's missing. When was the last time you saw her?"

"March, toward the end of it, I guess. We had a falling out."

"Sounds like you had a falling out with your fists."

"I was really messed up. I'd been doin' a lot of drugs. Lisa was with me when I was in a really bad place. I felt bad. I tried to reach her. She wouldn't see me, wouldn't talk to me."

"Sounds like you treated her like shit on more than one occasion, Sanderson, my boy. And, you never quite got around to takin' her home to meet the folks, now did you?"

"I tried. The last time I talked to her, I was gonna take her to meet them. I'd talked to my parents and told them all about her. They wanted to meet her. They weren't thrilled of course, but they were willing to meet her. I told her, but she wouldn't believe me. Who are you anyway?"

"Ricky Steele."

"Look, Miss Steele. I don't expect you to believe me, but I love Lisa. Yeah, I started out using her. She's a hooker, how do you think I met her? But she's the finest person I've ever known. I know it sounds unbelievable, but that's how I feel. I told my parents I wanted to marry her, when I can get her to forgive me, that is. They said fine, but on the condition that I'd agree to come up here for the summer and think it over. This is their bargain. I'm going to get in touch with Lisa as soon as I get home, believe me. I promised for the summer I wouldn't write or call, but I'm going to write or call her in a couple of weeks, screw them."

"Are you aware that Lisa is only thirteen"

"Yeah, but she's more mature than any of the airheads that hang around the Club at home or here for that matter. I hate 'em. I don't mind waiting for Lisa either. I'm hopin' when my folks get used to the idea, they'll help out with school for her."

I couldn't quite picture Muffy writing out those checks.

"Can you think of anywhere she might be?"

"No, except maybe with that girl, Natalie, who she lives with. Like I said, I haven't seen her in over a month."

"Did you tell your parents Lisa's name and where she lived?"

"Yup, I told 'em everything. Funny too, they didn't seem too freaked out. The thing that got them the most riled up was where we used to go, you know, when we wanted to be alone. Right under their noses on the grounds of the Club. Dad was really ripped about that."

I could imagine. Muffy was a cool one.

"You mean Aquinessett?"

"Yeah, I was working there, till I got the job here. We didn't hang out where any members could spot us. There's an old barn out in the woods, used for the mowers and golf carts till they built the new building. Lots of the guys use it now and then, to take girls. Lisa and I always went alone. I kept our relationship pretty much a secret, till I told my folks."

"Yes, so I understand." He might be in love, but he was still a shit as far as I was concerned. "Where is this barn in relation to the main buildings?"

"There's a cart path halfway down the 16th fairway leading off to the right. It's at the end of that path. Pretty overgrown now, why?"

"I don't know, I just thought maybe she might have gone there to hide."

"Hey! What do ya think you're doin'?"

We turned to spy a red-cheeked man, who looked to be in his sixties, very fit and chipper, barreling down the path toward us. He was not sporting a S. L. leisure suit, thank goodness, but I bet he owned a closet full. I had no doubt that I was looking at Mr. Walker, in the flesh. I cringed, waiting for a verbal lashing. Ian Walker didn't actually grab me by the scruff of my neck, but it sure felt like it.

"Just what do you think you're doing? This is private property and you're trespassing. Sandy, rejoin your group immediately. You're needed at the Lodge."

"Settle down, Mr. Walker. My name's Ricky Steele and you know very well why I'm here. I'm sure your old college buddy gave you a heads up about me."

"That's none of your business, whoever you are. I want you off my property, now. Come along quickly."

"Look, Mr. Walker, I think we got off on the wrong foot. I'm sorry for trespassing, truly I am. If you'd been here I would have spoken to you directly, but you were gone."

"Keep moving, Miss Steele. I've got to get back."

"Five minutes, please?"

"What is it you want?"

He was out of breath and walking slowly.

"What can you tell me about Sandy Wilkerson?"

"Nothing."

"Can you at least tell me how long Sandy's been at camp?"

"Came week before last."

"Has he had much free time? Before the campers arrive are your counselors occupied, or do they kind of come and go at their leisure?"

"There's more to do now thaen when the camp opens."

"Would Sandy have had free time, to get away in the last week or so?"

"Not thirty seconds. He's been on the canoe trip for ten days and nights. In the back woods with no contact whatsoever with civilization. And there's no such thing as free time for the Sunrise employees. Every member of the team has to be contributing one hundred percent, 24/7. Our reputation depends on it."

"Thanks, Mr. Walker, you've been a big help. And, I'm sorry to have barged in."

We shook hands and he departed, waving as he disappeared down the path to the dock. I turned to find an empty car awaiting me. I looked around and spied them at the water's edge, wading. I whistled and they grabbed their shoes and came running, laughing and chattering like two kids away at summer camp.

As we drove away the sound of the sandy crunching gravel surrounded us once again, forestalling conversation. The Subaru got us on the road, but I didn't fancy an overnight stay in it, so I pulled into the Luxury Budget Cabins, ten miles from the resort, and called it a day. They had a small restaurant, kind of a truckers' joint, where we ate a quiet meal. I encouraged Nat to eat a tossed salad, and a bowl of chili. She gagged a couple of times, but got 'em down. Most of it came back up after we got to the room, but I figured some nutrients might've sneaked into her system. Teddy ate two burgers, fries and onion rings and yours truly, a veggie burger. We stayed up until midnight watching silly television.

I set my watch alarm for 5:45 a.m. and was just fading into dreamland, when she said, "Did you ever think about getting married, Ricky? Getting married and having kids?"

"I fear that time has passed me by. I was married for a very short time. Truth was, I wasn't very good at it. I'm pretty irresponsible and a lousy housekeeper."

"Just wondered."

"Night, Nat. Night, Teddy."

"Night," Nat whispered.

Teddy said nothing.

As I drifted off, my mind returned to Lisa. We still had nothing, but at least one mystery had been cleared up. I was relatively certain the "B" she mentioned in her diary entries was the barn in the woods. Not that it mattered much, but it was a loose end.

Chapter 36

Our flight home was rough and bumpy with Nat white as a sheet, shaking the whole way. Teddy didn't look much better. I had the airsick bag poised and ready, but miraculously it wasn't needed. The two-hour layover in Newark was loads of fun. I just love long, gray rooms with TVs hanging off the sides of the plastic molded chairs. Kinda makes you feel glad you're alive. I gave Nat and Teddy a bunch of quarters and they plunked themselves down to enjoy reruns of *Mr. Ed*.

I practically had to drag Nat onto the Providence plane. Fortunately, this flight was much smoother. I paid the parking and we headed home. As I approached the city, I longed to turn off at the Grove and go home for a hot bath and clean clothes, but I needed to get into the office, at least for a little while, then I wanted to head out to the Aquinessett. It would probably be a waste of time, but I wanted to see the maintenance shed. Maybe we'd find Lisa camping out. Unlikely, but one could hope.

I dropped the kids off at the apartment, telling them I would phone later. My watch read 2:08 p.m. as I drove into the parking lot of my building. I'd had quite a time maneuvering past the hordes that had amassed for Sidewalk Days. Sidewalk Days happen about once a month at the outlets starting in mid-April and on through November. Racks of clothes and tables piled high with clothes, lamps, pocketbooks, knick-knacks, glassware, whatever the stores wanted to sell fast, spilled out into the parking lot area, some under tents, some taking a chance on the weather. Almost nothing puts me in a fouler mood than Sidewalk Days.

Finally, I broke through, parked the jeep and climbed the stairs to the office two at a time. When I reached the landing, there it was again. Silence. Peering down the hallway, sure enough, the office door stood open. I could almost feel the fists on my poor little face and my gun was in the glove compartment. I turned to go back and retrieve it and decided I would bring the security guard back up with me.

The security guard was swamped, but he assured me he would be right up. I headed up alone and inched my way along the hallway, stomach in knots, cold sweat dripping down my back, adrenaline in overtime. I wasn't ready to die and I certainly didn't relish another beating. I reached my door and raised my leg to kick it in when a sound broke the silence. I stood listening, my back to the wall until I heard it again. Snoring.

"Oh, for Christ's sake," I moaned, letting out a huge sigh. "Jesus Christ, Iry!"

I toed the door open and she stirred, but did not wake. Sleeping off a good one no doubt. I was tempted to shake her silly after the scare she had given me when I gazed around the room. Flowers? Everywhere I looked on tables, refrigerator, desk and every inch of floor space were flowers. Wreaths, bouquets, potted plants; the scent was overpowering and the colors against the drab office furnishings incredible.

I turned around and saw that the door had been forced, not Irene's style. The florist sure hadn't done it. I walked through to the inner office and was greeted with an even denser jungle of blooms. A vase with at least three dozen pink roses sat on my desk along with three or four bouquets and a gardenia plant in full bloom.

I picked a rose and was sniffing deeply when the phone rang.

"Ricky Steele."

"So?" Did I remember all your favorites?"

"Who is this?" The voice was sickening familiar.

"Rick, doll, we all make mistakes. Here I was thinkin' one of my guys iced that Phillips prick as a personal favor to me. Then I find out he was outta town. A big laugh, huh? Can you believe a fuck up like that? Here me and my guys went and messed up that pretty little face of yours for nothin'. But, no one's gonna say Rollo Duffy don't know how to say sorry.

"What, no smart remark? No, thanks Rollo, let bygones be bygones, I forgive you?"

"Fuck you! And I'm sending you the bill for repairing my door too, asshole!"

I slammed down the receiver, grabbed the roses, and threw them in the waste basket.

It took me a half an hour to throw out the entire lot. I kept the potted plants, but the rest went out the window into the dumpster in the parking lot below. Irene woke halfway through my tantrum and rescued a few bouquets mid-air, which she carted away after receiving her allowance. I give her ten dollars a week, if I have it on me. By the time I'd disposed of every last bloom, my anger at Rollo Duffy had subsided enough for me to get down to work. Forgive him indeed!

After a brief perusal of my mail, now wet and soggy from plants dripping all over it, I threw it aside and got out my notebook. While sitting in Newark, I had jotted down a few scribbles about my conversation with Sandy Wilkerson, and I wanted to get them straight. I flipped back through my notes over the past few days and realized I needed a serious organization session.

Once I got started, it took over an hour to type everything, print it out and read through it. What did I have? A whole lot of nothing. I needed to talk to Billy Linden and Agnas Brown again. Yuck.

I called Natalie, no answer. Where the hell was she?

Chapter 37

I dialed Mark's number. While I waited, I draped the phone on my shoulder and continued with my paperwork.

"Hey, you're back. Still in one piece?"

"Fine, thanks. I need another favor though. Nothing major."

"You okay? You sound awful."

"Discouraged, that's all. This case is goin' nowhere and even if it were, I don't think it would be somewhere happy."

I gave him a brief description of my conversation with Sandy Wilkerson.

"I'm sure it's nothing, but I'd really like to get out and take a look in that cart barn at the club. Do you know it?"

"No."

"You busy tonight?"

"Kind of. Why don't you just go to dinner with your dad and stepmother, or that boyfriend of yours, Harp? I'm sure he could get you to the 16th fairway. You could sneak out over cocktails and be back in time to slurp up the escargot."

"No, thank you. How 'bout Don, the pro? Couldn't you say I was coming and he'd let me in, leave me directions? I can probably sneak in as a service person, bribe a laundry truck driver, something like that, but the easier the better. You seem to slip in whenever you feel like it."

"It's not Fort Knox, Rick."

"Can you please make the call?"

"No problem. I'll call Don and call you right back."

"Soon?"

"Right away, but, Rick?"

"Thanks, I'll be waiting."

I hung up before he could say another word. I really did need a vacation.

I got up from the desk and wandered into the outer office. My stomach was growling and I realized I had not eaten since our motel breakfast, a measly corn muffin and tepid tea. There was nothing in the fridge, but a few sodas and a carton of vanilla nonfat yoghurt, out of date by three months. Disgusted, I grabbed a coke and tossed the yoghurt in the trash. No doubt I'd forget it was there and in a few weeks my whole office would reek of sour milk. My clients always notice the smell before I do. Bud empties the garbage on his way out, all the while lecturing me on the correlation between office housekeeping and a sold client base.

I found a half eaten box of Triscuits in my desk drawer. They were limp, but I grabbed a handful and sat down at my desk again. I was just reaching for the pile of soggy bills when the phone rang.

"Hi, it's me."

"And?"

"Don will leave your name at the gate. He's gotta leave early, but he'll draw you a map and leave it at the gatehouse. He hasn't been out to the barn in a couple of months. Says it's never used any more. He didn't think the kids had even been using it for a while. Said he'd go out himself and check it out tomorrow, but he's too busy this afternoon, Member Guest Tournament tomorrow."

"That's okay, I kinda want to see it."

"Sorry I can't join you, but I got this shitload of work and tonight I have another commitment."

"Fine, no problem. Thanks for calling Don. See you."

I tried Nat's cell again.

"Hi, it's me, Ricky. You okay?"

"Yeah. Just got off the phone with Billy. He wants me working or he's gonna drop me. Says Lisa's through even if she does come back. I don't know what to do without her. She's all the family I got and now with Billy pissed off…"

I let her cry for a few minutes, then said, "Where's Teddy?"

"He gone to Ronny's for the night. His parents are away and his sister is babysitting."

"Nat, I've got some things to take care of, but I'll come by later and pick you up. We can grab some dinner. Sound good?"

My instincts told me it was dumb to bring her along, but Nat was good company and there was not any danger involved. Truth be told, I didn't want to go out to Aquinessett alone. Having Natalie tagging along would be a distraction, forestalling ruminations about past wounds and my unfortunate experiences with the country club set.

I told her I'd pick her up around 6:30 p.m. and recommended she wear blend-into-the-woodwork-type clothes. No bright colors, no sparkles, no fluorescent headbands or flashy jewelry. She had been pretty toned down on the trip, but you never know. Left to her own devices she might whip together a doozy of a get-up for a trip to the country club.

"Later, Nat. Take care and don't worry. No work either."

Easy for me to say. I hung up making a mental note to drop in for another chat with Billy Linden. It was 4:30 p.m. and I wanted to go home and wash up. The outlet crowd had thinned, but I still had a near miss with a bag-laden woman, two unruly children in tow. In the midst of what looked like a serious double tantrum, the kids stepped right out in front of the jeep. My window closed, she was spared my screamed epitaphs, and I hers. She would have a tale to tell hubby tonight of their narrow escape from the jaws of death.

I stopped by Ally's for a quart of red chowder and two spinach pies. At home, I poured the chowder into a bowl and popped it and one of the pies into the microwave. Once again, I ignored the meal I had so dutifully planned for this evening, eggplant parmesan. Next month, I would discover a squishy, wrinkled eggplant stuffed against the back wall of the fridge. Beaky followed me from room to room, yowling and meowing, her way of expressing outrage at my neglecting her. I replenished her food and water dishes and patted her head. She hissed, clawed at my sneaker, then disappeared into the laundry room. Such an affectionate sweetie pie.

A hot shower and clean clothes and I felt like a new woman. On edge for days, I longed for a day of idleness. A little reading, a little resting, a passionate encounter with the opposite sex. I craved the warmth that suffused my body after sex. I'd been so cold and jumpy lately. But with who?

I ate the soup and pie slowly, reading the paper. As usual, the chowder was delicious, the broth spicy and rich, lots of clams and vegetables. The pie was its usual bland self, but I dipped it into the chowder before each bite. Yum! I hadn't read the news all week, never mind the sports page. Not much new, at least according to the *Providence Journal*. The Red Sox had slipped into fourth and the world's problems raged on.

Reluctantly, I roused myself a little after 6:00 p.m., washed the dishes and shoved them into the overflowing drying rack. I heated the other pie and reheated the remainder of the soup, then poured it into a wide mouthed thermos. I wrapped the pie in tin foil and put it and the thermos in an old picnic basket. I threw in a banana and a couple of napkins. Nat would no doubt turn up her nose at the lot of it, but if she did, we could stop somewhere on the way back from the Aquinessett.

Chapter 38

As I pulled up, I spied Nat on the sidewalk dressed in acid washed jeans and an oversized navy sweat shirt. Her sneakers looked suspiciously glow-in-the-dark, but overall she had dressed for stealth. I had on my dark blues and grays.

The gatekeeper handed me a note from Don and waved us in. He gave a curious glance at Natalie, then pressed the button and the gate swung open. He told me to park by the pro shop. As I parked a red sports car pulled up on our left near the main building. They could see the jeep, but our faces were deep in shadow as Lola emerged from the Mercedes sports coupe.

Light shone on her shimmering form, a soft white shawl over pink evening dress. The rays of the setting sun reflected off the jewelry, dripping from her neck and ears. From our vantage point it almost looked like she was wearing a turtleneck of diamonds, so brilliant and bejeweled was the slender high neck of her dress.

"Holy shit, look at that!" Natalie exclaimed, gaping as the vision swished toward the front door. Big Tony, impeccable in a dark evening suit, held out his arm and they waltzed in, all flash and glitter. We stood and gawked, unable to tear our eyes away.

The performance, staged for the benefit of the goggling doorman and several others lurking around the entrance, was suddenly interrupted by Mrs. Richards's stumble. Lola appeared to catch her heel on the doorstep, but ever the trooper, she made a quick recovery and they disappeared into the sumptuous recesses of the Club.

"Totally awesome. Is she someone famous?"

I shook my head, wondering what it would be like to be Lola.

"Come on, Nat. Let's get a move on."

In the envelope from Don, I found an Aquinessett score card with a map of the course on its back side. He had marked a line directing us from the pro shop to the 16th fairway. We started walking. As we crossed several fairways, we interrupted one foursome preparing to tee off in the growing darkness. A beautiful spring night, the sky was suffused with rosy colors as the sun set. A gentle breeze whispered through the tall fir trees bordering the fairway.

As we walked, birds chirped, the pungent smell of freshly mowed grass intoxicating, I remembered what I liked about the game of golf, the surroundings. No matter how you putted or chipped, the backdrop was always serene and magnificent, especially at this hour.

We crossed a bridge and walked the length of the 15th fairway, finally arriving at the tee marked ACC-16. It was one of those long, winding stretches with a dog leg to the right. We checked the map again and proceeded down the path Don had marked. We were at the edge of the woods, skirting a long stretch of sand traps, when I spied an opening in the thicket. A path led into the woods, overgrown, but still visible.

"That's it. Come on"

We plunged in as darkness fell. The little light remaining was obscured by tall, thick hemlocks. I had brought my heavy duty flashlight, which doubles as a weapon in a pinch, but we didn't need it yet. The grass was tall, and I made a mental note to check for ticks when we emerged. I certainly didn't need Lyme Disease to add to all my other problems. Natalie followed, stepping gingerly. Woods were clearly not her thing. She asked about snakes and I don't think my answers were entirely reassuring.

As we pushed farther on, the brush became almost impenetrable. I was on the verge of turning around to head back for my heavy duty pruning shears, when we spied a structure ahead of us. Painted a dull gray, it looked more like a barracks than a barn. This had to be the place.

Chapter 39

Dark now, we headed for the door following the flashlight's beam. I gave it a shove and it swung open with a loud screech. Cautiously, we stepped in. I don't mind spiders, but I do not like their webs plastered across my face. Visions of arachnids rushing down with evil intentions toward destroyer of their home, fill me with dread. I took the brunt of the webbing. Nat hung back, in mute horror as I flailed away at my face and hair.

The interior smelled of mold and rotted grass. It was divided into various cubicles and what looked like an enclosed office at the far end. As we moved forward, a new fouler stench assaulted us. Dead rats in the wall? Just thinking about long, stringy tails and sharp yellow teeth gave me the shivers.

We made our way toward what looked like an office, which was empty save for a couple of metal chairs and a rusty file cabinet missing both drawers. A stained mattress was on the floor in the corner. Rusted beer cans littered the floor. It had been a while since the grounds crew had partied here. Then, I shone the light on a green and yellow box of heavy duty trash bags, which, by the look of it, appeared to be a recent addition. The box was on a wooden crate in the middle of the room. No dust, no cobwebs, no nothing on that bright, shiny green and yellow box. Nat was behind me, whining, holding her nose against the stench, which had grown much stronger.

"When can we go?"

I walked farther into the room and picked up the box. As I did, I noticed four tiny brownish red spots, more like little lines really, less than an inch long and a quarter inch wide, in a row on the top of the crate. I've seen dried blood often enough to recognize it. Next to the spots, the crate was gouged with a deep rut, about five inches long. I had a very bad feeling about the stench as it no longer smelled like dead rat. Natalie hung back, cowering so she couldn't see the crate.

"Listen, Nat. It's pretty grungy in here and the stench is unreal. Why don't you go out and take a breather."

"What's the matter?"

"Nothing. I'll finish up in here and be right out. We need a lookout anyway. Never know who might be around. Go on now. Knock three times if you hear anyone." I pushed her toward the door. "Wait right outside, okay?"

After the last bit of nudging, she gave in, thrilled to escape the cobwebs and smell. "Yuck," she muttered, voice trailing into the darkness. "How could Lisa have stood this fucking stink?"

I went back to the office and shone the light around. Nothing. I moved farther down the hallway, where there were a few more stalls, empty save for a few bits of broken machinery and old tools. Pitch black, the flashlight's strong beam danced around cobwebbed walls as I proceeded. The stench grew even stronger as I rounded the last stall and I directed my light into its depth. My hand shook and I was fixing to retreat when the beam fell on the shiny black trash bag in the far corner. Full, its yellow drawstring was tied in a neat yellow bow.

I knew I should leave. Go back, phone the police and wait until they arrived, but, I was here and felt I should see it through. The stench overpowering now, I paused, and rifled through my pocket, pulling out my Swiss army knife. I opened the blade and stepped forward, flashlight pointing on my target.

Heavy duty trash bags do not tear easily. I kept the bag pulled away from its load while I cut a fairly long slit down the side. I tried not to breathe as I worked. I kept telling myself, just a little more, then it'll be over and you can run out and fill up your lungs with fresh air.

I had intended to confirm that there was, indeed, a body inside, then go out and have Natalie run for the police while I waited by the barn door, but the bag shifted suddenly and dropped to one side. I had been holding it more tightly than I thought and as it shifted she fell into a very small heap on the cold cement floor. It was difficult, but not impossible to recognize the bloated features, the damp matted hair. Lisa Brown. We had found her at last, about a week too late.

She wore the tight, green pants Natalie had described, a pink jersey with studied rhinestone jobbies, and the tiniest Reebok high top sneakers. Almost baby shoes. She had been strangled. An ugly black and blue mark encircled her neck like a snake. Otherwise, she appeared to be unscarred, until I turned her over. Her arms had been pinned underneath her. As the body rolled over I saw that one hand held a revolver. I didn't touch it or make any effort to extract it from her grasp.

The other hand had been mutilated, and as I stared at it in horror, I realized where the tiny, four lines of blood had come from. The four fingers of her right hand had been chopped off, below the middle joint. After death I reasoned, remembering how little blood there'd been on the crate.

I turned and started for the door. When I reached it, I called, "Nat."

No reply. I started to panic, and then spotted her behind a bush.

"Sorry, had to pee." She emerged, buttoning her jeans. She looked almost happy and my heart did a painful flip flop.

"Do you think you could find your way to the gate without me?"

"Sure, why?"

"My cell is in the car and I need you to get the gate keeper to phone the police. When they arrive, you can lead them back here, okay?"

"It's Lisa, ain't it? She's in there!" She reached for the door handle.

"Whoa, Nat, no!"

I grabbed her birdlike shoulders. "I can't let you go in. It's a crime scene now. We need to leave it as undisturbed as possible. Okay?"

"But, I—"

"No, Nat, please. We need help and I don't want to leave you here alone. Go on now, run, please. Take the flashlight and remember to tell the guard, 16th fairway, the old cart barn. Hurry! Tell the gate keeper to ask for Sergeant Roberts."

She hesitated a few seconds, then took off, sprinting away at a fast clip. I waited until I could no longer hear footsteps rustling through the woods, then leaned over to cry and puke my guts out.

It took forever for them to arrive. I didn't go back into the barn. The light was gone and my job was over. I'd found Lisa Brown. Miserable, I slumped against the side of the barn.

Fortunately Douglas had been on duty. He brought five officers, and spotlights that flickered as they approached. They managed to get a small pick-up down the path. It came crashing into the clearing ahead of the flashlights and Douglas hopped from its cab.

While the police went about their work, I held Nat in my arms, and she sobbed, gut wrenching, heartbreaking sobs. She had forced down her spinach pie and chowder on the drive out to Aquinessett, but they came up as soon as she returned. While she cried and vomited, I held her the way my mother had held me as a child, wiping her face with the sleeve of my jacket.

The next few hours were a blur, the usual endless questions, over and over. The body was loaded into the back of the pick-up, as a couple of the officers walked Natalie and me back to the car. She was a basket case and I wasn't much better. For once, Douglas took pity on me and sent us home with, "I want you at the station house first thing, Steele. You got that?"

I nodded.

Natalie sobbed and screamed all the way to the house. I insisted she come home and sleep in my guest bed. It was almost midnight before I got her into bed and forced her to drink a glass of milk, heavily laced with brandy and two sleeping pills I had unearthed from the recesses of my medicine cabinet. Then I lay down beside her until she fell asleep.

I took a bath, administered the same milk concoction to myself, minus the sleeping pills, and got into bed to sleep a heavy, dreamless slumber.

Chapter 40

A car door slammed and I woke with a start. I felt damp and clammy, but the room was cool. My head ached and try as I might I could not remember what day it was. Was I sick? Brain damaged? I dragged myself out of bed and plodded down the hall. After splashing water on my face and brushing my teeth and tongue, to get rid of the disgusting taste, I crawled back into bed. The clock read 7:30 a.m. I knew I needed to get going, but I lay back and closed my eyes. I must have drifted off to sleep again, because the phone's ring startled me.

"Hi, it's Mark."

"Uh huh?"

"I'm sorry. I really am. If I'd only known I never would have let you go out there alone."

"Mark, I'm okay. No need to feel guilty. All's well. How'd you find out anyway?"

"Don called. The club's in an uproar. They had to cancel the "Member Guest" today and there are cops crawling all over the place."

"Poor darlings."

"You want anything? Want me to come over? We could fly down to Mexico for a week or two. My sister and her boyfriend just came back. It was real cheap and they had a great time. We can lie around the beach all day sipping Marguerites, have some leisurely dinners and spend the rest of the night, as ours.

"Mmm, this cougar will need to pass on that one."

"You're not a cougar, just incredibly sexy."

"Don't be ridiculous. I've gotta go."

"Why? Your case is closed. You've found Lisa Brown. Let Roberts and his boys do the rest. No one hired you to find a killer."

"No, they didn't, but I have a young kid, sleeping in my guest room. She needs help and maybe I can provide it. There are lots of loose ends."

"Ricky, listen to me."

"Mark, stop right there. I have a few questions, that's all. Maybe a trip downtown will give me the answers I need. I'll talk to you later."

"Promise me you'll take care, will you? I heard through the grapevine that your boyfriend, Harp, offered to get you some kind of bodyguard. I'd take him up on it."

How was it in a city of 90,000 people, everyone seemed to know my business? "First of all, he's not my boyfriend, and second I do not need a bodyguard."

"I'll call you, okay?"

I rang off, squashed the thought of a run, then showered, dressed and ate a small breakfast of bran flakes with a banana on top. I didn't bother with tea since I would have plenty during the hours I would be sitting around the station house. I gathered my stuff and tiptoed in to peek at Natalie. If she was asleep I intended to leave her a note, but I found her sitting at the edge of the bed, staring at the floor.

"Hey, Nat."

"What am I gonna do?"

"We'll figure out something."

Tears streamed down her sunken cheeks. "I don't know how I'll live without Lisa. Why would someone kill her? And, why there? How did she even know about that place?"

"I don't know, Nat. It could have something to do with her boyfriend, Sandy, but more likely it's because she was with Peter Phillips the night he died. She might have seen his killer, or the killer thought she could identify him. I don't know. We might know more after I talk to the police."

"You going now? Should I come with you?"

"No, you stay here and rest. They'll need a statement from you, but I'll come back and pick you up later, okay? And listen, we need to find Teddy and fast. He's gotta be told, but he's also gotta get off the streets now. Don't you open the door to anyone today, unless you know 'em okay? I'll call later."

"Do you think I might be next?" she wailed. Oh, God, Miss Steele, what am I gonna do?"

"Nat, relax. I don't think you're next. I'd just rather be cautious, okay?"

She calmed down a little, but started rooting around for her clothes, telling me she would not be left alone. I told her to hold on, ran next door and knocked on Vinnie's door. I crossed my fingers, praying he was home. I was so happy to see his rumpled visage several minutes later that I almost hugged him.

"Hey, Rick. A little early, ain't it?"

Vinnie spends many days home, working nights. I'm not sure where they need night time mechanics, but I don't ask. Using my fawning, obsequious voice, I learned that yes, he would be home today, and no, he wouldn't mind sleeping in my bed to give Nat some company. Clearly naked under his short terry robe, he retreated into his bedroom to throw on some shorts, before following me home. After quick introductions, he was in my bed, sound asleep again."Remember, just wake Vinnie, if anything strange happens or you're nervous, okay?"

She nodded, visibly perked up at the prospect of spending the morning with Vinnie.

CHAPTER 41

I parked near the station house in a space reserved for police vehicles. The desk officer, who I did not know, was busy wrangling with some woman about a speeding ticket so I walked straight back to Douglas's office without speaking to him. Douglas didn't appear to have been home since I'd seen him last. Styrofoam cups were everywhere and empty fast food containers littered his desk and the overflowing wastebasket beside it.

I took the only seat not covered with trash. "Hey, Doug, you okay?"

"Steele, it's about time. What happened to first thing?"

"Give me a break. It's only nine-fifteen. Besides I got a kid now. Takes time to arrange for babysitters."

"Cottrell will take your statement. He needs the kid's statement too. She should've come with you."

"I'll bring her later. Have you got anything at all?"

"Not yet. Lab isn't through, but cause of death was strangulation. Been in the shed about six days. Ernie thinks she died sometime late Saturday."

"What about the severed fingers? Did they turn up?"

"Nope and they won't. You know the routine. She probably scratched the guy, got some skin under her nails. Those fingers are fish bait, long gone."

"They were hacked off after she was dead, right?"

"Looks like it."

"Any idea what was used?"

"Some kind of ax, a pretty small one. We went all over the place and area around it didn't find it. Ernie thinks that maybe the fingers were chopped off a couple of hours after death. Killer went away, got the ax and came back to finish the job. Why the hell she ended up there is another question. We'll know more when we talk to the other kid."

"What about her things? Anything on her that might help?"

He shrugged. "Body's down with the lab boys. Her effects are upstairs. Tell Cottrell I said it was okay for you to look through the stuff, and tell him every detail about your last couple of days. I mean it, Steele. I hear you took a trip to New York? I can still throw you in a cell so don't leave anything out."

The phone rang.

"What about the gun?"

He answered, asked the person to hold on, and covered the mouth piece. "Cottrell has it. Go on up."

Since he was already barking into the phone, I didn't think I should interrupt to ask for Tim's exact location. The second floor of the station was mostly storage rooms, but there were a couple of offices with tables and files where one could spread out and sift through stuff. I figured I would find Cottrell in one of these. After climbing the stairs, I started down the hall and found a room at the end with boxes and folders stacked all around and papers spread out all over the table. No sign of blue-eyed Tim. As I peered in, I heard a toilet flush at the end of the hall, twenty seconds later Tim emerged from the men's room, adjusting his belt.

"Hey, Rick. Been waiting for you. Come on. I gotta get to the lab, check on things, then we can talk."

"Can I come along?"

"Okay, but be cool. It's been a rough night for everyone, especially Ernie."

He smiled that beautiful smile of his, blue eyes twinkling. Maybe being a cougar might not be so bad, or was cradle robber the more appropriate term? I really did need to get a life.

Chapter 42

Until the previous year, all the preliminary lab work, autopsies, blood work, whatever, had been done at one of the local hospitals, or was sent to the State forensics lab in Boston. Now the city had its own lab, adjacent to the station house so they were able to capably process most routine evidence. Lisa's body had been sent there. It was still possible that she would take a trip up to Boston, or at least some of her would, but time would tell.

We exited the building and walked twenty yards up the street to the lab. A one story, pre-fab job, it resembled a small clinic. Ernie was on a break, stretched out on the couch in his side office, drinking coffee. He looked worse that Douglas. Tim Cottrell, on the other hand, looked like he hadn't lost a wink of sleep. Us old guys fare worse with sleep deprivation.

Short, with dark thinning hair, Ernie usually plastered what remained of his scant locks across the top of his head in a nasty comb over. This morning he had neglected his personal grooming and so his hair stuck out all over the place, uneven and scraggly, his baldpate in full view. The imprints of a surgical mask and cap still showed on his cheeks and forehead.

"Hey, Ern. Whatcha got?"

Ernie gave Tim a cursory glance, gazed over at me, then proceeded, as if it was perfectly natural for me to be there. Ernie never was a go-by-the-booker.

"Not much I haven't told you already. Just sent some tissue samples off, but it was definitely strangulation. Fingers severed a couple of hours after death, no other visible marks of abuse. Looks like she was strangled with a scarf, long soft cloth, something like that, not a rope or anything coarse 'cause there were no scratches on her neck."

"What about the gun?" I asked.

"We're running a trace on it. No prints, but it looks like the same gun that killed the Phillips guy. Same gun that's killed four or five guys this past year. Should know more in an hour or so."

I stepped forward, staring at the sad little face on the table. "And her effects, did you find anything special?"

"Not much. Her clothes are bein' worked on. The rest of the stuff's over there." He pointed to a table in the next room. "Have a look."

I looked down at the pathetic array, mostly the contents of Lisa's pockets and purse. Makeup, brush, comb, various slips of paper, and a tiny change purse that she used as a wallet with twenty-two dollars and change stuffed in it. It was one of those beaded leather jobs with "Niagara Falls" and a picture of the falls worked in tiny, plastic beads.

I unraveled the slips of papers. A couple were receipts from CVS and Stop and Shop. I was just tossing the last receipt, for thirty- eight dollars from Cherry & Webb, back into the pile when I noticed the back. There was a number scribbled on the back. I didn't have to think twice to recognize it. It was the number of "Friends On The Line." Could she have wanted to call that day and never got the chance?

I thought back to Sandy Wilkerson's description of his parents' reaction to hearing about Lisa. Somehow it didn't add up. Muffy and Sanderson calm when their darling boy was dating a hooker, a preadolescent one at that, and proposing to bring her home for dinner? I decided to pay them another call.

We chatted with Ernie for a while, then I went back to give my statement to Tim. This took most of the morning between the trip home to fetch Natalie and my statement. She had a difficult time tearing herself away from Vinnie, who was entertaining her with card tricks when I arrived. While they played he had her laughing at his ridiculous stories, laced with expletives and lots of exaggerations. They were both in heaven.

Nat gave Tim her statement and as we were leaving the station house we stopped by to say bye to Douglas and a call came through. He took it and raised his finger, indicating we should wait. A minute later, he hung up.

"That was ballistics. They've traced the gun. Stolen a year ago January from Manny's Garage, bottom of President Avenue. We'll check it out. I know Manny. I'll stop by on my way home."

"Want me to check it out? I'm heading out now. I could swing by?"

"Not unless you want to be swinging from some gallows next. Look, Steele, you're finished. Your M.P. is found. You're done. I mean it. No more running around claiming you're workin' with the police either. Tony Richards isn't your naïve, little suburban housewife. He knows bullshit when he hears it and he's not above giving us trouble. Now you stay the hell out of this, you hear me?"

"Douglas, I'm sorry, but I have a responsibility."

"Fuck your responsibility. No more, nothing. You'll just screw things up. This guy's a sicko and much as I'd like you outta my hair, I don't want no more dead bodies on my hands."

"Aw, you really do care, Douglas."

"Get the hell outta here before I throw you in a cell."

I blew him a kiss and turned away.

"Steele, did you give Cottrell all of it?"

"Of course, what do ya take me for?"

"Steele?"

I turned to face him. "Yes."

"I mean it."

"So do I. I told him everything, Girl Scout's honor."

"Steele."

"Yes?"

He shook his head. "Never mind, thanks. Now get the hell outta here."

Natalie and I walked out arm in arm. I was smiling, despite all the loose ends I wasn't allowed to pursue. Truth be told, I felt relieved to be out of it. There was also Natalie to think about. Her skinny, little arm felt so fragile wrapped in mine, like a twig ready to snap in a strong wind.

My tentative plan was to give her a few days to recover and then ease her into Ruth's hands. She couldn't go back to her father, or Billy Linden. What other choices did she have? And there was Teddy, once we found him. I hoped we'd find him soon.

Chapter 43

Before heading home, we decided to swing by the apartment so Natalie could pick up some extra clothes. As we pulled up, I saw Teddy curled up in a corner by the front door. I let Natalie out and waited in the car. I figured Teddy would rather hear it from her and didn't want to intrude on their grief. I watched him recoil from her tearful embrace, his expression perplexed as she began talking.

He took it calmly. No tears, no hysterics. I wondered if he was numb or just resigned, but then how does a ten-year-old process death anyway? Maybe the finality of it hadn't even sunk in. Maybe after all he'd been through, he just didn't care.

"Come up, if you want, Ricky," she called as they disappeared into the building.

I locked the car and followed. Carl was not home. Teddy slumped on the couch while Natalie collected her things and I made a call to "Friends on the Line."

"Hi, this is Friends On The Line, Martha speaking. How can I help you?"

I explained who I was and a brief rundown on what had happened to Lisa Brown since we had last talked. She expressed words of shock and sorrow as I questioned her about Lisa's recent phone calls, most notably a week ago Saturday. She asked me to hold and went to check.

Moments later, she clicked back on. "That night's calls have been logged, but none from a Lisa. Sorry. Maybe she used an alias or intended to call, but never got the chance?"

"Yeah, I'm afraid that's just what happened. Any chance a call would have been missed or not recorded?"

"No way. We're required to record everything, even a wrong number or a no name. Lesley Parker was on that evening. She would've written it down. She's incredibly careful."

"Is she there now?"

"Sorry, she quit. Hold on a minute, I'll look and see if I have her number."

She was back almost immediately. "Nope, sorry, thought I might have a phone number, address, something, but we don't. She wasn't here long. I was surprised when Mrs. Richards told me she quit. She seemed to be happy enough, but then we've had a lot of trouble keeping people this past year or so. Turnover is always heavy in this line of work."

I thanked her and rang off, giving her my number again and asked her to call if she found a phone number or address for Lesley Parker. After stopping at the Somerset Burger King drive-in window, I dropped the kids off at my place, laden with junk food. They could spend the afternoon resting and watching the tube with Vinnie next door to keep an eye on them.

I headed to the office to get organized and check messages. The first message was from Ron Cathers, Peter Phillips's friend.

I grabbed the phone and dialed. On the sixth ring, he answered, sounding out of breath. I explained who I was.

"Yeah, hi. Sorry, just finishing my run. Don't usually keep my phone with me, but here we are. Katie told me you were lookin' for me?"

I gave him a quick summary pertaining to my interest in Peter's death. I then asked if there was anything he could tell me about who Peter was working with, or what case he was working on before he died. He related much the same kind of story as Steve White, Peter's tennis buddy.

"How about lately? Anything out of the ordinary, maybe an after hours deal? His wife seemed to think he was keeping something a secret and neither she nor I believe it was cruising for hookers."

He was silent for several minutes.

"Mr. Cathers?"

"Yeah, I'm here. What the hell, I didn't tell this to the cops 'cause they got no respect for the dead, barging in the day my pop died. Pete swore me to secrecy, but I don't guess it matters now.

"I don't know all the details, but Pete thought he'd nailed the guy who's been bumping off the Summer Street Johns. As I'm sure you know, there've been three or four murders down there within the past year? Peter was getting close."

"Did he give you a name?"

"Nope. He had a pretty good idea, but didn't want to give anything away until he had proof. Said it might be dangerous for me to know. I'm sure that's why he didn't tell Rachel. He was scared, Miss Steele. He'd set up a meeting with the guy just before I left. I was getting ready to call him from Montana when Katie called to tell me he was dead."

"Did he give you a time or a place where the meeting was taking place? Anything?"

"He didn't say. I got the feeling he'd talked to the guy, but I'm not sure when and where. One thing's for certain, though. That's why he's dead. Count on it."

"You need to tell all this to the police. It's important and I'd rather they hear it from you, not me."

"I was planning to go in tomorrow, after I talked to you. No one wants them to catch the bastards more than I do. It's a fucking shame, excuse my language. A guy like Peter Phillips, quiet, friendly, a loving father. He was my closest buddy and I really miss him."

"I'm very sorry for your loss. Thanks so much. You've been a huge help."

I asked him to call if he thought of anything else, rang off and pushed the button on my machine again.

"Miss Steele, this is Sanderson Wilkerson. Please return my call immediately. Thank you." He gave his number twice, but he needn't have bothered. It was his home number and I already had it.

"Yes, sir!"

I saluted the machine and punched in the number. His dibs answered, voice several decibels lower, but recognizable.

"Mr. Wilkerson, this is Ricky Steele. I understand that you are upset, but perhaps I could explain the situation to you?"

"I have no wish to hear anything about your situation. Were you not Ralston Steele's daughter, I'd have you thrown in jail for harassment."

I mentally counted to ten. "Whoa, Mr. W., my father has nothing to do with my affairs. And, with my connections to law enforcement, I doubt even you have the clout to have me thrown in jail."

"Stay away from my son. Do you hear me?"

"I'm sorry, Mr. Wilkerson, but I have a job to do. Your son, by the way, was only too happy to speak with me. It's you and your wife who seem to be obstructing justice. Have you got something to hide? Where were you last Saturday night, sir, if I might ask?"

I figured he'd slam down the phone without answering, but it was worth a try.

"What business is it of yours?"

"Sandy's girlfriend, or rather his fiancée, Lisa Brown was murdered last Saturday night."

"How dare you insinuate that my son had any connection to that filth. And my whereabouts at any time are none of your business!"

"She was a child, surviving on her own, Mr. Wilkerson, not filth, and you should be ashamed of yourself for such judgment. And, if your whereabouts are none of my business, they'll soon be police business. I've yet to inform them about your son's involvement with Lisa Brown, but now that she's turned up dead, and you are so incredibly uncooperative, I have no choice."

"How dare you! What are you implying?"

"Sandy told you all about Lisa Brown and his intentions regarding her. He actually thinks you were supportive of his idea of him and Lisa being together. If that was ever going to happen. I have no wish to pry into your family's affairs or to drag your name through the mud, but I need answers. Now, where were you last Saturday night?"

"My wife and I know nothing about Lisa Brown, except the little Sanderson told us. We've never met her and know nothing about where she lives. And, as for last Saturday, we were attending a fundraiser for the Animal Rescue League out at the Aquinessett. It was a dinner and dance. Is there anything else?" His voice had lost some of its bluster.

According to what Mark had learned from Don, Sandy had caused his parents a shitload of grief the past few years. Wrecked cars, pregnant girlfriends, expulsions from several prominent preparatory schools, drugs, alcohol, you name it. Maybe Mr. W. was weary of being dragged into yet another of Junior's messes.

"No, that's all. Thanks, Mr. Wilkerson. I'm sorry if I—"

"Goodbye, Miss Steele."

He hung up, sounding defeated, but was he a murderer? I made a note to check out his fundraiser story.

The last message was from Bunny. "Hey, stranger, did you make it back from New York in one piece? Call me."

Smiling, I dialed Coles River Travel and Realty. Bunny was gone for the day so I tried her cell.

"Oh, my God, you're alive!"

"Hey, Bun, what's up? Not tryin' to sell my house out from under me are you?"

"No, but I haven't seen anything but your back running out of the office for ages. Let's have dinner. Whatcha doin' tomorrow night?"

"Nothing. I'd love to have dinner, but I have a suggestion."

"Uh-oh. I know that voice. Forget it, I'm not crawling through a rat-infested sewer or scaling a barbed wire fence before dinner. No way, Jose! Last time you "made a suggestion" I nearly lost my job, not to mention wrecking my best suit and heels. Forget it!"

Bunny's real estate connections have proven useful from time to time, gaining me entrance to forbidden places, mostly connected with insurance claim investigations. We've had a few close calls and the going can get dirty. Bunny wasn't much of an investigator, but she had a great sense of humor.

"Hold on, dearie, it's nothing like that. I was just going to ask if you'd mind eating out at Aquinessett. My treat if you like. You still belong, don't you?"

"Now I know you're up to something. You hate that place. Fess up, why do you want to go out there?"

"Just call it old times' sake."

"Bullshit. Either I get the facts, or I'm not getting you in."

Briefly summarizing the case without mentioning names and I ended with, "Please, Bun. I promise, no trouble."

"Well, okay. It's the Sunday night buffet. They're always great. If you promise to behave, I guess it'll be okay."

"Bunny, I love you!"

"Humph."

"I'll pick you up." She lives only two blocks from me and I'm a better driver.

My calls completed, I sat back. Who was left? If the Wilkerson's alibi checked out, who was behind all of it?"

Billy Linden? What was his motive? Natalie claimed he had been in Boston the previous weekend. I could check that out. Carl? He was strange, but a killer? And besides, what possible motive would he have for killing Peter Phillips?

Nothing made sense and my brain was getting fuzzier by the minute. I still hadn't checked out Mike Correiro, the breaking and entering case that Phillips had been working on, not to mention the connection to Rollo Duffy, but somehow I didn't think Duffy, sleaze that he was, was involved in Lisa's death.

Vinnie and I cooked supper and we all sat around, watching an ancient Indiana Jones movie on Vinnie's giant flat screen. Rather, the three of them watched and I stewed over my notes in the background. Vinnie was great with the kids. They instantly took to him and I became invisible, an arrangement that suited me fine and did not hurt my feelings in the slightest. After we got back from Vinnie's, the kids went to bed, leaving me alone on the couch in the living room, fiddling with my notes, working myself into a depression. I was just gathering my things to head off to bed when Natalie appeared in the doorway.

"Got a sec?"

"Sure," I said, settling back. "Come sit." She sat beside me on the couch. She was shivering so I tossed a blanket over her legs.

She seemed self-conscious, uncertain of where to begin.

"What's up?"

"Have you ever thought about having kids? I mean adopting?"

I knew where this was leading, but I played dumb, not sure what to say. "'Member we talked about this before? First of all, I'm too old to start now and besides, I doubt I'd be very good with kids."

Swallowing hard, she said, "Why can't I live here with you?"

"Natalie, I, you, we."

"I wouldn't be no trouble. You know me, I'm quiet. And I can cook a little, and clean. I could take care of things for you when you're at work."

I leaned over to touch her arm. "Nat, listen to me. You're a great kid. If I had a kid, you'd be the one I'd want. I'm just not the mother type. Look at me. Look at the way I live. Even if I wanted to, and I don't, Social Services wouldn't approve me as an adoptive parent. I'm too old and I'm single. I'm also irresponsible and I lead a dangerous live. What kind of a home could I possibly give a kid?"

Tears welled in her dark eyes. "Couldn't be any worse than what I've had so far."

"Maybe not, but you deserve better."

"Never mind, forget it. Was a bullshit idea, anyway."

She jumped up and dashed out of the room.

"Nat, wait."

I wanted to follow her and tell her I was not abandoning her, that I would find her a good place, but I did not want to make promises I could not keep.

I did not sleep well.

Chapter 44

The next day dawned sunny and warm, in sharp contrast to my somber mood. When I got back from my run, the kids were still sleeping. I usually take a longer run Sunday mornings, eight miles on the roads, ending with the last mile or so on the beach. The Sunday papers were waiting upon my return so I cooked breakfast and settled in. I allow myself a fried egg on Sundays, sprinkled with parsley, Cajun garlic spices and parmesan cheese. I have English muffins with it. Heaven on a plate.

Several hours later, I was on my third cup of tea and had just started the *Times* crossword when Vinnie knocked at the door.

"Hey, Rick. What do ya say, me and you take the kids to Rocky Point later? You know Teddy's never been there? Imagine that, never been to Rocky Point!"

Rocky Point, an amusement park in southern Rhode Island, is one of my least favorite spots. I love the Shore Dinner Hall with its clam cakes, chowder and steamers, but the rides make me nauseous and the people that lurk around the arcade give me the willies.

"I don't know, Vin."

"Then, how 'bout I take 'em? Debbie's comin' over later. She loves kids and we'll take good care of 'em. Give you a break."

I couldn't conjure up a picture of Debbie, but no matter. "Well, if they want to, I guess it's okay. Might be nice. The funeral is tomorrow, you know."

"I'll come get 'em around 3:30 p.m. We'll eat out there and I'll have 'em home by 10:30p.m., sound okay?"

"Thanks, Vin. If you don't hear from me, just assume they're keyed. I'll send them with some money, thanks."

"You already said that, and don't worry about the money."

He pecked my cheek and disappeared.

The city was burying Lisa. Her body wouldn't be ready for burial for a few weeks, but at my insistence, a small service had been scheduled for tomorrow. Ruth Channing had arranged for the service to be held at the little chapel next to her church. The minister spent some time speaking to Natalie, Teddy and me about Lisa and had even attempted to contact and visit Agnas Brown. I don't believe he was successful there.

When the kids had left, I called Ruth Channing. I wanted to talk about Nat and Teddy's future while they were still within my grasp. After the funeral, when the shock of Lisa's death wore off, no telling what they'd do. After a few minutes of silence on the phone, Ruth said, "I have a family that will probably take the boy. They're looking for an older male child, to adopt. If it works out and they click, it'd be a great situation. They live in Touisset, not far from you as a matter of fact. They have two teenagers, a huge house and a couple of dogs. It's an incredible opportunity for a boy his age. They'd give him a good home. 'Course he'd have to stay here with me at Belmont House for a little while, until the adoption papers are finalized and his biological mother signs off her rights."

"I'll take care of Agnas Brown."

"The adoptive parents would like to meet and visit with Teddy a number of times before taking him home."

"That sounds great, Ruth, but what about Nat?"

"The father's signed papers releasing her. He wants nothing to do with her. He claims she's not even his. He's signed her over to us. Mom's dead. She died when Natalie was just a baby. "We could go after him, Rick, and make him support her, at least temporarily, but that's not the best solution under the circumstances.

"I've got to be honest, my dear, we're trying, but finding a home for Natalie Remy is going to be difficult. Not impossible, but difficult. Her history in foster care is grim, running away, fighting with siblings, failure to bond with family members."

"Maybe it was the other way around, Ruth. I mean, maybe the families failed Natalie. She's a good kid."

"Ricky, I know you care about her, but I have to tell you the realities. Even if Natalie had been a model foster child, there's her history as a prostitute to consider. What family with other children is going to welcome her with open arms?"

"She wants to live with me, Ruth. Can you believe it? Can you honestly imagine me as a mother?" I laughed, without much enthusiasm, waiting for her to chime in, agreeing with me that the idea was ridiculous.

"How do you feel about the idea?"

"Whoa, Ruthie. This is where you're supposed to say; 'ha, ha,ha,ha, Rick, good joke. What crazy notions you get!' Besides, who in their right mind would approve me as a foster parent? June Cleaver, I am not."

"I don't imagine Natalie Remy would hit it off too well with June Cleaver, Beaver, she ain't. If you were looking to adopt a baby, I'd say you'd be out of luck, but a teenager? Who knows?"

"Ruth, just keep tryin', please."

"Will do, my dear, and don't worry. We'll find someone."

"Thanks, I gotta go."

We agreed to meet at the church the next morning before the service to arrange the flowers, then we hung up. I was picking up Agnas Brown. I was not looking forward to that drive, sure to be filled with light-hearted, stimulating chit-chat.

Bunny and I arrived at the Aquinessett a little after six, our entrance not nearly as dramatic as Lola Richards's several nights earlier. Before we hit the Sunday buffet, I excused myself, pretending to visit the ladies room. Instead I went directly to the reception area to inquire about the benefit the previous Saturday.

The girl at the desk, Ginny, her name tag read, directed me to Lou Barnsley in the dining room. Lou, a tall, severe looking woman dressed in a three-piece black suit, with lapels that spread out like bat wings, was busy directing the affairs of the large dining hall.

"That's Lou." Ginny pointed, then returned to her post.

I'm almost five ten, but Lou towered over me, six feet at least, with three inch stilettos. Her ash blond hair was swept back and she wore a cream-colored, linen sheath that hugged her slim, curvaceous form. Where do people get these gorgeous bodies and where was I the day they handed them out? I would not permit myself to be intimidated by Lou, the magnificent giant. I waited until she was free keeping out of sight of Bunny across the room.

"Ms. Barnsley?"

"Yes?" She looked me over, her gaze cool, appraising. Her expression screamed, 'I don't know you, do I? And where did you get those clothes?' She held the reservation book in front of her, which partially concealed her dress' plunging neckline. Closer now, I noticed the starvation chest, popular with many of my Newport clients.

I endeavored to draw her aside, affecting a cool, business-like tone to match her own. I explained my interest in the Wilkerson's whereabouts last Saturday and ending my recitation with, "You understand of course, the need for absolute discretion, Ms. Barnsley. Everything I've told you is strictly confidential, as your words to me shall remain."

"I'm sorry, Miss?"

"Steele."

"Oh my, are you any relation to Ralston and Rita Steele? I believe I see the family resemblance. Daughter perhaps?"

I smiled through gritted teeth. "Yes, Ralston is my father. Now about the Wilkersons?"

"Truthfully, Miss Steele, our members' business is private and never subject to gossip. However, as Ralston's daughter, I see no harm in telling you that, yes,

Mr. and Mrs. Wilkerson attended the benefit last Saturday. I served them myself. They arrived quite early to help set up, and of course, as two of the League's biggest supporters, they stayed until quite late, dancing and so forth. Now, if you don't mind, I have a great deal of work to do."

"Thanks, Ms. Barnsley. You've been a big help."

As she turned away so did I and ran smack into Bunny.

"A big help with what?"

I smiled my most ingratiating smile, as I propelled her toward the buffet line. "Let's eat, Bun!"

"Did you find out what you needed?"

"Yup, now let's forget it. I don't want to think about the case or anything. For one night I just want to enjoy your company without someone pumping me with a zillion questions, okay?"

Bunny took my arm and gave it a squeeze. It was not a friendly squeeze.

Chapter 45

The buffet table groaned with tantalizing choices and I managed to cram a little of everything on my plate, then waddled back to our table. I went back for seconds too. Like they do at a potluck, the entrees all blended into one another, one delectable mass of calories and carbs. I skipped the salad, except for a few florets of broccoli. I could graze a number of decent salad bars in the city anytime, but who knew when I would get back to the Aquinessett and Chef Jarrard's cuisine? Lobster Newburg over fresh puff pastry, beef ragout, seafood cassolet, chicken piccata. Yum, out of this world. Maggie, my doctor would die on the spot if she saw me.

Bunny shook her head. "I just hope Jarrard doesn't venture out of the kitchen and see what you've done to his food! He'd be horrified to find it all mushed together like that."

"It's delicious, Bun, and Jarrard shouldn't line up his masterpieces on a buffet table if he doesn't want to see 'em mushed together."

Bunny opened her mouth to reply, when something behind me caught her eye.

"Hey, gorgeous. I see you haven't lost your appetite."

I would recognize that silky voice anywhere. I nearly choked on a jumbo shrimp.

"Jay, hi!" Bunny beamed up at him, hand extended.

"Hi, Bunny, haven't seen you out here lately. Two businesses must keep you hopping."

He turned to me, eyes more serious for a second before the twinkle crept back. "Hey, Rick."

"Hello."

I gazed up to spy his most wolfish grin. Gorgeous as always in pale pink sport shirt and khakis, beige linen jacket slung over his shoulder. He wore a blue silk tie, but it was loosened, as if he took a somewhat cavalier attitude to the Club's dress code.

"How've you been?"

"You mean since we spoke several days ago?"

"You know what I mean."

"No, I do not."

Gazing from one to the other of us, Bunny decided to end the Mexican stand-off.

"Join us. We're about to have dessert."

I kicked her under the table, but she ignored me.

"Tempting, thanks, but I'm meeting a client. Only time I get out here nowadays. I've considered dropping my membership, but would miss Jarrard's cooking."

Bunny shook her head, gazing up at him with adoring eyes. "I wouldn't advise that, Jay. You and I joined years ago when the initiation fees were cheap. Now, they're through the roof."

"Don't I know it. It's just this life doesn't suit me any more."

He directed this remark toward me, knowing my antipathy to the club life. Could he be anymore transparent?

"Don't golf much and tennis I can do anywhere and I'm finding the atmosphere a little stifling."

"Don't be ridiculous," she said, waving her hand. "This is where most of the city's business is conducted."

"And, speaking of that, I see my client now. Ladies, great to see you both. Bunny, let's have lunch and talk real estate."

Shamelessly batting her eyes, Bunny leaned toward him. "Anytime."

"Ricky, I'll call, okay?"

I shrugged. "Your choice."

As he pecked us both on the cheeks, his scent nearly made me swoon.

As he turned and headed for his client, a very attractive woman, I noticed, Bunny whispered, "Well, that was interesting. What a gorgeous hunk of man."

"Humph."

"You weren't very nice, my dearest. How long has it been?"

"Six months."

"Want to talk about it?"

"Absolutely not."

"He's still crazy about you, that's obvious."

"Didn't I just say I didn't want to talk about it?"

"Give the guy a chance. He's wealthy, incredibly hot and available. Besides, as I recall, you never let him explain."

"That's talking about it. I love you very much, Bunny, but I swear I will walk out this minute if you do not change the subject."

"Fine, let's get dessert."

We returned from the dessert buffet, Bunny with a small dish of fruit and yours truly, a plate piled high with gooey confections. We ate in silence for a time, then Bunny started talking. For the remainder of the meal, she regaled me with the latest travails of the real estate office, her stories laced with sarcasm and wild exaggerations. She had an endless number of anecdotes concerning her coworkers, none of whom she was particularly fond of, and then she switched to her live-in boyfriend, Elmer. Who would ever name their kid Elmer? Poor Elmer did not fare well in most of Bunny's tales, but I was still laughing as we pulled up in front of her house.

"Elmer didn't have the decency to put on the porch light for me!"

Elmer was at least twenty years younger and probably didn't even know there was a porch light.

"Night, Bun. Thanks."

Chapter 46

Vinnie's car wasn't in his driveway when I pulled into mine. The Rocky Pointers had not returned. There were a number of cars parked along the street and it looked like the Silvas across the street were having a party. I parked, walked toward my door and gazed up at a clear sky filled with stars.

If I had been looking ahead instead of up, I probably could have avoided the blow. As it was, I saw a glint of metal, like the chrome piece on a rearview mirror. As I fell, I remember thinking, what the hell is a rearview mirror doing in the forsythia bush?

When I woke, everything was white. My face stung, like I had been badly sunburned and I waited, expecting the top of my head to blow up. I remembered the rearview mirror, but it was nowhere in sight.

What I did see, when I finally focused, was Jay Harp asleep in a chair beside the bed. I was in the hospital and he was there, sitting with me. I tried to get up, to call to him, but my head gave a resounding thunder clap and I blacked out. I must have gone back to sleep because the next time I woke he was standing over me, holding my hand.

"Happy Birthday, hard head, how are you?"

"What happened to "hi, gorgeous," or are you trying to tell me something? Am I permanently disfigured, have I lost half my face? What?" God, my head hurt and talking set it to pounding again.

"No such luck, gorgeous." He drew out the word, holding the "r". "Just a couple of superficial scratches and bruises and a nasty knock to the head. You'll be fine in a couple of days."

"What happened?"

"You're the one who's supposed to tell us that."

"Us?"

The police want to talk to you. It was the Swansea police that answered your neighbor's call. Maddie rang 'em up, but Fall River cops have taken over now, I guess. Roberts and Cottrell have been in a couple of times. Want me to see if they're around now?"

"Why do they want to see me?"

"Your visitor left you a note, saying, 'Stay out of the Lisa Brown case.' It was one of those with letters and words are clipped out of magazines."

"Is that it? That's why I'm here?"

"Looks that way. Looks like someone wanted to scare you, or maybe worse. If Maddie hadn't come out when she did, you'd have been dragged who knows where. That's what the guy was doing, dragging you down the driveway, when she spotted him. You got a nice case of "shell burn" on your cheek."

He was referring to my driveway's surface, crushed up quahog shells. I winced, thinking about my poor face, scraping over them. "You mean Maddie actually saw him?"

"Sure did. The old girl was out on the porch checkin' out the guests comin' in and out your neighbor's party. Anyway, she went inside for a bit and hadn't seen you drive up, but when she came back she spied someone dragging you off. She yelled, and he dropped you and ran off. She's pretty shaken up poor old gal."

"Did she see a car?"

"No. Calm down, PI, the police are handling it. With all the cars at your neighbors' party, she didn't notice what kind of car he drove off in."

"Did she get a look at him?"

"No, but she described a long coat, wide brimmed hat, pulled down, not sure of the color, nothing else."

"What hit me? It looked like a rearview mirror crashing down on my head."

"They have no idea. Nothing was found at the scene. Now you better rest."

"What about the kids?" I tried to sit up, but the pounding in my head started again like gangbusters.

"Relax, they're with Uncle Vinnie. He seems to have adopted them."

There was a hint of derision in his voice. Jay had always been a tiny bit jealous of Vinnie's and my friendship.

"They're happy. Don't worry."

"Lisa Brown's funeral?"

"Kids took it okay, according to Vinnie. He drove them and the mother got a ride from a neighbor. Last outing of her life, I'm afraid."

"Why?"

"She's dead, Rick. She died last night. Police think it was an overdose. There was enough heroin in her apartment to keep her happy for months."

"Not possible."

"Well, slight exaggeration, maybe, but they found a lot, that's all I know."

I wondered where Agnas Brown had gotten so much cash, but not for long. Thinking made my head hurt too much.

"Listen, Vinnie's filled me in on what you've been doing, the long version, not the skimpy one you gave me. Rick, this is nuts. At your age, hookers, heroin addicts, multiple homicides. This is a far cry from trailing cheating spouses or helping a friend in need, which I might add, also almost got you killed."

He referred to a case where I had helped my dear friend, Karen Harp, Jay's sister-in-law, to learn more about how her husband Ron had died. Murder, it turned out.

"What were you thinking?"

I raised my hand in the halt position. "Except for our chance meeting at the Aquinessett, I haven't seen you for six months so you are in no position to lecture me, my friend."

"Well, I disagree. Finding you lying in your driveway, bleeding from head to toe is a kick in the gut to anyone, especially someone who cares about you."

I gazed up, remembering how much I love his beautiful dark eyes, then shook myself. "And, what were you doing here anyway?"

"Well, I thought you'd given me a 'come hither' look at the Club. I thought I'd stop by to say hello, never expecting to see your poor neighbor screaming and you lying all bashed and bloody."

"Come hither? Now who's nuts? If anything, I'm sure I was giving a 'get lost' look."

"Well, whatever, I'm here and you are not getting rid of me. Once you recover and things are settled with the kids, you and I are going to talk."

"Humph."

I drifted off to sleep and when I woke again, I found Jay still there along with the police. Douglas and Tim hovered over, more mother hens to add to the roost. I told them everything I knew, which wasn't much. They said they were bringing Rollo Duffy in for questioning. I told them about the flowers and Rollo's apologetic phone call, but they were unmoved, and still intended to grill him.

Finally, Douglas stood. "Look, Steele, rest up. I mean it. That's a nasty bump. You're lucky to be alive. Let me know if anything's missing when you get home."

I smiled wanly and drifted off again, noticing that Jay had settled back into his chair with a briefcase of work.

When I next woke, it was dark, and a doctor was standing over me. He informed me that I would be staying at least until Wednesday and departed. Soon after Doctor Gloom exited, Jay came in. He'd been waiting in the hall and he had a bag which he plopped down and proceeded to empty. It contained dinner, linguine with clam sauce, my favorite, crusty bread and salad.

"You missed your hospital supper, so I whipped this up for us. Nurse vetoed the wine, but the rest is okay. Couldn't have you turning another year older without some kind of celebration, could we?"

He propped up my pillows, swung my meal table over the bed. I didn't say anything, I was afraid if I spoke the tears would start and never stop.

The light delicate sauce, laced with garlic and fresh basil, complimented the sweet, succulent clams. I used the bread to sop up every bit of leftover sauce. We ate in silence as I savored every mouthful.

I wished to be home. This meal deserved a sensuous aftermath. I wondered how sex in a hospital bed would feel, the Johnny sure made undressing easy, but even though the heart was willing, the flesh was weak and beaten. I glanced over at him as he finished cleaning up, and paused to survey his work.

"Thanks." I reached out and he took my hand.

He kissed me softly. "Ricky, we'll talk when you're better. I've been thinking a lot about us."

I drew him down and kissed him again. Who knows where things might have led had the night nurse not interceded. "Visiting hours are over, I'm afraid. Sorry."

Jay left, and I slept soundly.

Chapter 47

After his rounds, Phil drove me home Wednesday afternoon, lecturing me nonstop about my lifestyle.

"Get a real job, Rick, please. The people who care about you can't keep going through this."

I listened, still too weak for a snappy retort. Maybe a change in career, wasn't such a bad idea.

My head hurt, but overall I felt much better. The scratches on my face had healed and the redness from the friction burns faded each day. I was still an ugly sight so I avoided glancing at my reflection as we passed the plate glass windows on the way out of the hospital.

As we drove up Fairview, my street, I thought about the three days lost from my life and for what purpose? We were no closer to Lisa's killer, we had no leads to speak of and I was forbidden to take any further part in it. I had to admit I was ambivalent about Douglas's edict. On the one hand I was eager to catch a murderer who had almost added me to his list. On the other hand, I longed for the boring, but safe routine of my bread and butter investigations. Snapping a few photos, trailing a harmless philanderer, typing a bunch of bullshit and sending it off to Bud. These occupations, while boring, did not result in bodily harm. My face felt like grated cheese and I had the kids to think about. If only my head would quit pounding.

"Thank God for Vinnie," Phil said, changing the subject. His charm worked its magic and he convinced Natalie to check into the hospital. She loves him, thinks he's Adonis. She's okay. Relax. I got her into a program. Takes about four weeks, maybe more to get the bulimia under control, and then, we'll see."

"Why didn't anyone tell me about this? When did all this happen?"

"Yesterday. We didn't want to bother you and Vinnie was afraid you'd feel guilty and insist they wait until you got home."

"Jeanie'll be here in an hour or so. I met her yesterday. She's a love, you'll like her."

"Who the hell is Jeanie?"

"She's Jay Harp's cleaning lady. She'll come, cook some supper, and straighten up anything you want her to. Don't worry, Harp says she's low key. Would you rather he cancel her?"

I was about to yell a resounding "yes" but my head was throbbing too much to speak. We walked through the kitchen, dishes piled high, floor a mess, and into the living room where I felt the need to recline immediately.

"Bring Jeanie on, I surrender!"

"That's the spirit. Want me to stay till she gets here?"

"Nope, I'm all set. Thanks." My eyes were already closing.

"Rick?"

"Umm?"

"While you're recuperating get out the classifieds. Take some time. See what's out there. You are a great teacher."

"Bye, Phil."

I was already dozing off.

An hour later, Jeanie arrived. She worked fast and seemed undaunted by the mess as she moved from room to room, leaving cleanliness and order in her wake.

Vinnie came by not long after her arrival with a bag of groceries. He stayed long enough to check on me and put away the food. While I took a nap, Jeanie cooked several meals with the supplies he had dropped off. She froze two chicken pot pies, several casseroles of noodles and chicken and left a large pot of chicken noodle soup simmering on the stove for my dinner. It's my absolute favorite comfort food sick or well, and Jeanie had loaded her version with fresh vegetables.

After my rest, I pulled out my notebook and flipped through it. Maddie had picked up my purse and brought it into her house, rather than allowing the police to find it. While I had been sleeping, Fulty had dropped it off along with a gigantic tuna casserole.

Jeanie finished up and peeked in to say goodbye. I waved gratefully, going for my purse. She smiled shaking her head, "You know Mr. Harp better than that. It's covered. Bye!"

I slept on and off the rest of the afternoon. Vinnie came over at dinner and heated up a bowl of soup for me, serving me in bed. I wasn't that hungry, but I sipped it slowly while we chatted about the kids, the attack and what I was going to do with myself. He was singing the now familiar, "get a new job rap." I listened patiently and thanked him for dinner. I intended to plan out the next day, but fell asleep instead.

Chapter 48

Thursday morning dawned dark and cloudy. After my early retiring, I woke around 6:00 a.m. The clouds threatened rain so I roused myself and pulled on my running stuff. I was determined to run, or at least walk. I needed to get back into familiar daily routines. By the time I dressed my head was pounding. My answer was four Advils. I wasn't going to quit. I started a slow jog and never made it past that. In fact the entire "run" was more of a slow walk, but I did it, two miles out and two miles back.

When I opened the back door, I actually felt pretty good. The blood was flowing to most of the cells and my head had cleared. I sensed all this euphoria was temporary, but I took advantage of it while it lasted. I showered, dressed, ate a quick breakfast and was out the door by 7:45 a.m.

The building was quiet as I climbed the stairs to my office. I thought back to the morning I met Natalie and how much better I had felt then, even with a monster hangover. It seemed like years since that carefree day. I didn't even check the hallway. If someone was lying in wait to kill me, fine. Put me out of my misery.

The mail had piled up inside the door and I gathered it and plopped the lopsided stack on my desk. This was the kind of work I needed today, mindless and easy. I spent a long time sifting and sorting the mail, drinking tea and reading the newspaper. I took a break to call Phil, to check on Nat. Then, I phoned Ruth to see how Teddy was adjusting.

It was nearly noon when I finally got around to turning on the machine to get my messages. There was a call from Bud, with a gentle reminder about the work he'd left last week, a call from Holly Stevens, a lawyer I work for time to time and two calls from people I'd never heard of. Both the numbers they gave me were Newport exchanges so I figured it was more spouse trailing. I put them last on my list. The Randy Andys could dally a little longer without my attention. What was a few days when infidelity was a way of life?

I checked the folders Bud had left. A couple of routine claims; one a basement flooding, the other a squabble between neighbors about a dead tree. Bud's client's neighbor had cut down a tree in the client's yard, claiming it was a hazard to his kids, and Bud's client had sued him and lost. Now Bud's client was putting in a claim to his insurance company for reimbursement for the loss of a historic old elm. I was supposed to run out and look at this tree, assessing its longevity and approximate value. Bud's firm was prepared to pay three hundred dollars, not a penny more.

I dialed Bud's number to check on a few details. We talked awhile and he ended by saying, "Gotta go, Rick. I know it's a bunch of bullshit, but I'd appreciate your write-up soon. The Bellows are getting tired of that dead tree lying across their front yard. Pretty soon they'll be submitting a claim for the dead grass underneath it!" I promised quick action and hung up.

Next I spoke to Holly. She had a medical malpractice case against one of the city's top gynecologists. She doesn't use my services too often as her firm employs a couple of its own investigators, but she was desperate. The case was going to trial soon and the prosecution's chief witness had disappeared in the depths of the North End. Perfect. I promised to get on it that day when I learned that the witness lived fairly close to Manny's Garage. I didn't think it would hurt to drop in while I was in the neighborhood.

I called the first of the Newport numbers and got an answering machine. "Hi, this is Carla and Jim Peterson Can't come to the phone right now. We're otherwise engaged—tee-hees in the background. Please leave your name and number after the beep—more tee-hees—and we'll get back to you real soon. Byeee!" I almost hung up, but listened for the beep and dutifully left my name and number, and a "brief message" suggesting that next week was a better time to connect.

The second number, Paula Yost, rang a bunch of times and then a kid answered, "Yeah?"

"Could I speak to your mother please?"

"Nah."

"Isn't she home?" I used my best, kid-friendly voice.

"I hate her."

Oh, swell, a mother hater. I decided to humor him. What if he dropped the phone and screwed up my telephone for the rest of the day? "That's too bad. Do you think I could speak to her anyway?"

"I hate her. She's a penis breath."

"I know how you feel. Maybe I could leave a message, then we'll both hang up?"

"Who is this? Are you one of her gabby friends, 'cause if you are, I hate you too."

I was about to respond, when I heard a woman's voice in the background.

"Bobby, what are you doing? Give me that phone. Oh, dear, hello, I'm so sorry. Who is this please?"

I gave her my name and explained that I was returning her call. "Oh, Miss Steele, I apologize. Bobby's going through such a hostile stage. I don't know where he gets it from. We've had him in therapy for months, but it doesn't seem to be helping."

I could think of some therapy that might do the trick, but I held my tongue. Since I've never had kids, what do I know?

"Thessaly Martin gave me your name. It's about my husband. He's, well, you know. I'm pretty sure he's, you know, fooling around. I just have to know for sure, so I'll know how to proceed, if you get my drift. Do you think you could help?"

I explained my fees, one hundred and fifty dollars an hour plus expenses and that I could not start work until the end of next week. I also told her that I would need certain information on her hubby, Jerry. Place of business, clubs he frequented, the usual stuff. She thought everything sounded 'just dandy' and agreed to email the information on her hubby. I explained that I usually billed through PayPal and took down her email address. After explaining that an invoice for the thousand dollar retainer would be forthcoming, I rang off. A small infusion of cash at this point in time would be very welcome.

Chapter 49

My calls completed, I contemplated my next move. I did not feel like tackling the feuding neighbors today. My pounding head could not take a bunch of yelling. I decided to put them and the flood damage off. Those would be an easy morning activity tomorrow, when I would hopefully feel better. I decided to visit the North End, then call it a day.

After a filet 'o fish and a coffee milkshake from McDonald's, I headed for Connelly Blvd, the address Holly had given me for her witness. I parked and waded through the rubble to the tenement steps, checking the mailboxes. No Ida Goodson listed, but Holly had said Ida was living with a man whose last name was Wordell. I walked into the front foyer, knocked on the first door I came to. An oily, little man answered, opening the door a crack. "Anha, anha," was what I think he said. I decided to treat it as a friendly greeting.

"Hi, I'm looking for a friend of mine, Ida? Ida Goodson? You know her? It's really important I find her. Or maybe, Mr. Wordell?"

He pointed up and slammed the door. "Thanks," I said to the closed door, then headed up the stairs. When I reached the landing, a man, burly, dark and hairy, emerged from a door on the second floor. It was a tight passageway and I didn't relish being caught in a corner with him, but I screwed up my courage and asked about Ida again.

"Who wants her?"

Something in his eyes told me, this might be Mr. Wordell. I took a deep breath, decided to tell the truth. Honesty can be the best policy once in a while. He listened to my babbling, regarding me with complete disdain.

"She's been here waiting, but no one called."

"Did she receive a subpoena?"

"Nope."

Not wanting to argue, I asked, "So she is here now? Ready to testify when someone calls her?"

"I told you that. What'a ya deaf?"

"Sorry, and your name is?"

"None of your goddamn business. You know, we don't go in much for nosy broads around here." He stepped closer. It was not a friendly gesture.

"Sorry to intrude, I'll be on my way if you can point out where they can find her when they need her?"

He pointed to the door he had just closed.

"Might I speak with her, just for a minute?"

"You're a slow learner, ain't you, lady?"

"Not a good time? I hear you. Thanks anyway."

As I retreated the Hairy One followed, close at my heels. After I climbed into the jeep, I turned back to wave, old friends parting after a reunion. He didn't return my wave.

Chapter 50

Manny's Garage was around the corner so I drove up and parked in front of the garage doors. I peeked in the office and spied a wiry middle-aged guy behind the desk.

"Hey," he said, as I entered. At least he was friendlier than Mr. Wordell.

"Hi, my name is Ricky Steele. How are you?"

His navy jump suit had his name and a patch with "Manny's Service" in red lettering, stitched on the breast pocket. A very dirty baseball cap was pushed back from his forehead, revealing a line of grease and dirt. Dirty strands of gray hair stuck out from the sides of his cap in a helter-skelter fashion. He had a mad dog look that reminded me of Charles Manson, but his eyes were friendly.

"Fine and dandy. Car trouble, Miss Steele?"

"Always, but that's not why I'm here. You the owner?"

"Yup, Manny Barboza. You sellin' something?"

Ignoring Sergeant Roberts's stern warning, I sallied forth into my assisting the police lie. Besides, Manny didn't look like the type who would tattletale to the police after I left. If I was gonna use the lie, what better time than now when I could still reasonably plead insanity due to head trauma.

"Hey, there's not much to tell. Like I told the cops, the gun just disappeared. I'm not even sure of the exact day. I kept it in here, in the back of my drawer, but I never look back there. It'd been three weeks since I last remembered seein' it, when

I noticed it was missing. Anyone coulda took it. I don't lock up till closing, and plenty of guys cruise in and outta here, hangin' around, usin' the phone, you know."

"What kinds of cars do you work on?" I asked, idly thinking of the exorbitant prices I paid to have the jeep serviced.

"All the foreign jobs no one else wants. My main business is the German cars. Volvos, occasionally Morris Minors, there aren't many of those around now, even had an old Hillman up until 'bout a year ago. What a beauty she was. Why, whatcha got?"

"An old, tired jeep Wagoneer!"

"No problem, bring her in. I have a couple of those Woodies I service regular."

"Thanks, Manny." I left quickly wanting to make my getaway before the sun went down.

Chapter 51

The sun was bright crimson as I turned into the hospital parking lot. After checking at reception, I proceeded directly to the third floor. Natalie was on the phone when I entered the ward, sitting slouched in a chair, feet propped on an empty bed at the far end of the room. Four of the beds in the eight bed ward were occupied. Hers was at the other end of the room, nearest to the window. A huge vase of flowers stood on the bedside table beside it.

The minute she spied me she said, "Gotta go." She hung up and hopped up to greet me. "Ricky, you're finally here. Please, get me outta here, will you?"

"No can do. Nat, let's get you back into your bed, then we'll talk. Softly though, okay? No shouting, my head's still in rough shape."

"Oh, shit, that's right. How you doin'?" Her concern was perfunctory at best.

"Better, thanks."

"Good, now, get me outta here! This place sucks. The nurses are fucking bitches. They won't let me have anything to eat, 'cept some disgusting cereal shit."

"Nat, you're sick."

"Fuck that. I feel great."

"Well, you're not great, and you won't be for at least four weeks."

"Four weeks! No fucking way I'm stayin' in here for four weeks! How can you pull this shit?"

"Listen to me. This is where you belong, and please get that mouth under control."

"I thought you were my friend. Now you've got me locked up like I was in jail! Bitch down the hall won't even let us go past the nurses station for a walk or nothin'."

She shouted this last part as a nurse, presumably the 'bitch' in question, wheeled a patient by the doorway to the ward.

"You're really sick, Nat. The doctors think you belong here to get the vomiting under control and I do too."

"Well, you're not in charge of me. You, or the fuckin' doctor."

"Do you believe that I care about you?"

She crossed her arms over her skeletal chest and turned away, staring out the window. This conversation was going nowhere and my head was screaming bed.

"Do you think if I didn't care I'd have gone through all the trouble of finding Lisa, getting you into the doctor, getting you into treatment so you can get well, worrying about you? All this?"

She shrugged.

"Believe me, I know hospitals are shitty, but you're gonna have to trust me on this one. Right here, in that bed, is where you belong. I'll come and see you every day, Vinnie too, but you gotta try to stick it out and get better. You hear what I'm saying?"

"What do you care anyway? You're just gonna get me well, then shove me into another foster home like you did with Teddy."

"Now, don't go getting yourself all worked up. Let's just take things one step at a time. You get better and in the meantime we have a whole month or so to plan what's the best situation for you, okay?"

As we chatted, I'd been toying with a card attached to a vase of flowers on her bedside table. Idly, I read the message on the card that lay face up in my palm and cringed. *Hey, love, get better quick. Everyone's been asking for you. Love, Billy.* I ripped the tag off, threw it in the trash.

"And no contact with Billy Linden, is that clear?"

"I gotta think about the future."

"You have no future with that creep!" I shouted, instantly regretting the outburst, my head threatening to explode.

Nat looked as if I'd slapped her. "I ain't got no future with you either."

She turned away again, gazing out into the night.

There was nothing more to say. I patted her shoulder and promised to return in the morning. I was close to tears by the time I reached the parking lot and I broke down completely once inside the jeep. I pressed my forehead against the steering wheel, a futile attempt to drive the pain away. Shit, the whole thing was shit.

It was nearly seven when I got home. I cooked myself an omelet with scallions, cheese and avocado slices. Jay called just as I was finishing the last mouthfuls.

"How you doing?"

"Fine, never better." I was hoping that if I ignored it, the ringing in my ears would stop.

"Hey, listen, Rick. I've got this fundraiser at the Marine Museum tomorrow night. Wanna go with me?"

"I'm actually going with someone," I said, remembering Mark Fallon's invitation.

"Oh?"

"Yes, I do have a life."

"Of course, well, I'll see you there? Maybe I can steal you away from him?"

I hung up and dialed Mark Fallon to see if we were still on for the fundraiser. He apologized for being out of touch.

"How about I pick you up at six-thirty tomorrow night? I've gotta be there early to help John set up. Besides, we've got the whole night after that."

"Down, tiger. See you tomorrow night."

I took a hot bath and hopped into a freshly made bed. Jeanie had hung the sheets on the line and they smelled like fresh air and cool breezes. Thoughts of tomorrow evening made me smile as I drifted off to sleep. Mark Fallon, Jay

Harp, a few drinks, nice dinner? Lots of possibilities. What did it matter if I was a mangled mess and they were both hopeless lotharios? Something interesting might come out of it.

Chapter 52

The following morning I felt almost human. I ran at a reasonable pace, ate breakfast without feeling nauseous and got to the office in good time. Before going out on my calls for Bud, I phoned Ruth Channing to check on Teddy. She was optimistic. The potential parents were paying him a second visit that afternoon and the first had gone well. Tonight Vinnie was coming to take him to the movies. Ruth asked me to stop by around one and I hung up.

By 11:00 a.m. I was in suburbia wrangling with the Bellows about the elm tree sprawled across their front yard. I stopped by a nursery on my way to Somerset, before going to the other job, the flooded basement. The nursery felt three hundred dollars was reasonable given the size and age of the tree and possible deterioration due to disease, Mother Nature or whatever.

The flood damage claim had been filed by the Tuttles, who lived in the Shady Acres subdivision off of Route 138 in Somerset. In the middle of remodeling their tract house, several weeks of steady rain had poured into their basement and wrecked the furniture stored down there. Bud's company was going to pay, but they weren't sure how much. I walked through the mess with Mrs. Tuttle.

She got really worked up wading through all her priceless junk. I have a houseful of priceless junk myself, so I was sympathetic. I guessed five thousand, eight hundred dollarsbased on what I saw, but couldn't share the numbers, that was Bud's job. I took photographs and an inventory of most of the items and said goodbye. She was pushing Danish and coffee at me, but I declined.

It was after 1:00 p.m. as I headed back to the city. I caught Ruth at the table eating her lunch. She insisted on making me a sandwich, chicken salad on whole wheat and poured me a tall glass of iced tea.

"This what the kids eat?" I asked, with a mouth full of chicken salad just like my mom used to make it."

"Nope. Wouldn't touch it. Modern eating habits are so unhealthy." She sat down beside me at the kitchen table. "What's up? You feeling better?"

"Yup."

"Ricky, have you seen your dad?"

"How's Teddy?"

"Great. He'll be going home with the Ervins, mark my words. They're good people. I've had several nice chats with Natalie. We'll work something out there."

"She's a good kid."

"I'm sure she is. That's why I asked you to stop by. I have a couple, Bill and Janet Anderson. They should be here any minute."

"Foster parents?"

"Well, not exactly. They're from my church. They are preparing to take charge of the UCC Mission in Zaire and they are looking for an older child to adopt."

"Missionaries? Ruth, you can't be serious. Nat, living with a couple of missionaries? I suppose they're reborn types?"

"Now, Dorothy, don't be intolerant.

"But, Ruth, do you really think they'd be a good match?"

"These are good people. They especially want a teenage girl."

"Free labor, no doubt."

Ignoring my comment, she said, "I've told them quite a lot about Natalie and her circumstances and all. They're willing to meet her. This is them just driving up."

I spied a battered station wagon pull up in front of the house. A young couple, mid-thirties, emerged. She waved and smiled as they approached. Ruth hurried down to greet them; yours truly trailed behind.

"Janet, Bill, I'd like you to meet Ricky Steele, an old family friend."

"Hello, Miss Steele." Janet Anderson extended her hand. "Ruth has told us so much about you and what you've done for Natalie." Her husband nodded hello, but said nothing and took a seat beside his wife on the old porch glider.

"Ruth tells me you're looking for a teenage girl?"

"Yes. She would be such a help at the mission."

"How much have you heard about Natalie, Mrs. Anderson?"

"Quite a lot, really. She sounds like she needs us as much as we need her."

"Forgive me, but do you really think a thirteen-year-old prostitute would be an asset to your mission? Do you even think you can handle her?"

"The Lord will help us, Miss Steele, and we've worked with many troubled adolescents."

"With all due respect to the Lord," I interrupted. "Natalie Remy is a very needy kid. She needs love and attention. She's also unwell and perhaps not up to doing the Lord's work right now."

He leaned forward. "Miss Steele, I'm afraid you have misunderstood. We're not looking for cheap labor for our mission. We are looking for a daughter. A child we can love and raise as our own. Janet is unable to bear children. Yes, our life can sometimes be harsh, that's true. We fret a baby might not survive, so far from medical facilities, but a teenager. There are so many older children waiting for adoption, who need a good home. Janet and I are far from perfect, but we are ready to try and we would like to meet Natalie."

I felt like a complete jerk. I mumbled apologies, which they accepted gracefully. We chatted for a few more minutes before I rose to depart. Ruth walked me to the car.

"Don't worry, I'll let you know what happens. The Andersons will go to the hospital and meet Natalie. Then, we can take it from there. One step at a time."

"Thanks, Ruthie, I'll call you."

Chapter 53

I drove back to the office and spent the remainder of the afternoon typing up reports for Bud, then dialed his number to find out how soon he needed them.

"Monday is fine. I'll come by sometime in the morning. Thanks, Rick. Want to come for dinner tonight? Mary told me to ask you yesterday and I forgot. She's pissed at me, so how 'bout it?"

"Sorry, I'd love to, but I've got a date, if you can believe it!"

"Not Harp?"

"Nope, I'm playing cougar tonight and going with Mark Fallon, remember him?"

"You're kidding."

"Yes, about the date and cougar part. He's just a friend who did me a favor so I'm returning the favor tonight, going to a Marine Museum fundraiser."

"Oh, right, I forgot all about that."

"Shall I make a donation in your name?"

"Put me down for a hundred and I'll send it in."

"You got it. Say hi to Mary and tell her to call me directly next time instead, than relying on you."

I cleaned up and locked the office, then swung by the hospital for a quick visit with Nat. She was on her way to exercise therapy, her least favorite activity, for which she blamed me.

I decided not to mention the Andersons. Let Ruth handle it. When I said goodbye, she turned away so I headed for the door. When I turned back, I expected to see her rounding the corner with the nurse, but instead she was on my heels. She threw her arms around my neck and clung to me.

"Hey, what's this?"

She shrugged, dropping her arms. "Nothing, just thanks, that's all. I'm sorry, Ricky."

"Hey, sweetie, no apologies necessary. You've been through hell. You're entitled to be pissy. I'll see you tomorrow, okay?"

"Okay."

I leaned down and kissed her forehead. The next few weeks were going to be rocky.

I arrived home at 5:00 p.m. with plenty of time for a bath and a nap before my evening with Mark. Bath first. Then I dried my hair and slipped on a robe. Lying down I wrapped myself in an eiderdown and set the alarm for 6:15 p.m.

By the time he knocked, I was dressed in my "go-anywhere dress," a blousy, gray number that can be dressed up or down with jewelry. The drop waist and silky material make me feel slim no matter what my poundage. I'd swished my hair back and fastened it with faux tortoise shell combs. A touch of mascara, a dab of blush and I was all set.

"Hey, you look sensational!"

Before I had a chance to return the compliment, he stepped in and put his arms around me.

I pried myself away and grabbed my coat. "You look pretty sensational yourself. All the *young* maidens will be swooning."

He did look drop dead gorgeous in a navy sport coat, khakis and a faded blue oxford shirt that picked up the blue in his eyes.

I grabbed a shawl and my purse. "Come on, let's get cracking. John will be frantic if you told him you'd be there by 6:30 p.m."

By the time we arrived, John was half finished with the bar set up and running around like a lunatic.

"About time, Fallon. No, I've got someone to tend bar. You just need to get the rest of this set up. He's gonna be a little late. Hi, Rick, long time no see. You here to help? Great, get the projector outta the office and set it up on that table."

Someone was giving a short talk on the history of the steamship line. A booming business at the turn of the century, the ships had shuttled wealthy mill owners and their families to New York and back, in luxurious comfort. After retrieving the slide projector, I wandered through the museum as Mark completed the bar set up.

Everything ran smoothly. When the speaker began her presentation at 8:15p.m., people were still trickling in. She gave a talk I've heard many times. Lots of anecdotal accounts of voyages descriptions of elaborate dinners, and photos of the ships' ornate interiors. She showed slides at various points, mostly from the museum's own collection. In fact, everything she told us could be picked up by a visitor, who took the time to read the blurbs in the display cases. The crowd applauded appreciatively at the conclusion of her speech, after which she took a few questions.

During the question and answer period, Jay Harp appeared, an extremely tall woman on his arm. Even in flats, she towered a good three inches over him. She had to be at least six three. They arrived with a noisy bunch of latecomers, who tittered and carried on loudly in the front foyer. They quieted as they came round the corner and realized the talk was in progress. Among this glittering assemblage, I spied the Richards. Lola was decked out in soft rose organdy, over-dressed, in my opinion. She didn't see me and I didn't bother to flag her down.

After the presentation, Mark disassembled the equipment and I chatted with the speaker. After bidding her goodnight, I ambled around the museum, peering into the various displays, which is where Jay and Amazon woman found me.

"Hey, Rick. You look lovely, as always. Where's your date?"

"Working, and he's not my date."

"Fallon?"

"Yup, he's just a friend."

"Does he know that?"

"I tell him that regularly."

"Maybe tonight it won't be necessary. He seems to be pretty chummy with that babe by the bar."

I turned to spy Mark with his arm around a beautiful blonde. In her twenties, or maybe late teens, her little black dress appeared to have been sprayed on a figure you don't usually see outside of the tabloids.

"I'm glad he's found a friend," I said, peering over Jay's date.

Jay noticed me craning my nosy neck. "I'm sorry, where are my manners? This is Wilda. I've been wanting for you two to meet."

Wilda extended her hand, taking mine in a firm handshake. "I hear you are in need of protection, Ms. Steele."

Low voice, silky soft, like the fabric of her shiny, deep blue capris, which clearly did not come from Target. I felt sure I'd find a designer label if I peeked inside the pants or matching bolero jacket. Under the jacket, she wore a plain, black jersey and her long, almost black hair was pulled back in a lustrous braid that curled down her back. Her shoulders, broader than her date's, strained the jacket's expensive seams. She had an amazing body, all curves and muscles. As I gawked at her dark, flawless skin, I realized she had asked me a question.

I shook my head. "Sorry, recent head injury. What were we saying? Oh, yes, *some* people think I need protection. It's an age thing. How old are you, if you don't mind my asking?"

"Twenty-nine."

"Lucky you. No creaky knees, no aches and pains."

She smiled. "You look great for your age. Are you and Jay contemporaries?"

Somehow, I was pretty sure she knew the answer to her question, but humored her nonetheless. "Oh, heavens no. Jay's miles older than me."

"Two years," he replied, drolly, clearly not happy with the change of subject. "Wilda is a martial arts expert in many disciplines, holds a black belt in karate, and is now on retainer to me. Her sole responsibility is watching you."

As I wondered whether, in addition to being a lethal weapon herself, Wilda carried a gun, she moved to extract a business card from her jacket pocket and I spied the bulge of a small gun, probably a .22, just visible under her left arm.

I took the card and smiled up at her. "Would you excuse us a minute, Wilda?"

I dragged Jay behind a display case, intending to chew his head off, when he pulled me into his arms and kissed me deep and slow. My knees buckled and I almost fainted.

"See, that wasn't so hard, was it?"

Before I could protest, he kissed me again. Breathless, I pulled away, shaking my head.

"Okay, you asked for it."

He kissed me again, trailing kisses down my neck. My whole body lit up like a firecracker. We stood in front of a display case of one of the steamship staterooms. If I had a hammer, I would have broken the glass and dragged him into bed.

"I'm not stopping till you say yes to Wilda for one week."

He kissed me again and again until finally, I nodded my head.

"Is that a yes?"

Another nod as I shoved Wilda's card into my purse.

"Good, let's rejoin the party."

Chapter 54

As Jay mingled, Wilda and I chatted. We agreed we would meet for breakfast sometime in the next few days to go over my schedule.

"My job is to remain unseen, Ms. Steele."

"Ricky, please."

She nodded. "If I'm doing my job, you will not even know I'm there."

We were interrupted by his voice behind me. "Why, Miss Steele, you do get around."

I turned and stepped on Wilda's foot, nearly spilling my wine. She moved away to retrieve a napkin. "I could say the same about you, Mr. Richards."

I turned back to search for Wilda, hoping Tony would sidle away, but she had vanished. At that moment, Jay returned, gazing from one to the other of us.

"Have we met? Tony Richards." He held out his hand.

"Jay Harp."

"Of course, thought you looked familiar. Striking woman you're with, Columbian?"

"She's actually from Guatemala."

Tony's eyes scanned the room, but if he craved another ogle at Wilda, he would be disappointed. "I knew your father."

"Oh?"

As they conversed, I gazed into a nearby display case filled with silver once used in the steamship dining rooms. Silver was not a big interest of mine, but I wasn't going to give Mr. Big Shot the satisfaction of my hanging on his every word.

I caught snippets of their conversation, fuming with each passing minute at the intrusion. It had been months since I'd been kissed like that and, forgetting all of my prior resolve to stay away from Jay Harp, I wanted more, now.

Oh, Lord, now they were talking cars. I would never get Jay away.

"Got rid of my MG a few years ago. Too much trouble. It was a great car though." Blah, blah, blah.

"We have a Mercedes sports coupe now," Tony said, his chest puffed up like a peacock. "My wife's, she loves it. Was all I could do to get her to part with her old Hillman. Belonged to her favorite uncle. Loved that old thing, but it was getting dangerous. Bitch to find parts too."

He continued to talk, but I heard nothing. My knees were weak and I felt light headed. Without realizing it, I leaned heavily against Jay. He grabbed my waist. "You okay?"

"Oops, yes, fine. I mean, I'm okay, but I've got to get going. Our reservations are for nine, aren't they, sweetie?"

"God, is it that late?"

I pulled at Jay's sleeve. "Sorry, Tony, gotta run."

He nodded, regarding me strangely. "Nice to see you, Harp."

"Same here, goodnight."

As Richards walked away, Jay grabbed hold of my arm. "What's the matter with you? Is your head still bothering you? You were incredibly rude to Richards. What's he done to you?"

"He did it, Jay. He did it."

"What're you talking about? Did what?"

"Richards did it. He killed Lisa, Peter Phillips, all those guys the past year. Don't you see? Phillips was investigating him, he caught on and killed Phillips. Lisa got in the way so he killed her too. God, why didn't I see it before?"

"What are you talking about? Where did this come from anyway? Was it his aftershave? The cut of his clothes? The way he lit his cigarette? What tipped you off?"

"He drove a Hillman. He used to own a Hillman!"

"Oh, now I see. Of course, it's a well known fact that all Hillman owners go around shooting people and strangling young girls. You should be home in bed. How much have you had to drink?"

"Where's Wilda anyway?"

"Forget Wilda, she's gone, and don't change the subject. You're talking craziness. I'm taking you home."

"If you'd shut up for a minute and let me explain it won't sound so crazy."

"Fine, I'm all ears."

At that moment, Mark found us.

"Ready, Rick?"

I introduced them, then asked Mark to hold on for one sec. He regarded me quizzically, but graciously stepped aside as I drew Jay off.

"Manny's Garage, the place where the gun was stolen, services Hillmans. Or they did till about a year ago. Lola Richards had a Hillman. Tony stole the gun when he picked up the car after it was serviced. I don't know why he was killing all those other guys and I don't care, but I'm sure Peter Phillips must've guessed something. Why else would he meet someone in that warehouse? Or maybe he never knew it was Richards until it was too late."

"Interesting theory, but don't you think it's a little on the thin side? Where's the proof? Sounds like a lot of coincidences to me."

"I need proof and I'll get it."

"I don't like the sound of that."

"Let's forget it tonight, okay? Besides, Mark's right, we've got to run."

I gave Jay a quick goodbye peck on the cheek and joined Mark in the foyer. Before we headed out, I excused myself for a pit stop. As I washed my hands, my phone vibrated and I saw a text from Jay. "I want to c u, 2 night."

"Yeah, right, tiger."

I slipped the phone in my purse without responding and headed out.

We got to *Stella's* at 9:45 p.m. and ate at the bar. *Stella's* is a Portuguese restaurant. They started small but have expanded several times. Their mariscada is to die for and Stella makes amazing, crusty bread to swish around in it. The décor is simple and they never rush you. Lingering over dinner is encouraged and Stella, herself often lingers after hours with her patrons.

As usual, the mariscada was superb, loaded with squid, mussels, lobster and fresh fish, the broth rich and garlicky. We shared it, yet never saw the bottom of the bowl. The wine, recommended by our waiter, a Portuguese vinho verde, was crisp and cool, and complimented the seafood perfectly. By the time we paid the bill and wandered out arm in arm, I was feeling pleasantly tipsy. Mark suggested after dinner drinks or coffee at the Hot Club, but I declined.

On the drive back, I opened my windows, leaned my head out, and let the cool wind blow on my face. As we drove up Fairview, I felt almost sober, my skin tingly, like it feels after a long run on a cool day.

Mark wanted to come in, but I begged off. I knew he offered easy, uncomplicated sex, but Jay Harp had, once again, turned my world upside down. Besides, when have I ever sought uncomplicated when it came to men? I texted him as soon as I closed the door. Within five minutes, he appeared on my doorstep. Certain of my weakened resolve, he had eaten at the Rainbow and been nursing beers for the past few hours.

Beaky, who had not been fed all day, jumped on her food, then meowed piteously as she followed the clothes trail from the kitchen down the hall. When she reached my bedroom to find that Jay had shut the door behind us, she let out a bloodcurdling scream, to no avail. By then, naked and breathless, our bodies had come together in the passionate heat I had missed for six, long months. Oh, my goodness, had I ever missed it!

I'm clearly not the investigator I think I am as I haven't a clue how the man knows how to push my buttons, but he did not miss a one. I may have dreamed it, but I thought I heard "I love you," as his kisses trailed down my stomach toward the promised land. Oh, my!

Chapter 55

He was up early.

I glanced at the clock, 6:15 a.m. "It's Saturday," I groused, squinting up at him.

"Sorry, love, gotta go. I promised to help my parents move a bunch of stuff."

"How are they, anyway?" Jay's dad was wheelchair bound, his mom, his wife the sole caregiver, with some help from visiting nurses and family.

"Trucking along, you know. We keep begging her to get more help, but she refuses." He leaned down to kiss my nose. "You rest and we can do something quiet tonight, how about it? I'll call, okay?"

"Two nights in a row? That's got to be a record."

"Ricky, we've got to talk." He looked down at me, eyes dead serious, not a trace of humor.

"About you and Marty?"

"Very funny. Marty's gone, I promise."

"When have I heard that before?"

"This is different. I want to explain."

"Not necessary."

"Maybe not, but I'm going to anyway. And, you, my love, are going to listen."

"Humph."

"I love you." He leaned forward for a deep kiss.

With Herculean strength, I pushed back. "Jay, we haven't seen each other for six months. This is too fast, too much to take in right now."

"Okay, fine. We'll go slow, if that's what you want. Listen, I've gotta run. I'll call you later, okay? Should be free by 8:30 p.m.; I'll meet you here, okay?" He bent down and kissed my forehead.

"I might be busy tonight. You didn't even bother to ask."

"Well, are you?"

"Humph."

"Eight-thirty then?"

"Fine."

"And?"

"You know how I feel about you. I don't have to say it."

"I'd still like to hear it."

"Tonight," I said, returning his kiss.

"Remember, no work today. Rest and don't even think about Richards till Monday. There's nothing you can do anyhow."

After Jay left, I sat for a long time thinking about the past year. I loved him. Of that, I was certain, but he had also hurt me. Deeply. Twice.

Eventually, I pushed ruminations about my love life aside and rose, turning my thoughts to Peter Phillips and his connection to Tony Richards. There was nothing I could do, at least until I checked with Manny on Monday. I hoped he kept some sort of records. I rolled over and pulled out the Fall River phone book to look up his number. Not too many garages are open Saturdays unless they sell gas, but it was worth a try. I dialed the number. He answered on the first ring.

"Manny?"

"Nope, Man won't be in till 9:00 a.m."

"So he's working today?"

"Until two, but he's full up. Can't take anyone else. If your car is in trouble today, better stay home 'cause we can't help you. Up to our armpits."

"Thanks, anyway."

My head throbbed, but I suspected it was the wine, not the concussion. Slowing down my pace, I dressed in my running gear, careful not to bend over too far. After a run, a shower and breakfast, I hung around drinking tea and reading the paper. Suddenly I wasn't in a hurry. If I found anything at Manny's, it would only get me into trouble.

When noon rolled around I knew it was now or Monday. In record time, I was sailing down Route 6 towards the bridge, the adrenaline pumping. When I reached the bridge it was open, cars stopped to let a small tanker pass through on its way to the power station up the river. I always love to watch the boats go through. It's something my dad and I used to do, watching the huge boats pass silently through the narrow opening. It always sends a chill up my spine.

Chapter 56

When I pulled up, I spied Manny emerging from one of the pits and waved.

"Hey, Jeep Wagoneer, 1986, right?"

"That's me all right, but how'd you know the year?"

"Watched you take off. Hope you're not having problems today."

"No, I'm still working on the gun case, and I have a favor."

"Shoot."

"Do you keep records of the cars you service? When they come in and what you did to 'em?"

"Sort of, but they're not what you call in order. Haven't yet entered the computer age. Used to keep a file on each car when I first started, years ago, but gave that up. Too many customers, too much turnover. People don't keep their cars no more. Five or six years max, ya know?"

"What kind of records do you have?"

"For the past three or four years I just been throwing all the receipts in a folder each month. I give my customers a little record book to keep in their glove compartment and they keep track of the servicing that way."

"Would you mind if I looked through your receipts for the last year, for the months around the time the gun was stolen?"

"'Spose it'd be okay. The cops already went through 'em and didn't find nothin' though. He led me back into his office and opened the third drawer of a rusty, four drawer metal file cabinet.

"Here ya go. Knock yerself out. Gotta get back to work. Don't go messing up my filing system, you hear me?"

I laughed, then pulled up a wobbly wooden swivel chair. I sat down squarely in the middle, afraid if I shifted my weight to either side it would topple over.

He was right, the files were a mess and it took several minutes to orient myself. Manny had reported the gun stolen on March 26th of last year. To be on the safe side I went back to the January receipts and started there, sifting slowly. Most slips were dotted with greasy fingerprints and blurred scribbles. Manny's prices were very reasonable. If he could work with the jeep and all its idiosyncrasies, this was going to be my new garage.

I was halfway through the February slips, reveling in all the money I was going to be saving with Manny as my mechanic, when I came across it. The "R" on the name was slightly smudged, but there was, "Richards, February 18, Hillman. Oil change and tune-up."

I slipped the paper into my purse. Manny would never miss it and the Richards no longer had the car, so what did they care? I stuffed everything back in the folders and closed the files. I waved at Manny on my way out.

"Any luck?"

"Nope, but thanks!"

"Will I be seeing you and your old tank around?"

"Count on it. She's due for an oil change soon."

I waved and pulled out of the lot, adrenaline in overdrive now.

Chapter 57

I thought about swinging by the office, but headed to the hospital instead. I wanted to see Nat and hear how things had gone with the Andersons.

When I arrived she was watching *Mr Skeffington* a movie with Claude Rains and Bette Davis. I loved that movie and was tempted to pull up my seat and settle in. Seeing me, she clicked off the set, and declared the film to be "a flipping bore." So much for common interests.

We walked down the corridor to the visitors lounge which was empty. When we had settled ourselves on the orange naugahyde sofa, I said, "So, how's your day been goin'?"

"Okay."

"Anything out of the ordinary happen?"

She looked at me funny, her eyes questioning, "You know about 'em, huh?"

"How'd it go?"

"Okay."

"Just okay? I mean, were they nice?"

"Sorta."

"What did ya talk about?"

"Nothin'."

"Are they comin' back?"

"Maybe."

"Maybe."

"If I want 'em to."

"Well, do you?"

"Maybe."

The conversation went on like this for some time, but at least she wasn't screaming and swearing. After circling the floor, I said goodbye and promised to visit the next day. Vinnie was coming later in the afternoon to play cards.

Driving home I stopped by the Parrot's Den for a late lunch, stewing over a bowl of minestrone. By the time I reached home I'd made my decision. After combing the phone book, I discovered the Richards number was unlisted. I dialed the number for "Friends On The Line," gave my name and asked for Martha.

"Speaking. How's the investigation coming along? I can't get over that poor girl's death. What a horrible tragedy."

"Actually it's not my investigation anymore. The police have kicked me out, and to tell you the truth, I'm relieved."

"What can I do for you, Ms. Steele?"

"This is strictly a social call. I'm trying to reach Lola for lunch tomorrow. We hadn't seen each other in years until last week and we had such fun reminiscing." Gag, gag. "Problem is, she gave me her cell number and I've lost it. Just can't locate that slip of paper."

"Pain huh? They had to go to an unlisted number last year 'cause Mrs. Richards was getting some pretty raunchy calls. Got a pencil?"

Martha read off the number. I jotted it down and thanked her.

"Uh-oh, I just thought of something. The Richards are out of town until late tonight. They went to Boston for a meeting and then were going out to dinner. She may have her cell switched off. Do you have her home number?"

"Also on that missing slip of paper."

Super accommodating, Martha rattled off the Richards home number.

"Hope you catch her."

"I can wait until they return, no hurry."

"Have fun catching up." Was there just a touch of sarcasm in her tone?

I thanked her and rang off, first dialing Lola's cell. Voicemail picked up. Same thing at the home number. Oh, goody, looked like the coast was clear.

Chapter 58

I fiddled around till 7:30 p.m. waiting for darkness. I had dressed in dark clothes, gathered my things, left a note for Jay explaining what I was doing and promising to be back by 8:30 p.m. I pulled my big flashlight out of the utility closet and slipped it into my bag.

Lola and Tony lived in one of the huge historic homes on Highland Avenue. Last month the *Herald News* had done a big photo spread of the house. One memorable shot depicted the happy couple waving from the front portico of the manse.

I pulled up several blocks past the house and parked. The house was lit up here and there. Maybe timer lights? There was almost certainly an elaborate alarm system, but with luck that needn't concern me. What I was looking for was probably not in the house. I thrashed my way through the rhododendrons to the backyard and surveyed the scene. The garage doors were shut, electronic openers for sure. To the left of the doors the building jutted out, at least eight feet, with a lean-to-roof over it, probably a tool shed. I slunk toward the shed, praying the alarm system did not cover the garage. The side door was locked with a padlock.

I whipped out my set of lock picks and wrangled with the heavy duty Yale lock for several long minutes before it gave way. I then hung the padlock on a nail to the side of the door and pocketed my picks. Lock picking looks a lot easier on TV.

I groped along the inside wall, but couldn't find a light switch. I turned on my flashlight. The shed was open to the garage. I spied a huge, black sedan parked in the far stall, obviously Tony's. They'd take Lola's coupe tonight. The tools were all neatly hung on the wall or stacked in a corner stall. There was also a bench with pots and trowels scattered around it.

I'd searched everywhere, turning over empty buckets and peeking behind barrels and pots, under covers, until I came upon a bushel basket stuffed in the corner under the potting bench. A variety of tools protruded, helter-skelter, like they had been used recently and had not yet been returned to their proper places. A couple of trowels and a small cultivator, some clippers and something with a curved wooden handle.

As my fingers closed around it and drew it up, I knew what I'd found. A small ax, with a five inch blade. The blade was wrapped in burlap and brown stains were visible along its edge. Stupid, stupid. Tony should know better. Should've thrown the ax in the river, along with the fingertips.

I didn't hear the car until it was too late. Shit. I returned the ax to its place. One of the garage doors rumbled. With luck I could slip out the side. Too late. I didn't hear his footsteps until he was practically on top of me, barring the door of the shed. Framed in the light from the exterior floodlights triggered by the garage doors opening, he looked enormous.

"Why, Miss Steele, you turn up in the oddest places. Last night it seemed you couldn't get away from me fast enough. Yet, here you are, in my tool shed. What a pleasant surprise! I'm sorry to disappoint you, but we already have a gardener. He's very good. Not as attractive as you, but much younger. Now, if you don't mind."

"What is it, dear?"

Lola appeared at his side. As she spoke, she switched on the tool shed light revealing a gun in his hand pointed at you know who.

"Ricky, what on earth?"

"Lola, your husband's a murderer."

"My dear, Miss Steele, is that the best you can do? Here you are snooping around my tool shed, for God only knows what reason, and suddenly I'm a murderer? Sergeant Roberts will have a field day with this one. Maybe, a career as a gardener isn't a bad idea. Now suppose you tell me what the hell this is all about."

"You know full well what it's about. It's about Lisa Brown, Peter Phillips, and who knows how many others, killed over the past year."

"Tony— I—" Lola was trying to put in her two cents but he wasn't listening. He grabbed my arm and shoved me toward the back door of the house.

"I don't know what you're playing at, but I've had enough. Roberts will have your ass, before I'm through telling him about this."

"But, Tony, wait!"

Lola grabbed at him, but he brushed her off. I was relieved that the ax was still in hiding. Maybe Douglas would humor me and take a look before he hauled me off to jail.

When we reached the kitchen, he pushed me through the door. His iron grip hurt and I felt my arm growing numb. Pissed off now, I turned to him.

"Where're the scratches, Tony?" On your neck? Your chest? Where did Lisa Brown claw up your DNA making it necessary to hack her fingers off?"

Abruptly, he let go of me and swung around, stunned for an instant. Surely he had heard about the fingers from the cops. Then, I noticed his gaze directed at his wife. Shock, recognition, disgust, and resignation registered in the cold, black eyes.

"Tony, honey, don't be angry."

Instinctively, she reached for her neck, covered with a soft green lamb's wool turtleneck. It matched her wool skirt perfectly, and she'd dressed it up with a single strand of pearls. He stepped toward her and I suddenly realized how wrong I'd been. Wrong about everything. The cops hadn't told him about the fingers, there's been nothing in the papers about Lisa's mutilation. The cat hadn't scratched her, or whatever lie she had used to explain away the marks. I thought back to all the times I'd seen Lola over the past week. She had been draped in a variety of fabrics and styles, but from cashmere to organdy, every outfit she had worn shared something in common—a high neck.

I backed slowly out of the kitchen and inched toward the door. I didn't have my gun and I wanted to make tracks while they were still locked in their staring duel. One could only hope Tony would do the right thing and turn his wife in, but I decided it was best not to stick around to witness the heart wrenching scene. I had reached the door when he came out of his trance.

"That's far enough, Miss Steele."

He turned, pointing the gun to my head. So much for Tony's civic-mindedness.

"Get some rope."

"But we—"

"Lola, shut up and get the rope. Now. There's clothesline in the hall closet."

Lola leapt into action and appeared with the clothesline in no time flat. He handed her the gun and pushed her toward me, grabbing the cord as he did so. Her hands were shaking, but she managed to keep the barrel pointed in my general direction. He tied my arms behind me. The ropes cut off the circulation and my hands quickly went numb.

He shoved me into a chair.

"What are we gonna do, Tony? We can't keep her here."

"Shut up and get a shovel. Throw it in the Buick. Hurry up."

"But—"

"For once in your life will you shut the fuck up and do as I say?"

They both left the room and I tried to wriggle up. He'd tied the rope around my arm, then through the back of the chair and onto the refrigerator door handle, leaving no room for wriggling.

I listened to their muffled voices in the hallway and caught the word "reservation." I knew exactly what they meant. At the northeast end of the city there is an area known as the "Reservation." An old Indian reservation, the property surrounds the county's largest reservoir, the largest open, undeveloped space within the city limits.

Beautiful as it was, its lush pine woods were no longer safe, especially at night when the area became a haven for gangs and wild parties. The police patrolled, but there were too many dirt roads leading into the deep woods. A cat and mouse game could go on half the night while the rowdies remained undiscovered.

Jay and I had spent many fall days riding bikes along the Reservation paths and roads. On one of our last visits before we broke up, we had stopped in a clearing, making frenzied love on the soft moss covered ground. Afterwards, we carved a tiny heart and our initials into an old maple. Ashamed and afraid we had damaged the tree, we resolved to come back and nurse the wound at a later date. Two days later, we broke up and the maple was forgotten. Thinking back to that day, I could almost feel the sun on my face, as its fingers reached through the tree tops to warm us, naked and breathless, entwined on the mossy ground. I wondered if I would ever see the sun again.

Chapter 59

I needed to think fast. The chair upon which I sat was old, and covered with vinyl. It didn't seem classy enough for the Richards' swishy digs. Come to think of it, the whole kitchen was rather shabby, but there was no time to wonder about that now. I felt around the back of the chair, running my fingers over the upholstery tacts until I found a loose one, tugging and twisting I managed to pry it loose and grasped it in my fingers.

I could just reach the refrigerator's stainless steel front from my position and I ran my fingers along the smooth surface. I hastily planned the design and scratched slowly. I scratched the letters first, then the heart surrounding them. I'd just completed my artwork and pushed the chair closer to the fridge, when Tony returned.

He unhitched the rope from the fridge and yanked me to my feet.

"Come on, let's go."

Fortunately, his back was to the fridge and Lola was already outside somewhere, no doubt searching for the shovel. The ropes dug deeper as he dragged me along.

Lola had pulled the Buick out of the garage and the back door was open. I said a silent prayer that it wasn't the trunk.

"Get in." He shoved me in and slammed the door. Lola drove and Tony kept me company in the back seat. How cozy.

"You'll never get away with this you know."

How many people had uttered those ridiculous words before meeting their end?

"I have friends. They have my notes. They'll be banging down your door before you get home. Why make it worse for yourselves by killing me?"

"That part will be a pleasure, believe me. Where are your so-called friends now?"

Ignoring him, I asked, "Why did you do it, Lola? What possible reason could you have? Life not exciting enough with old Tony here?"

"Ricky, you don't understand. Those men were awful people. They deserved to die. And Tony, he has so much on his plate."

"Lola, shut up!"

"No, I want Ricky to know. We're killing her anyway, so what's it matter?"

Seemed logical to me. Tony sighed and remained silent as she babbled on. Maybe he wanted to catch up on Lola's extracurricular activities himself.

"I did it for the city. All those girls, out there. And those awful men, hanging out of their cars, calling. You should've seen their eyes, Ricky. Horrible eyes that make you shudder inside. For the good of the city. Tony's always talking about cleaning things up. Well, that's what I was doing. Cleaning things up."

"Very civic-minded of you, only one problem, Peter Phillips wasn't one of those awful men. He didn't need cleaning up and neither did Lisa Brown."

"Peter threatened to expose me. He'd seen me with Colin Fletcher, one of the vermin. Even in my disguise, he knew me. Somehow he knew about the gun too. I don't know how he knew, but he did. I had to kill him. After all, there's my reputation and Tony's. I couldn't let my husband's career and all his important work be ruined by that snoopy nobody."

I heard Tony groan and wondered absently what he'd do with her after he'd taken care of me. At least that was one problem of which I need not concern myself.

"So, Tony, why are you doing this? You don't have to be involved."

"Oh, Ricky, you're so naïve. Tony doesn't mind killing. He's done it before, why he—"

"Shut up!"

"And what about Lisa? Why did she have to die?"

"She saw me, of course, or at least I think she did. The night with Peter, I never would've known she was there if she hadn't called. Stupid really, we're a suicide hotline. We don't get mixed up in murder."

Now, Lesley Parker's hasty resignation made sense. Lola had answered the phone that afternoon, probably even offered to help. Lesley hadn't even been on duty.

"She was only a little bit of a thing. A couple of twists of my scarf and she was gone. Shame to ruin an expensive silk scarf. Everything was easy, except for the scratches. I gave her a little too much leeway before I twisted and the little bitch clawed me."

Old Tony was going to have his hands full. Murder sounded like a new hobby for Lola. Maybe he could redirect her into golf?

"When she suggested the barn as a meeting place it was perfect. She had no idea who she was dealing with. She thought she'd have the advantage, knowing the place and all. What a stupid little fool. The Aquinessett's my second home and that barn? Well, let's just say it's not unknown to me."

"For God's sake, Lola, would you shut the fuck up!"

Tony was close to meltdown. Maybe when we reached our destination, he would decide on a double homicide?

Ignoring him, she prattled on, "I hated to waste all that time with those fingers, but it couldn't be helped. Only took an hour to get the ax and the bags. I intended to bury her, but when I was cleaning up I heard something. So I figured, what the heck, I might as well leave her there. I wore gloves, burned 'em, I left no traces, nothing."

"Very efficient," I mumbled, as we turned onto the reservation.

Tony sat up and began directing her. Ignoring me, he watched the landscape, searching for a familiar turn-off. He's done this before, I decided, glumly, and practice makes perfect.

The clock on the dash read 8:53 p.m. There was only darkness behind us.

Chapter 60

I'd been digging for about a half an hour, trying to go as slowly as possible. You can probably guess what fun, little project Tony had given me. Let's just say we were not preparing for a campfire sing-along. Lola watched from the sidelines, rubbing her hands and pacing. She had been totally useless since parking the car at the end of a very long, very isolated dirt road. Tony kept the gun pointed at my head.

Mr. and Mrs. "Rub-em-out" and I were in a small clearing. Thick woods surrounded us. Not a sound broke the silence. No wild parties tonight. On the horizon, I could make out hazy light, hovering like a halo over the city.

What a way to go. I always thought my demise would be more glamorous, a shoot-out or something where I had a fighting chance. Not gunned down and buried unceremoniously in a crudely fashioned, self-dug grave. I thought about Nat and Mark and my muddled life. Was it to end here, alone, in a dirt hole?

"Get the hell outta there," he snarled, interrupting my reverie. Apparently work was not progressing fast enough. "Here." He thrust the gun into his wife's hand. "And don't take it off her for a second."

I stepped up out of my pathetic little six inch depression. It couldn't even be called a trench yet. I waited, not sure quite where he wanted me. He grabbed the shovel and started to step into the hole, then hesitated.

Thrusting the spade into the ground near the edge. "Where's the rope?"

Oh, great, I thought sadly, I have to die trussed up like a turkey too.

At that moment, sirens sounded in the distance. They were headed our way. He heard them too and turned to listen, shielding me from the gun for a split second. It was all I needed. I grabbed the shovel and whacked him hard on the side of his head, careful to stay behind him as I swung. He cried out in pain and slumped over. Lola screamed and ran to his side.

"Shoot, you idiot!" he cried, but Lola continued to crouch over him, apparently unable to comprehend what he was asking.

Oh, thank you, God, and thank you, Lola, I thought, as I crashed into the woods.

For what seemed like a long time, I was alone. In actuality, it was probably only thirty seconds. Long enough for Tony to recover from the blow, pick up the flashlight and take up the chase. I ran wildly at first, trying to put some distance between us. Then, I paused, listened and peered into the blackness, trying to figure out the location of the sirens and headlights so I could run toward them.

My pause allowed him to gain on me. He caught me several times with the beam of his flashlight. Did he have the gun? No shots yet. On we ran. He was in pretty good shape, barrel chest and all, and yours truly was not in top form. I knew I couldn't keep running much longer. Either my heart or legs would give out before long. The lights and cars appeared to be in the reservation now. They peeked in and out of my line of vision, but it was impossible to discern whether they were drawing nearer or moving farther away.

I tripped several times, which slowed my progress, but the going wasn't easy for him either. My sides hurt. I felt dizzy and my ankles had been wrenched and twisted painfully, from stepping into holes and tripping over roots. Then, suddenly, I was running on dirt, then gravel. The road. I had reached it at last. I could hear him behind me. He, too, was out of the woods and showed no sign of giving up the chase. I ran along the side of the road, keeping in the shadow of the trees and he gained on me. My ankles were shot and all that digging had sapped my strength. Suddenly, I heard a car behind us. The Buick, Lola at the wheel. As she bore down, he yelled for her to stop.

My strength was gone. If he hadn't had it before, he now had the gun. I jogged onward, headlights blinding me. As the Buick started moving again, I turned and stumbled over a root and fell flat on my face. In a flash, he was there, standing over me.

"Goodbye, Miss Steele."

Suddenly Tony was flying through the air, the gun too. Wilda's strong arms lifted me, throwing me into the bushes and she turned back to subdue Tony. Lola screeched on the brakes and the Buick swerved, coming to rest straight across the road. Two cars appeared in front of us, their comforting, red and blue lights flashing. It was over.

Out of the second car, Jay flew, catching me as I tried to stand. "It's okay, sweetheart. You're safe."

Chapter 61

The post-chase details are a bit fuzzy. I vaguely recall Jay helping me into the car and the glare of the lights as Mr. and Mrs. Richards were led away, but that's about it.

The police recovered the ax the following day. The lab found traces of Lisa Brown's blood on the blade. Manny's gun was also in the tool shed. Dumb, Dumb! Having been declared too unstable to stand trial, Lola was sent to Waterbridge, a hospital for the criminally insane. Turned out she had been masquerading as a prostitute for several years in order to further her new career as a murderess. She stole the gun from Manny's after spying it in his office drawer one day while using the phone.

While running down a client in a seedy part of the city, Peter Phillips had spotted Lola street walking. Even with the blond wig, gobs of makeup and outrageous clothes, he had recognized his boss' gorgeous wife and had confronted her. How he connected her to the dead Johns was never made clear. She stole and destroyed Peter's briefcase and diary. Lisa had been with Phillips the night he died and had, unfortunately, revealed herself to Lola through a call to the help line she trusted.

Agnas Brown knew about Lola. Lisa had told her she was meeting someone from Friends On The Line and stupid Agnas had called the morning after Lola had knocked me out with a five iron, not rearview mirror after all. Agnas called

Friends, demanding to know whom Lisa had met and where the money was. No one knew what she was raving about, but her call had been written up. Lola read the log and acted quickly before Agnas could call again. With her connections, it had been a piece of cake for Lola to rustle up the heroin. We never learned if Agnas administered the fatal dose herself, or if she had help.

Anthony Richards's trial starts next month. He'll do some time for attempted murder, but I doubt they'll get him on anything else. I heard through sources that Tony's gun might or might not be the murder weapon in an unsolved homicide from several years back, but that's just police station gossip.

I spent a week taking care of the business and working things out with the kids. Teddy was set up with his new family and they were awaiting the adoption papers. They had hit it off from the start and he was spending days and even a couple of nights at his new home. The doctors wanted to keep Nat in the hospital for at least another three weeks to build her strength. The vomiting was under control and she was filling out nicely. The Andersons visited her every day and miracles of miracles, they were hitting it off too. They had begun adoption proceedings and were already talking passports, inoculations and plane tickets. I stopped in to see her just before I went away.

"So, how are you?"

"Okay."

"You're really goin' huh?"

"Yup, the shots are fuckin' bullshit. They hurt like hell and I got three more to go."

"Nat, you gotta start watchin' that mouth."

"Oh, I don't swear in front of Janet and Bill. Hell, no, they're too nice."

"Thanks a lot. What am I, an ogre?"

"We're friends, that's different. You know what I mean."

"What do you think? Do you like them?"

"They're okay. I mean, yeah, I like 'em. They're not like the others, only in it for the money, you know? They want me, Rick, they really want me."

"I know they do, Nat. Who wouldn't? You're a great kid, and smart too."

"I'll miss you."

"Me too. Don't know what Vin's gonna do. He'll be lost without you guys."

"He says he might come for a visit next year. Think he means it?"

"Probably. God knows he has the money. Listen, Nat, I gotta go. I've got a plane to catch."

"Ricky?"

"Yup?"

"Thanks." Before I knew it the damn kid had her arms flung around me and we were both crying. If Vinnie hadn't come in for their afternoon card game, I might never have gotten away.

I had a round trip ticket to Nevis, an island in the West Indies I had visited as a teenager. There is a small, quiet inn where I could read, relax and let go. Walks on the beach, hikes in the rain forest and late night suppers in the cool shade of the veranda, all awaited me at the other end.

After six days on my own, Jay arrived to keep me company. A glorious week of warm days in the sun, cool nights, passionate, tender lovemaking. Definitely not reality, but it sure was nice. We flew home together. No promises, but an affectionate closeness had developed. Things felt different than before. Time would tell...

At this moment, life was sweet, indeed.

A Note From the Author

Thank you so much for taking the time to read my *third* Ricky Steele mystery, **Lost in Spindle City**! Thirty years ago, when I began this series, this was book #1, but Ricky has grown in so many ways and the prequels to this seemed the more logical to publish first. Time and my readers will tell if this order makes sense. For the first time, Ricky is home in this book, sleuthing in and around the fictional, but recognizable to locals, **Spindle City**. I had a great time including some of the vibrant color and history of this amazing city, even if actual persons and places are figments of my imagination.

Many authors have a favorite character, and, I must confess, Ricky is mine. Her strength, spunk, resilience, and tenacity at this stage in life, make me smile, laugh, and applaud her sometimes bumbling, but always-heartfelt investigative style. I've always envisioned the Ricky Steele series as films and can think of some wonderful, *mature* actresses to play Ricky and her cohorts. The physical comedy would come alive on screen in the way it does when I picture scenes in my mind, but perhaps am not quite able to capture on paper.

If you like **Lost in Spindle City** and would be willing to write an Amazon review, I would very much appreciate it! In fact, I will be happy to send my first 25 reviewers a free e- copy of **another of my titles**! If you submit a review, just email me at *mleeprescott@gmail.com* and I will see that you receive your free copy of whichever title you choose!

If you would like to sign up for future book releases and occasional notices about my books, please email me at *mleeprescott@gmail.com* and I will add you to the list. I promise I will not share your address, nor will I flood you with emails. Do visit my website at *www.mleeprescott.com* to read more about my books and to hear what's next. I am really excited about the launch of my contemporary romance, **Widow's Island** this summer (2014).

This book has been revised, proofed and edited many, many times, but I, and my intrepid assistants, are human so if you spot a typo, please email me at *mleeprescott@gmail.com* and I will fix it. If you'd like to know more about my other books, please scroll ahead to the next section that is followed by sample chapters of **Jigsaw**, a mystery where Ricky appears in a supporting role.

Finally, I continue to be grateful for the manuscript wizardry of the Formatting Fairies, and the unfailing good cheer and encouragement they bestow upon this author. Most importantly, I would like to thank my dear family and friends, who are always there, no matter where life's travels take me. I love them all beyond words. Finally, a huge thank you to my readers for picking up my books, for writing to tell me you love them, and for continuing to come back for more. It is heartwarming to know you are out there!

Warm wishes,
Lee

About the Author

M. Lee Prescott is the author of numerous works of fiction for adults, young adults and children, among them **Jigsaw, A Friend of Silence**, and **Song of the Spirit**. Her newest contemporary romance **Widow's Island** debuts in summer of 2014. **Lost in Spindle City** is third in the Ricky Steele mysteries and her middle-aged sleuth shows no signing of slowing down! Expect Ricky's fourth adventure sometime in 2015.

In her other life, Lee publishes extensively – books and articles -- in her field of literacy education. She is a professor of education at a small New England liberal arts college where she teaches reading and writing pedagogy (theory and practice). Her current research focuses on mindfulness and connections to reading and writing.

Lee has lived in southern California, North Carolina, and various spots in Massachusetts and Rhode Island. Currently, she resides on the waterfront, where she canoes, swims, gardens, and swings in her porch glider watching the ever changing spectacle of a tidal river. She is the mother of two grown sons, and spends lots of time with them, their incredible wives and her beautiful grandchildren.

Aside from writing, Lee's passions revolve around family, yoga (Kripalu is a second home), teaching, swimming, bouncing, and walking. She loves to hear from readers. Visit her website at *mleeprescott.com* and on Facebook page at (mlee. prescott). Her email is *mleeprescott@gmail.com*.

Contemporary romances and mysteries by M. Lee Prescott include:

Mysteries

The Ricky Steele series

Book 1: Prepped to Kill
Book 2: Gadfly
Book 3: Lost in Spindle City

Also featuring Ricky Steele:

The Juls and Tuck Mysteries
Book 1: Jigsaw

Romantic suspense

The Roger and Bess Mysteries
Book 1: A Friend of Silence

Contemporary Romance

The Well-Loved series
Book 1: Well-versed in Love (coming soon!)

The Morgans Run series
Book 1: Emma's Wish (coming in spring 2015!)

Single titles

Widow's Island (coming soon!)
Hestor's Way (coming soon!)
Glass Walls (coming soon!)
Placecards (coming soon!)

Young Adult

Song of the Spirit (coming soon!)
Asamaran (coming soon!)
Madeline, Call Me Meem (coming soon!)

Please note: If you are wondering why so many of my titles have the words "coming soon" after the title, this is because they are written and awaiting copy-editing, proofing and formatting. One book at a time, I am trying to launch them so thank you for your patience!

Sample: Jigsaw
Prologue

The gloves snapped as he slipped them off, disposing of them as he always did after an outing. A deeply satisfying sound, the snapping of latex, powdery dust feathering up into the air. Brother loved it. Just as he had loved Rosie in those final moments as she begged for her life. "Oh sweet Rosie," he crooned lying back on the musty cot in the darkened room, his lair. "You made me soooo happy."

Already the euphoria was ebbing away, sucked into the insatiable maw of time, eroding his pleasure, washing away his joy. Try as he might, Brother was powerless to stem the flow, the precarious happiness seeping away only hours after the outing until all that remained were powdery smudges dotting his furrowed brow.

Chapter 1

July 27, Thursday

"Alright ladies, take the field!"

Bobby Gagnon, coach of the Flint Flames of the greater Fall River Women's Softball League, frowned watching 'his girls' take their positions. In his forties, a twice-divorced, recovering alcoholic Gagnon still looked like the triple A ballplayer he had once been. While his hair was thinning on top, his wiry, muscular frame looked much as it had in his twenties thanks to years as a brick layer.

"Jesus Christ Peters! Put something into your throw-- anything! I haven't seen a rag like that since--

"Souza! The catcher, Souza, the catcher, for Christ sakes! Her mitt's where it always is, at the end of her goddamn arm!

"That's the way Gladys-- stretch for the throw.

"Wilson! Center field's that way! Atta girl!"

As Gagnon continued yelling, coaxing and browbeating, the occasional compliment thrown in, his eyes scanned the street. Finally the person he'd been waiting for hopped out of a dark green pick-up, J & T Limited lettered in black and gold on the cab's door. The pick-up took off and Bobby turned back to the field, feigning indifference as the latecomer jogged onto the field.

The explosion came as she reached the bench, stooping to tie the laces of her cleats. "Whitman, it's about goddamn time you showed up! I wanta talk to you!"

"Hi Bobby, nice to see you too." Julia "Juls" Whitman smiled, straightening to her full height, gray blue eyes regarding him without a hint of consternation. She stood at least six inches taller.

"Where the hell's Mikawski?" Bobby resisted the urge to hop up on the bench to continue his harangue. He didn't much care for women looking down at him.

"Isn't she here?"

"No, and if she doesn't show in five minutes, you're pitching."

'But I--"

"Put a sock in it and start throwin'. I gotta a date tonight and we're starting on time for a change. Belles have been warming up for forty-five goddamn minutes."

"Rosie'll be here. She'd never miss a game," Juls called over her shoulder trotting out to the mound.

Fifteen minutes later the game was underway with Juls pitching-- still no sign of Rosie Mikawski.

By the third inning, Juls, agitated and distracted, allowed three runs to score, two of them on errors.

Gagnon blew up. "What the hell are you doin' out there, Whitman? Jesus Christ!"

"Watch your language Bob, there are kids watching," called Dan Powers, husband of Ruby, the Flames second baseman.

Powers' words had little effect. After the next pitch yielded a triple, Bobby charged out to the mound, arms flailing, eyes bulging, curses punctuating the night air.

Juls endured his screaming for several minutes before exploding herself.

"Stop it Bobby! I didn't want to pitch and you knew it! How do you expect me to concentrate when I'm worried about Rosie? This isn't like her, I talked to her this morning and she was psyched for this game. Something's wrong."

"You got that right, and you're it!" Gagnon snarled, worried himself, but unwilling to show it.

"Look, you've had it," he continued, turning towards the outfield. "Mendoza- get your fanny in here, now! And you, get out there where you belong."

"Fine," she mumbled, turning towards left field.

"Juls," he called after her, his voice softer. "She's fine. Forget about it and play ball. We'll go over to her place right after the game, okay?"

He watched Juls' retreat, her long straight back knit with tension. Even in league issue orlon, she was just short of gorgeous with those long, thin legs and slender hips. Juls Whitman had commanded his secret admiration since the day he'd volunteered to coach the Flames. Her hair had been long then, tied back in an unruly braid that reached her waist. Shoulder length now, the auburn hair was tied back in a ponytail that stuck out above the strap adjuster on her cap. A smile to die for and lips that begged to be kissed, the woman had no idea of her effect on men, least of all, middle-aged Bobby Gagnon.

Tuck Potter, Juls' partner in a suburban caretaking business was a boyhood friend of Bobby's younger brothers. Tuck had coached the Flames for five years, but the business had grown to the point where it was impossible for both partners to be unavailable three or four nights a week during the summer. Tuck had described the team as a "great bunch of ladies" and he had been right. Coaching the Flames had been Bobby's salvation.

Years earlier, the J and T partners had had a brief affair, but nowadays, Tuck described Juls as "one of the guys." It was bullshit, of course, since Bobby knew damn well that Tuck still harbored more than friendly feelings for his partner. Juls had prevailed, and she now kept Tuck, and most men for that matter, at arm's length.

Gagnon hadn't failed to notice the tears rimming his pitcher's eyes and she was right, it wasn't like Mikawski. The Bedford Belles were their biggest rivals and Rosie would never have missed this particular game voluntarily. All the punch knocked out of him, Bobby withdrew to the bench, glumly taking his place alongside his players.

The game dragged on, Juls' dread mounting with each inning. The Belles finally put them out of their misery, burying the Flames under a merciless barrage of hitting. The ump called the game in the seventh, Belles-12, Flames-1as darkness descended over the Globe Corners field, the headlights of passing cars a distraction the Flames would no longer have to endure.

Juls gathered her things scanning the crowd. "Where's Tuck?" she asked to no one in particular. "He was supposed to pick me up! He should have been here hours ago. The one night I really need him!" She waved at her teammates who were heading for a beer at Archie's across the street.

"Go in and call Mikawski," Gagnon yelled, tossing the equipment bag into his trunk. "If there's no answer and Tucker isn't here by the time you're back, I'll run you over."

"You sure?" Juls asked, dropping her bag at his feet. "What about your date?"

"Screw that, now get goin'. Give her hell so we can go in and get a goddamn beer to drown our sorrows after this fuckin' game from hell."

"Thanks Bobby, watch my stuff okay? Be right back."

Gagnon threw her bag into the car, starting the engine and pulling the Impala up in front of Archie's. Knowing Rosie Mikawski as well as he did, there was no way he'd be havin' a beer in the foreseeable future.

Two minutes later Juls appeared, "No answer," she said, hopping in. "Let's go."

"You know she's probably all fucked up, three sheets to the wind at the Bluebird right now doncha?"

"No way."

Gagnon didn't believe it anymore than she did. Softball and her teammates were Rosie's whole life.

Bobby had spent many evenings with Juls, Tuck and Rosie drinking, playing cards, enjoying cookouts on the beach, going to concerts, out to dinner. Just last weekend they had all sailed to Nantucket on a friend's boat, camping on the beach, all the men in one tent and Rosie, Juls and two other women in a tent up the beach, giggling all night long.

Mutt and Jeff he called them. When the two friends walked into a room one was first struck by the contrasts-- Juls' tall, slender beauty, alongside the handsome, but shorter, stockier Rosie. The latter's coal black curls wild and unkempt, her dark eyes dancing with light mirrored her personality. Rosie was gregarious, loud and physical in her affections, whereas Juls, although friendly, was quieter, more reserved. Beneath the facades, however, dwelt two kindred spirits and together, they created a whole, distinct from their individual selves, a palpable warmth radiating from the pair that enveloped all around them in its warm, comforting embrace.

Their easy camaraderie was nearly impossible to resist and people were drawn into their circle of friendship. For Bobby Gagnon-- to whom women had always been strange, elusive creatures-- the friendship with Juls and Rosie had been a revelation.

The "girls" as Tuck called them, had known each other since grade school, remaining close friends through high school and college despite long periods of separation. Bobby never tired of listening to the stories of their growing up years. The Whitmans had never approved of Rosie Mikawski from the Flint, but that hadn't mattered a wit to their daughter. During her high school years, Juls was sent away to a boarding school in the Berkshires, while Rosie stayed at home, but the friends wrote, sometimes five or six letters a week, calling as often as they could. Weekends, if Rosie could get away, she'd coerce a friend into driving her up to visit Juls, sneaking her out of the dorm.

As he started down Willett, Bobby began praying. "God make everything be okay," he thought, as he pulled the Impala up to park across the street from Rosie's building.

"What?" Juls asked, looking over at him.

Not realizing he'd spoken aloud, he mumbled, "Nothing," adding hoarsely, "Come on let's go give her hell."

Chapter 2

Dan "Tuck" Potter walked into Archie's Tavern not three minutes after Bobby's Impala rounded the Globe Corner rotary, disappearing from sight. Spying the Flames clustered at their usual tables by the jukebox, he waved, grabbing a beer on his way to join them.

"How'd ya do?"

"We stunk up the field," Karen Ramos replied, her leg slowly extending, pushing an empty chair towards him. A come hither move if he'd ever seen one and he'd seen most of 'em.

"No?"

"Yup. Lost twelve to one," Ann Greeley said, rising to fetch another round. "It's okay. We have two more shots at 'em. Besides, we were missing players. We'll get 'em next time, you wait."

"Gagnon must be a happy camper. Where is the lad anyhow and for that matter, where's my partner?"

"They've gone to Rosie's. She didn't show for the game, Bobby's pissed and Juls is a basket case."

As Ann prattled on, Karen leaned back in her chair eyeing Potter, her eyes leaving little doubt as to her intentions. The team uniform-- baggy on most of the women-- fit Karen like a second skin. The top was stretched tight across her ample bosom, nipples clearly visible under the thin, white orlon. Reddish blonde curls--

frisky even after three hours shoved under a baseball cap-- ringed her heart-shaped face and her dark eyes danced with mischief. Karen was pretty and she knew it.

She had always had the hots for Tuck, but her interest had never been returned. He barely knew she was alive except when he needed to locate one of his buddies, Juls, Rosie or Bobby. Fuck him, she thought, not my type anyway, too preppy with all that tousled, sandy hair and sea blue eyes. His tan canvas slacks were worn and ripped, but she had to admit, they looked gorgeous on his trim athletic body. A faded blue work shirt fell loosely over the broad shoulders and although Karen had never seen what lay beneath the shirt, she could imagine.

"Well, ladies, gotta go. See you at the next game."

He had barely sat down and now he was rushing off, as usual, trailing after Juls. It was always Juls, more like a marriage than a partnership, Karen mused, grabbing his untouched Pabst, calling "thanks" as she turned back to her teammates.

"Phew," Tuck mused as he headed towards the North end, driving at least twenty miles over the speed limit. "Cat's on the prowl tonight," he said aloud, thinking that Karen Ramos was trouble with a capital T. He'd just broken up with one bitch and he sure as hell didn't need another.

After Gracie had packed up and left a year and a half ago, Tuck's lady luck had taken a decidedly sour turn until Marcia came into his life. In the beginning, their relationship had been sweet indeed. A friend of a friend, they'd hit it off from day one and Marcia had fit right into the gang. Then, she moved into the beach house he shared with J and T's office and things had gone downhill fast. Juls didn't like Marcia, but hell, Juls hadn't liked any of his girlfriends except for crazy Annie from Boston. Juls claimed he only dated bitches, but she and Annie had hit it off from the start until Annie had fallen in love with big Jim and run off to Colorado to run a saloon. They still sent Christmas cards.

He had to admit, Juls was right, he did attract bitches, no doubt about it. As soon as Marcia moved in she started screaming, a continual screech that never let up except when Juls was in the office, which wasn't often. During Marcia's residence, Juls had avoided the office as much as possible. Too much of an effort to be pleasant.

When the whole gang got together, it was easier for his partner to keep her distance, but in the office it was impossible. From day one Marcia insinuated herself into every facet of the business and once she grabbed hold of a project, there was no wresting it away from her. Tuck had initially encouraged his live-in's involvement, but things had quickly gotten out of hand. He smiled, remembering Juls' long overdue explosion after a particularly trying day with Marcia.

"That's it Tuck! Either she goes or I do! No… that's not right. I'm not going, Marcia is and you're telling her as soon as she gets back!"

"Telling me what?" Marcia purred, voice smooth as silk as she sauntered in from the kitchen.

Taking in the saucy stroll, the self-satisfied grim-- Marcia had a wicked smile-- and the haughty flip of her silky blond hair, Juls took a deep breath and let her have it.

"Marcia, I started this business with Tuck almost twelve years ago. It's a good business, we make a decent living, we get along and our customers are happy."

"So what'dya want, a medal?"

Tuck cringed, fearing he was about to witness a murder.

Juls ignored the sarcasm, "Then you come along and suddenly Mr. Longfield's calling saying you've insulted his wife. We've got dirty units that you were supposed to have had cleaned and we've got a phone bill that's three times what it usually is. The there's the--"

"Can I get a word in?" Marcia interrupted, her voice squeakier than usual.

"I'm not finished."

"You're just jealous, that's it isn't it? You can't stand it that Tuck and I are partners now and doing a great job without you!"

Tuck intervened at this juncture. "That's enough Marcia. Juls is right, it's our business, hers and mine and you've been screwing up. It's my fault, I take the blame for encouraging you to become involved in the first place. Stupid move on my part. Sorry hon, you're gonna hafta bow out. It's not working and if Juls hadn't spoken up, I would have. The Longfields are two of our oldest customers; they've been with us since the beginning. There was no reason for you to treat Janet like that, calling her dog---"

"A fucking guinea pig! I can't believe what I'm hearing! The little rodent bit me, for crying out loud, and all you care about is the old bat and that decrepit husband of hers! What's the matter with you people?"

"What's the matter with us is that J and T is built on good will and friendly service neither of which you seem able to deliver," Juls replied. Her voice had lost its fire, but her cheeks were flushed and blotchy, betraying the anger still smoldering beneath the surface. "And we don't have the money for all these hour long phone calls to California, New York and wherever else you're always calling."

Jaw set, her face flushed and angry, Marcia glared at the partners standing side by side behind the desk. "Fine, I'm outta here. Screw the both of you and your cozy little partnership. No one could step between you two and live to tell about it anyway! I've been offered a job in New York starting next week so good riddance!"

"What the--?" Tuck stared at her.

"That's right. I'm leaving Sunday so you can go back to your pathetically chummy existence."

So, Marcia had departed and Tuck had heard nothing from her and didn't expect to. Something told him that Karen Ramos would make Marcia look like Pollyanna. Best keep his distance from that one. Besides, it wasn't as if he needed lady friends. A coed working for J and T this summer had already caught his eye and if he and Kerry hit it off, the last thing he needed was Karen breathing down his neck.

Marcia had been right about one thing, he and Juls did lead a chummy existence. However, he doubted that Juls had ever been jealous of Marcia or any of his girlfriends, she just didn't have it in her. He had known his partner for nearly fourteen years. She was warm, funny, stubborn, practical in business matters, athletic, compassionate, opinionated, a fiercely loyal friend, a forgiving opponent, a hard worker, a loving daughter and sister, but jealous? Not Juls.

They'd met in Laguna Beach, California where they were both attending an advanced workshop on the craft of leaded glass construction. Amazed to find fellow Fall Riverites so far from home, they had sought each other out during the workshop, spending their free time together during the six week course. At the workshop's conclusion, they extended their stay for four weeks, traveling up the coast to Northern California, Washington and Oregon. A brief romantic fling during that trip had ended the day they stepped off the plane in Providence.

While a fierce attraction lingered, by the time they arrived at home, they had decided to go into business together and Juls had insisted romance give way to friendship if they were to work together. By his own admission, Tuck had already dated and discarded more women than he could remember and she wasn't about to start a business only to have it fall prey to his romantic whims. Tuck reluctantly acceded to her wishes, but more than once over the years he had regretted the promise made in the parking lot of Green Airport. He was still very much in love with Juls Whitman.

The past twelve years had been prosperous ones. They'd started with the glass shop, making windows and lamp shades on commission as well as restoring old windows in local churches and the turn of the century Victorian homes of Fall River, Newport and surrounding areas. While the business grew steadily, stained glass was not the booming business on the East coast that it had been out West. After three years, J and T branched out in another direction, becoming J and T Limited in the process.

Most of their business now was caretaking the summer homes, condominiums and multi-million dollar beach houses of Windy Harbor, a wealthy summer enclave fifteen minutes southeast of Fall River. The tiny coastal town had grown by leaps and bounds over the last twelve years as farmers sold out for millions to the affluent New Yorkers and Bostonians voraciously gobbling up the last stretches of virgin coastline. A sleepy little fishing and farming village for many generations, Windy

Harbor had finally been discovered. Like it or not, the locals had had to adapt and many did not do so graciously.

The hostility of Windy Harbor's natives had in fact been largely responsible for the initial success of J and T. Snubbed and shunned by their neighbors, the Harbor's newest residents had had no where to turn for help and services until Juls and Tuck appeared on the scene. With open arms and friendly smiles, the partners catered to their clients every whim with efficiency and discretion. J and T looked after clients' properties in winter and summer, handling all rental agreements and arranging to have services-- water, phone, electricity, trash collection and so forth-- resumed or terminated with the changing seasons.

Having spent the better part of his adult life in the Harbor Tuck knew the plumbers, electricians, carpenters, painters and various other service oriented people. One room in his weathered shingled beach house served as J and T's office. Thad Potter, Tuck's father had been left the house by a maiden aunt. Since the elder Potter refused to leave the Fall River home where Tuck and his brothers had grown up, when Tuck had approached him about starting the business, he had been only to happy to deed it over. Juls' house was ten miles away in Tiverton, R.I. just outside the Fall River city limits.

The partners took excellent care of their clients, running errands, searching for missing pets, investigating petty thefts-- trash barrels and mail boxes were the most frequent targets-- arranging for cleaning services, planning parties-- or hiring caterers -- and helping to arrange for clients' memberships in the area's yacht , golf and beach clubs and Windy Harbor's Ladies Literary Society, the most exclusive and selective of the all the 'clubs.' While not always successful in wheedling memberships for the newcomers into the Harbor's closed societies, the partners endeavored, if unsuccessful, to sooth bruised egos by suggesting alternative activities for their wealthy clients, many of whom had never heard the word "no" until they moved to Windy Harbor.

Business had grown so much that J and T now had a waiting list and while there were two rival companies proffering the same type of service, J and T was still the "agency of choice" for those lucky enough to "get on the list". Not a bad way to make a living if you liked people and both partners did. Marcia had not and it showed.

As he turned onto Rosie's street, Tuck spied the Impala and pulled up, parking behind it. Brushing thoughts of Marcia and Karen aside, he wondered what had been important enough to keep Rosie from the game, she lived and died for softball for Christ sake. Slamming the door, he cursed under his breath, angry at himself for missing Juls at the field, "damn the Willises and their fucked up lawn sprinkler!"

His heart-- already in his throat after taking the front steps two at a time-- nearly stopped as the first of Juls' screams pierced the stillness of the night.

CHAPTER 3

Racing up the stairs, Bobby puffing along in her wake, Juls reached the third floor in seconds. Rosie's unit was at the end of the hall, number sixteen.

The building was over eighty years old, but Gladys Kenney, the owner kept it in immaculate condition. The plaster walls had recently been white-washed and at the far end of each hallway, window seats had been built in, green and white awning striped cushions inviting passersby to linger. Despite its pristine appearance, the building was still in the heart of the roughest part of the city. In an effort to thwart thieves who continually absconded with her framed prints, Gladys had decoupaged fine arts posters along the corridor's walls. Wall scones bolted to the walls bathed the passageway in soft light, the overall effect one of peaceful serenity.

After several minutes with her finger pressed to the buzzer, Juls went to the window seat, rummaging under the seat cushion to find the key Rosie kept hidden there. "Shit! Why won't this work?" she cried, jabbing the key in, turning to the left and right. The lock refused to budge.

Hand on her shoulder, Bobby reached from behind. "Here, let me try babe."

"I'll get it," she said, shrugging his hand off. "It just... takes a minute to... there, finally!"

She flipped the light switch by the door as they stepped into the living room, into the warm inviting space where they had spent so many evenings drinking, watching movies, playing cards, talking and laughing together. Tonight the room smelled musty, the air close and still and she wondered why all the windows were closed on such a warm summer night.

Rosie collected Native American and Mexican textiles and favored the stark lines of the mission style in her furnishings. All of her pieces were reproductions of Gustaf Stickley designs, well-made, handsome and sturdy like the woman herself. Hanging from the cream colored walls were three Navaho rugs in bold patterns of red, gray and black. The floor was covered in gray wall to wall carpeting, clean and new like the rest of the building, another large Navaho rug lay across its center the same reds and grays slashed through it in a chevron pattern.

The large, comfortable sofa was flanked by two matching armchairs, all three pieces covered in off-white cotton duck; a number bright woven throw pillows echoing the colors of the rugs. Rosie's pride and joy stood in front of the sofa-- a massive oak coffee table, also in the mission style, built by Rosie herself in a woodworking class at the local community college.

The morning papers were scattered across the table's polished surface and Rosie's body lay at its far end. She was dead, no question about that. The body sprawled half in the living room, half in the bedroom, legs twisted back at unnatural angles, naked except for gray athletic socks which Juls recognized as her own, loaned to her friend several weeks earlier. Black curls obscured the face and aside from a few scratches here and there, her body appeared untouched, white and smooth in its deathly pallor.

Her good arm lay at her side; the scarred left arm-- burned in a childhood accident-- tucked beneath her. There was quite a lot of blood pooled beside the body that appeared to have come from her underside and pieces of a jigsaw puzzle were scattered around the floor, some floating in the blood like tiny amoebae.

Juls screamed, rushing to her friend's side. As she began to claw at the smooth white rope still wrapped around Rosie's neck, Bobby roused himself, leaping forward to yank her back. "Juls, stop it. We can't touch her!"

He pulled her back and Juls let go, the movement causing the body to roll towards them leaving the severed left arm on the floor behind her. Her arm had been amputated at the shoulder.

"Jesus," he whispered. Juls screamed again, beginning to shake violently.

"Oh my God, oh my God," she mumbled over and over as he dragged her towards the kitchen phone.

As she struggled, lunging towards her friend, he tightened his grip. "Cut it out, Juls, come on now for God's sake, we can't touch her. We've gotta call the police, they need to see her just as she is. You can't help her, babe, she's gone, now come on."

He reached the phone just as Tuck burst through the door. Juls crumpled into her partner's arms and Bobby turned away as the police dispatcher answered at the other end of the line.

The next few hours a blur. The three sat huddled on the sofa as the police went over the apartment, occasionally pausing to ask questions. Cameras flashing, their voices hushed and somber, a small army of men collected samples, searched through drawers and closets going over every inch of the three rooms. Occasionally neighbors peeked their heads in and were led to the window seat in the hall where an officer waited to take their statements.

"Make them stop," Juls moaned, almost incoherent as the hour approached midnight. "Rosie hated having her picture taken. Please, Tuck, please make them stop." In her Flames uniform covered with grass stains, blood and dirt, she looked like a small child inconsolable after falling off of her bike and skinning her knee.

"Juls, it's okay," Tuck said, drawing her to him. "Hush now, Rosie's past caring. How much longer officer?" he called to Jack Mederois, the homicide detective in charge.

"They'll be taking her out in about five minutes. I have just a couple of questions for Ms. Whitman, then you folks can take off."

True to his word, not five minutes later the photographers packed up their gear and Rosie's draped body was carried out on a stretcher. As his officers began sealing the crime scene, Mederois came to sit beside them.

"Where will they take her?" Juls asked.

"City morgue first. We'll have to keep her a few days, then we'll contact the family and see about the funeral home and all."

"There is no family, just me."

"Well then Ms. Whitman, we'll let you know when you can have her collected and--"

"Oh God, who would do this?"

"We were kinda a hopin' you might give us a hint. Some one with a grudge? Ex-boyfriends, disgruntled co-workers, whatever? Or someone new, that she just recently met?"

"There's no one like that. Everyone loved Rosie. No one who knew her would hurt her."

"How 'bout someone she might've met recently? A new boyfriend maybe?"

"None that I know of."

"Do you guys know what Ms. Mikawski was doing today, someone she might've been seeing? Mr. Gagnon says you unlocked the door and there are no signs of forced entry. No broken windows, jimmied locks, what have you. Seems like she must've known the guy. Had to have let him in."

"I don't know what she was doing today except for the game. Softball. We play on a team and we had a game tonight."

"So I see. What time was that?"

"Five."

"She was long gone by then, I'm 'fraid. Preliminary exam puts time of death around one, two somethin' like that."

"Oh, God, the whole time we were playing, Rosie was lying here." Juls crumpled against Tuck, fresh sobs wracking her slender frame.

"Sh, okay now," Tuck whispered, holding her tighter as if his grip might somehow stop the trembling

"I know this is tough, Ms. Whitman. Just a couple more questions, please. What can you tell me about her arm? Was she able to use it, the scarred one I mean?"

"Yes," she sniffled, regarding him. "Sometimes it stiffened up in the cold, got tingly at unexpected times, things like that, but it was only a scar. It happened when she was four. A kettle of hot water spilled on her. Her family always called it an accident, but her father was a drunk. Rosie had no memory of it, why?"

"Just curious. She's a big woman, strong, I mean. Seems like the type who'd put up a fight, but there's no sign of a struggle and I just wondered if maybe one arm was weaker than--"

"How did she die? I mean, was she--"

"Strangled. That white rope around her neck, guy brought it with him."

"And her arm?" Tuck asked.

"Happened after she was dead. Thank God for that at least." Mederois studied Juls, aware that she was fading fast, withdrawing into herself, unaware of her surroundings. He turned to Tuck. "How 'bout the apartment? Was your friend in the habit of leaving the door unlocked?"

"Never," Juls answered for him. "I'm sorry, but I have to know. Was she? I mean she was naked so was she--"

"Raped? Doesn't look like it, but we won't know for certain until forensics gets through with her."

Juls moaned.

Tuck gripped her tighter. "Look Detective, we're gonna split, okay? She needs to get outta here."

"Sure thing, I'm sorry Ms. Whitman, about your friend and all, and about keepin' you so late. Let's leave it for now and we'll talk in the morning."

He rose, joining his men a few of whom were still collecting their gear. "Oh," he called back over his shoulder. "One more thing-- did Ms. Mikawski like jigsaw puzzles? I mean, would she have been working on one do you 'spose?"

"Not that I'm aware of. I didn't even know she owned any jigsaw puzzles," Juls said, looking to Tuck for confirmation. He nodded at Mederois.

"I thought not."

"How's that?" Tuck asked.

"Can't be sure till we check a little further, but, well, we've seen this type of thing before."

"Jesus, a serial killer!" Bobby cried, instantly regretting his words.

Juls' face, red and blotchy from crying, froze in horror.

"We don't know that Mr. Gagnon. There are similarities to other cases, but we'll have to look further. Let's not go spreadin stuff like that around, okay?"

"Oh God," Juls moaned, as the two men half-carried, half-dragged her from of the apartment, driving her home.

Several shots of brandy and two sleeping pills borrowed from a neighbor and Juls settled down on tear-soaked pillow, a drugged, fretful sleep finally overtaking her. Tuck slept beside her bed in the chaise, Bobby on the living room sofa.

Made in the USA
Charleston, SC
06 March 2015